HOME TOWN

S. A. FANNING

IMMORTAL WORKS
SALT LAKE CITY

Immortal Works LLC
1505 Glenrose Drive
Salt Lake City, Utah 84104
Tel: (385) 202-0116

© 2024 Pete Fanning
www.petefanning.com

Cover Art by kingwoodcreations.com

All rights reserved, including the right to reproduce this book or portions thereof in any form whatsoever. For more information visit https://www.immortalworks.press/contact.

This book is a work of fiction. Names, characters, businesses, organizations, places, events and incidents either are the product of the author's imagination or are used fictitiously. Any resemblance to actual persons, living or dead, events, or locales is entirely coincidental.

ISBN 978-1-953491-79-4 (Paperback)
ASIN B0CYNSDMPR (Kindle)

For Nana

CHAPTER 1

The cannons boomed from the end zone as we sprinted out to the forty-yard line. One side of City Stadium exploded into cheers as we gathered there and huddled close, smacking helmets and shoulder pads, our arms slung around each other as we swayed back and forth, a tight, united circle of camaraderie. Our faces were flushed, eyes wild behind face masks as our helmets clicked and clacked. A trail of smoke spiraled into the dusky sky. Tonight, we squeezed a little closer, pressed a little harder. This one was for bragging rights.

Stonewall vs. Briggs. The battle for the city. The game was always scheduled down the stretch of the regular season—our home and away schedules staggered accordingly as we shared the stadium. And the hype was real. All year, the town had been counting down the days, clinging to an old rivalry like it was all they had left. Now it was finally time.

We were heavy favorites. It was a down year for B.D. Briggs, while we were undefeated and getting ready for the postseason. All week long, Coach had stayed on us, warning us to tune out the noise, not to look ahead to the playoffs, to ignore all that stuff in the news.

"That stuff in the news" meant the monument. A few weeks back, the town council had voted in favor of relocating the General Elijah Abner statue from its perch on the downtown terrace to a nearby museum or park. The story in our local paper went off like a bomb, with small protests popping up, scathing editorials, and all sorts of social media threats leading up to the game. The town was split in half when it came to the confederate monument—our differences as cut and clear as the teams taking the field.

A slap on the helmet jolted me from my thoughts. "Let's go, Ben."

Moose, our enormous defensive tackle, went down the line, barking orders, screaming at everyone about what we were going to do tonight. His glare lingered on me as he took his place beside me for the national anthem.

Moose and I were seniors, co-captains, the guys the defense looked to for leadership. Moose was always after me to be more vocal, and usually I was up for it, but tonight felt different, like it was charged. Like something was going to happen. Something other than football.

Everything quieted down for the anthem. Hats came off heads, hands over hearts. Our marching band stood frozen in place, facing the flag, when the entire Briggs team, their marching band, and even the cheerleaders dropped to one knee and raised their fists to the air.

Any hope this would simply be a football game vanished as a deluge of booing and jeers flooded the field. A slight pain found my head, thudding in my ears before it washed downstream to my arms and legs as our side of the stadium lost their minds in unison before the anthem flared to an end.

Coach called us in, his face a ripe shade of maroon. He shook his head and said, "Just one more reason to kick their asses."

We hadn't played a down, and I was already fighting for breath. I didn't have the heart to mention how booing during the national anthem might've been more disrespectful than kneeling in silence.

It wouldn't have mattered. A jolt of anger snaked through the stands like a hot, exposed wire. It was impossible to ignore. As the anthem came to an end, everyone on our side clapped louder, whistled harder, and put a little more heat in their words. They took it personally.

I was tight. The muscles in my legs clutched as we met at midfield for the coin toss. Big Moose and me—seniors, team captains, arms locked—same as we'd done all year. I'd been a captain since junior year, something my dad thought was a big deal. Like Moose's old man, my dad had played on this very same field. You know the story: small town, traditions, expectations.

I did my best to put it all away. I nodded at our opponents, the steam from our breaths lingering like the tension between us. Moose rolled his massive neck, like he always did, only the Briggs guys didn't seem all that intimidated by our neck rolls, our staring, or even our perfect record. Two of the guys stood straight, heads cocked and smirking, like they'd told a joke on the way out and couldn't get it together.

Fine, I thought, *let them joke. It's better for us if they come in unfocused, undisciplined, unprepared.* But mostly, I wondered how this 4-4 team was so confident.

The third captain wasn't smirking or joking. Devin Calloway was a guy I knew but didn't know. We were connected at the hip as far as the local news was concerned, had been since we were both named all-conference our sophomore years. Since we led our respective teams in tackles. Since we both committed early, Devin to Virginia, me to Virginia Tech. Rivals.

Devin was as fast as they came. Quick, strong, and always well prepared. He made a living in opposing teams' backfields, and when he wasn't there, he was laying out any receiver dumb enough to come over the middle. Coach Campbell didn't have to warn us about DC.

The ref continued his spiel about the toss as we faced off, glaring at each other while our families and neighbors and crazy aunts and uncles and cousins screamed across the field like lunatics. It was like we were locked into some contract whether we wanted it or not.

We won the toss, and our side got the cowbells going, doing that rebel yell thing. Yeah, the Rebels. Our team colors were red and white, a dash of blue down the sides of the pants, but most of our fans wore hunting jackets and camouflage, their bright orange stocking caps dotting the crowd. They usually arrived in a convoy of pickup trucks, some with hunting dog cages in blood-stained beds from all the deer they'd skinned and let drip off the tailgate. Most of the trucks were plastered in mud around the fenders, with confederate flags proudly on display in the windows or mounted to truck beds like they were just hoping someone would call them out on it.

And the Briggs side *was* calling them out. Like I said, they weren't intimidated by us. Not with the kneeling, their marching band, the drumline corps with the snares ricocheting off the bricks, tapping its way into my bloodstream as they advanced toward us—a single, amoeba-like body, weaving and taunting our side of the bleachers before worming its back to the corner. It fired up both sides of the stadium, for different reasons entirely.

Even still, I could hear this woman in the stands—on the Briggs side—screaming over it all, over the rat-a-tat drumming, the clapping, the whistles and clacks of the helmets during warmups. Her voice was like an air horn, cutting through the noise.

"Do the damn thing!" She leaned over the railing where a banner read GO 44!

She kept repeating it, over and over again. *Do the damn thing! Do the damn thing!*

I couldn't stop watching her as we lined up. I was hoping she'd stop—not because it bothered me but because our fans were having so much fun with it. Every time she screamed our side would whoop it up. They'd lean back then point and shake their heads. From the field, I could only guess what they were saying, but when I sprinted back over to the sidelines what I heard was more disgusting than I'd imagined.

I blinked it off, glanced away from the policemen at the exits, guns on hips, heads on swivels. But it was too late, I could no longer pretend this was just another game. It wasn't. Not this time. It was all about to boil over. Only the width of a football field—160 feet—separated our two sides, and it felt like the field was shrinking. I was just glad Mom was at work and Parker was at a friend's house.

Coach went down the line, smacking helmets and clapping. He paused when he got to me, forced me to look him in the eyes. I nodded a few times and he moved on.

I ran in place, blew some warmth into my hands. To my right, confederate flags waved against the night, but not for the first time. I'd gone to Stonewall Middle School before Stonewall High. We'd been the *Little Rebels* then, now we were the *Raging Rebels*. Until a few days ago, I'd never given much thought to the name—where it came from and what it meant. It was just sort of what we'd grown up *being*.

To top it all off, Jeff's dad, Gunny, was in full form. I'd known Gunny for years, although, how well can you know someone who's always blind drunk? He paraded with the stars and bars, waving it back and forth under the night sky like it was his finest moment.

All of this was spinning in my head. Devin Calloway, the screaming woman, the monuments. The flags. The kneeling. The machine gun drums. Gunny. The nervous laughter in the huddles.

But I wasn't laughing, I was kind of pissed. I mean, were they *trying* to get us killed down here? And when did our game became *their* game? The outcome some sort of verdict, some kind of grudge to settle once and for all.

It was like they'd stolen it from us.

The screams, the cheers, the throttle of anticipation—usually I put it away and played the game. All of us did. At nine wins and zero losses, we'd been killing it all season. We'd worked since summer—conditioning and camps—since last season's overtime loss in the state semifinals. Besides, we'd beaten Briggs two straight years, so no one would say it, but we were looking past this game and forward to our yearly showdown with Clearview before hitting the playoffs full stride. This was *the* year.

So the Briggs game shouldn't have been that big. Rivalry? Yes. Packed stadium? Always. But the sides, the monuments, the town, the game. The coaches might not admit that it had become a racial thing, but here we were. B.D. Briggs, the black school, against Stonewall High, the white school. Yeah, we had some Black guys on our squad, just like Briggs had a few White dudes, but as we kicked the ball into the night sky, everyone in the stadium knew that's what it was. They'd made it that way.

They'd wanted it that way.

When Briggs took the opening kickoff to the house, things went nuclear. It was all they needed to believe they could beat us. The Briggs side of the stadium ignited. A thousand people leaped into the air and came down with a crash. After he lit into us, Coach Campbell, his face like a strawberry, did the clapping thing he did when he was trying to keep us focused. We couldn't even hear him. We couldn't hear a thing over the Briggs crowd.

The very first play on our opening possession, Devin Calloway shot through the gap and crushed our quarterback. Brantley coughed up the ball, and Briggs was in business. We'd been huddled up, the defensive guys, going over things with Coach Stinnett when we heard the cheering on the other side. We strapped on our helmets and went to work.

We held Briggs to a field goal. It actually hit the post and bounced in. And just like that, ten-zip. They kicked off again.

Our offense got their act together—at least until they crossed midfield and stalled. We punted, pinned them deep near their end zone. The Briggs band played some hip-hop rhythm, and the entire Briggs side bounced to the beat. It was like their Super Bowl.

The only thing that helped my nerves was being on the field. The hitting tamed some of the jitters. But the quarterback for Briggs could move. He was tall but quick, and he liked to tuck it and take off and was hard to hit clean. He scooted around the end, and I zoned in on him, ready to make the tackle, to set a lick on him, but he shook me out of my cleats and scampered out of bounds.

The Briggs side went crazy. How had this team lost four games?

The quarterback took it again for twelve more yards. He danced his way back to the huddle, pointed at us, and nodded his head. Another first down. The celebration on the Briggs side continued, which got our side going again. Like my dad, most of them had played at Stonewall. They cupped their hands to their faces, yelling down at us as the defense took the field again—chanting stuff. Like, racial stuff.

I made the mistake of looking up to the stands, and I stopped cold. Someone had brought a noose.

The Stonewall faithful passed it around, laughing and having a good old time. I tried to shake it off when Moose called me back. It was third down and we needed a stop. And that was when the new chants started.

"Beat the *Briggs*... Beat the *Briggs*."

But they weren't saying "Briggs." What they *were* saying made me drop my head, ashamed to be wearing the Rebels uniform for the first time in my life.

The Briggs quarterback was under center when the chants caught on. He stood up like he was calling an audible and fiddled with his chin strap as he looked around, like he was wondering if it was real.

Moose egged the fans on, waving his hands around like a maestro, laughing like the whole thing was hilarious.

As the chanting grew louder and louder, the entire Briggs side went quiet, like they were shocked. Everyone was looking around like, "Are they for real saying that?"

The refs blew their whistles, stopping the game. Some guy in a suit trotted out and took the PA system.

He introduced himself as Mr. Ferguson, the B.D. Briggs principal, and did his best to be heard over the booing and chanting. "Please, I ask that everyone here tonight show some respect to the officials, each other, and most of all, the students on the field. Let's try and set an example for the students of our community."

The poor guy was speaking into a void, as trash, food, cans, bottles, dog bones—anything the Stonewall fans could get their hands on–rained down on the field. Between the announcement and the noise and the debris being thrown from the stands, it was clear this was no longer a football game.

The police moved in and escorted the principal off the field as a few beer bottles made their way to the gridiron. I turned to the Briggs sideline and found #11, Devin Calloway, staring at me. I wondered what it must look like from where he stood. Our side of the bleachers, with Gunny up there waving the flag, the noose, all that trash. I don't know how long we stood like that, with Devin seeing what was behind me and me seeing what was behind him, but it was like we knew it was all going to blow.

CHAPTER 2

On third down Briggs ran a quick draw. Their running back, a short dude who ran low and hard, started to hit the outside but lowered his head and bounced back inside. I was blocked but got a hand on him, enough to slow him down. Jeff came in like a missile and laid him out. Helmet to helmet.

The Briggs coaches stormed onto the field, screaming for a personal foul. It didn't help that Jeff stood over the kid, flexing like a pro wrestler. The refs didn't make a call, so on fourth and eight, Briggs lined up to punt.

Chris, our wide receiver, fielded the punt around the twenty and turned once, then got held up in a log jam. A Briggs player came in and nearly ripped his helmet off, causing Chris to fumble. Briggs recovered.

It was no accident, but the refs missed it. Moose didn't. He ran up on the guy and shoved him on his ass. His teammates came in pushing and shoving, nothing that didn't happened in almost every game, but our fans lost their minds.

Debris pelted the field. More bottles, seat cushions, some half empty drinks. A hot dog. The noose.

The refs whistled. Mr. Ferguson trotted out again. The cops inched closer as threats rang out. I wondered if they would call the game right there, but the fans wanted more. They wanted it more than we did.

Ten or fifteen minutes later, our defense took the field, and we lined up and tried once again to play a high school football game. But it was too late. The next play turned into a gang fight as soon as the ball was snapped and quickly forgotten, the guys in the trenches, offensive and defensive lines, started slugging each other. The running back skipped around the end. I closed the gap, but when I went to make a tackle, I was blindsided. The refs whistled, the benches cleared, everything else was a blur.

I rolled onto my side. From my spot on the ground, it was all cleats and legs and bodies stampeding onto the field. I wrestled my way to my feet, where Moose had two guys by the face mask. Coaches rushed the field, some trying to break things up, others looking to get a lick in. Shouting and whistling filled my ears. Everyone's faces were balled up with anger.

Fans from both sides of the stands leaped over the rails and rushed the field. Two Briggs guys hoisted a bench over their heads. The PA guy pled, "Good citizens of Ridgeton, please remain in your seats! Everyone, remain in your seats."

I turned toward the track, looking for Liv, my girlfriend, and the rest of the cheer squad. Coach Stinnett shoved me out of the way and kicked a guy in the back. Jeff grappled on the ground with one of the Briggs safeties. Others danced around, some with their helmets off, fists up like boxers.

Moms and dads, uncles and cousins—the bodies kept coming. They tore across the track onto the field, looking to hurt someone, all wild-eyed and ready for war.

My pads felt too tight. My helmet squeezed my head. I whirled around, trying to make sense of it, when once again, I found #11, DC, maybe twenty yards away, his arms at his sides, like me, taking it all in.

We locked eyes for the second time that evening. We were around the same height, about the same size. A local sports reporter once wrote about how similar we were, and for a brief moment I wondered if we were supposed to fight each other. I wasn't afraid of him, but I was afraid of what was happening.

Around us, our teammates were slinging helmets at heads, throwing punches, grappling on the ground, or kicking someone who was already down. Adults rushed the field—clerks you'd find at the grocery store or Walmart or at the drive-thru at the bank, hanging on to their pants by their belts and looking for someone to hurt. Even the bands had joined the fray.

The refs blew their whistles until they broke. The PA guy kept begging for civility. Coaches were caught between restoring order and ducking chairs hurled their way.

And I had no idea how to stop any of it. Devin and I only stared at each other, through the bodies and trash and screaming, our similarities once again on display as the look on Devin's face mirrored my own—the wide-eyed, blank expressions of two all-conference linebackers with no one to tackle.

I was standing at the edge of the war, caught between pulling guys off or getting the hell out of there, when the police got control of the field. Our tiny force, clad in black, with shields and helmets of their own, had their batons out as they strode purposefully onto the field, and people moved as the tear gas hung over the 50-yard line. Things had started to clear out when a shriek brought everything to a halt.

Not far from me, on our sideline, lay a crumpled figure. His feet twitched, arms wrapped around his stomach as he rocked back and forth on the field. I stood helplessly watching, unable to do anything more than stare at how his blood shined under the lights, like it was painted on the grass. Someone knocked into me, and I started toward the man as he wiggled around, side to side, his mouth an oval and his scream muted. His basketball shoes dug into the grass like he was trying to climb steps that weren't there. Drool and spit leaked from the corners of his cracked lips.

I knelt to check on him, and the police closed in and pulled me back. I staggered a few steps until someone caught me with a "Whoa there."

The medics arrived and huddled around the injured man. I stood motionless, gasping for breath, as they set him on the gurney and placed him inside the ambulance.

A coach turned me away from the glare of the ambulance brake lights as it drove off the track. His lips moved as, I'm sure, he said reassuring things into my ear, but I didn't hear a word, couldn't figure out where to go or what to say. I could only see the body on the ground, the blood, the guy's eyes as he lay writhing on the field, grunting and moaning. I still couldn't catch my breath.

My gaze landed on the scoreboard. We were down 10-0, it was still only the first quarter, with 5:42 left to play. We had all of our timeouts.

Coach Campbell corralled us, his face crazed, his goatee wiggling as he cursed. I'd never seen his eyes so wide as he shoved us toward the locker room, his voice breaking. "Now, get out of here, in the locker room, let's moooove!"

It was chaos. Little kids were crying. Parents were still screaming. Volunteers did what they could to help the small police force. I put one cleat in front of the other, my legs like noodles, as we headed to the locker room.

Moose punched a locker and I jumped. I didn't want to be there. I needed quiet, and the locker room was more of what we'd just seen.

Jeff had his helmet off, his hair matted down with grease and sweat. Jeff was always a little jumpy, but now he was pacing around the locker room, mumbling and talking to everyone and no one at all. "Anybody see my dad? I need to find my dad."

When he started on a rant about how the guy who got stabbed was in a gang and they were probably on the way over to retaliate, Coach Campbell snatched him by the shoulder pads, as though trying to jerk him out of a trance. "Son, listen to me. We'll find your dad, you hear? Just try to breathe. Deep breaths, okay?"

Soon as Coach turned him loose, Jeff got back to pacing. Coach turned to Coach Stinnett. "Where are those damn, buses? Place is going to be crawling with gangbangers. No one goes in or out of this locker room until the buses are here!"

We huddled there, barricaded in the locker room, refusing to come out, even when the Briggs principal came over to apologize. I perked up, catching bits and pieces of the conversation. The principal spoke to Coach in between breaths, about how he'd never seen anything like that, even in his Civil Rights days and all.

My phone buzzed with a text from Liv. She was okay. The cheerleaders had managed to escape in the van. The next text was from my little sister, Parker. Apparently, it was already on the news. I ran my fingers through my cold, sweaty hair. My breath cut short. Parker had been so upset with me because I didn't want her to come tonight. I don't know what I would've done if she'd been here.

Eventually, we got the all-clear to leave. By then, Moose had relaxed enough to make jokes. My hands shook, and I wanted to tell him it wasn't funny. I looked around when we got outside, waiting for something to happen. The stadium lights glowed, fog and tear gas settling over the field. The buses had pulled up over the curb onto the sidewalk for our safety.

All I could think about was the blood, how it shimmered under the lights. It drenched my thoughts until I had to slow and catch my breath. Bad move, the *News Team Six* lady rushed toward us, asking questions.

Moose wasted no time blaming her for all that was going on, how the news had been hyping up things. He shoved his way past her, and the guys followed his lead as the news lady swung the mike from person to person, searching for a soundbite. I was still reeling when the mike came to me.

"What are you feeling right now? What are your thoughts about the game, the fight?"

The team trudged on, leaving me behind with this news lady asking what I was feeling. I didn't think, just reacted. "What am I *feeling*? I'm ashamed."

Coach Campbell whirled back at the sound of my voice. He set his jaw and glared at me.

But the adrenaline was raging, and I was too rattled to filter my words. "I'm ashamed of our town, our team, the fans, the school. We just wanted to play football."

A hand found my shoulder pads with a slight tug as Coach cut in. "Ben, come on, let's move."

The reporter rushed to get in a follow up question. "Are you afraid, after being caught between the two sides? Are you worried about your safety?"

I threw my hands out. "There shouldn't *be* sides. I mean, yeah, two teams, but not..." I motioned to the field where I'd seen the blood, the medics...a war. I fought to free myself from Coach's clutches, blinking off the emotion flooding my eyes. "Not that. How does it end? What else has to happen?"

I said some more things, things I don't quite remember, before Coach hauled me off. I was dizzy with all of it, but I noticed some of the guys had hung around, watching, the younger guys who'd listened to me all year. They stood wide-eyed and gaping, as Coach ushered me away from the microphone.

Moose waited near the bus, still flushed and ready to hit someone, as Coach and I caught up. He shook his head like he was ashamed of me.

When we got back to the school, where the scene was only slightly calmer than the stadium, Mom and Parker ran up and nearly tackled me in the parking lot.

Parker, wiping back a blur of blonde flyaways, shook her head. "Ben, what in the hell?"

Mom shot my little sister a look. "Parker. Language."

I scanned the lot, my eyes still stinging from tear gas, and my body still buzzing on high alert. I glanced down at Parker. "And what are you doing here?"

Park was thirteen but thought she was Mom, Jr. She stayed after me about grades and football, but now, as she clutched onto me, I could tell she was no longer mad about me not wanting her to be at the game. "It was all over social media. The brawl. Did someone really get stabbed on the field?"

I looked around, parents and fans acting like we'd just come home from war. I had to get away. "Can we go?"

Dad called before we got in the door to our house, and he didn't hold back. He claimed the Black refs were in the bag for Briggs, then he called out the principal, said he should've taken responsibility from the start instead of blaming people.

And yeah, I'm seventeen, I'd heard him say things before, but not like that. I winced as he tossed around the N-word, poured it on thick like gas on a fire. It was almost like he wanted me to say it back.

I didn't say much of anything, though. Dad didn't want to hear what I thought—that both sides were to blame. If Dad wanted to talk responsibility, it was our side who had thrown the first punch. What about that chant they had going, that *Beat the Briggs* stuff? And how about that confederate flag? And the noose? They knew that was going to start shit.

But I let it go. There was no talking to my dad when he was worked up like that.

He didn't think they would reschedule. Not sure if that meant we'd won or lost. I knew my dad and Coach Campbell were worked up about our record, but I only saw the blood. It was still on my cleats.

Win or lose, it no longer mattered to me.

CHAPTER 3

I didn't even try to sleep. But I was too numb to be any company for Mom, who lingered nearby, biting her fingernails and refusing to go to bed herself. Her constant chatter helped, though, and kept me from getting too far into my thoughts. She'd been listening to the game at the packaging factory where she worked and thought I was going to die. She'd rushed out, left on the spot to go pick up Parker, and they drove straight to the school.

Thought I was going to die. Was that guy on the field dead? I kept trying to imagine who stabbed him—a parent, a fan, an uncle, maybe someone who'd been to our games all season. It was more than I could handle.

All week everyone around me had built this game up to something explosive. Our coaches talked about the monument as we studied film, urged us to be ready to hit someone. Briggs was our rival, and everyone made it feel like the world was at stake instead of just a high school football game. That we were the good guys, fighting for what was right.

Now someone might be dead.

Late that night, I finally drifted off into a skipping, dreamless sleep that left me feeling more tired than rested. The next morning, I climbed the stairs and found Mom in the kitchen, bacon and eggs sizzling in the pan.

I had no desire to eat. But seeing how Parker glanced up from her plate, I knew I had to go through the motions.

Mom turned to me, her voice soft and gentle like I was in the first grade. "Hey, baby."

Two identical sets of blue eyes scanned over me.

I shook my head. "Both of you, I'm fine."

Maybe not quite identical. Mom's eyes were red and puffy, while Parker's were laser-sharp and prodding. I could only imagine how I must have looked to them.

There were several new messages in the group chat on my phone—Coach Campbell was calling for a team meeting on the practice field at eleven. It was the last thing I wanted to do. I looked around the table for the newspaper that was usually there, as my mom still liked to read the actual paper version. But it was nowhere in sight, so I checked my phone.

Man Stabbed During Stadium Brawl

Mom leaned forward to say something, but I turned away, thumbing through the article. The guy's name was Reggie Watts. He was the uncle of the Briggs quarterback. He'd nearly bled out on the field after receiving three stab wounds from a tactical knife. As of midnight, he was in critical condition at Ridgeton Memorial Hospital.

I dropped into my seat at the table. Mom slid breakfast in front of me, but the morning sun was no longer warm and bright. The smell of bacon and eggs was nauseating. I couldn't stop seeing Reggie's blood glistening on the 32-yard line. His vacant eyes. The screams echoed in my head. The bite of tear gas lingered in my mouth.

My stomach churned. I pushed away my plate, feeling Mom's careful gaze on me. Her silence was too loud, too strange. Mom was never short for words.

"You need to eat, Ben," Parker said, tossing back a strand of hair, getting back to her phone, and trying to pretend it was just another morning.

Mom took the seat next to me, clutching her coffee mug.

I winced when she set her hand on my shoulder and she quickly pulled back. Great, that wasn't going to help things. And things only got more awkward as we sat in silence, my mom and sister waiting at the edge of their seats for me to open up about last night. But I couldn't do it—I couldn't get the words out. I was afraid of what would happen if I tried.

I forced down a bite of toast, but even that threatened to come back up. It was no use. I gave up on breakfast and went back to my room to lie down.

A COUPLE HOURS LATER, I forced myself to take a shower, get dressed, and drive over to the practice field. Down the steps, walking the worn dirt path to the field like I'd done a million times before, I felt like an outsider, like I no longer belonged there. I wasn't ready for the lighthearted joking with the guys or talk of the playoffs. The weight of my steps became heavier as I forced one foot in front of the next.

Most everyone was there already, huddled tight in portable bleacher stands. Shorts and t-shirts, red eyes and blank stares. I didn't see Jeff, which made me think of Gunny and everything else.

Coach Stinnett sipped coffee and checked his phone. He nodded at me as I approached, while Coach Campbell paced, rubbed his goatee, and grumbled under his breath. He saw me coming and started for the bleachers.

"Guys bring it in." Coach motioned for us to come closer. The metal bleachers clicked and clanged as we tightened up, hip to hip. "So, first of all, rough night. I've encountered some hostile environments over the years, but never anything like what we saw last night."

I looked around. Everyone was staring at their feet. Ryan Buckley and the rest of the defensive guys looked exhausted, with tight mouths and tousled hair, like they hadn't slept either. I wondered if my eyes looked as vacant as theirs did.

Only Moose seemed comfortable, sitting back on his elbows, his enormous body shifting the bleachers. "For real," he snorted.

Coach nodded. "I've contacted Russell—Mr. Howard. He's going to have this game expunged."

Some groaning behind me. I knew Moose and a few others wanted another shot at Briggs, but Coach held up a hand, his state championship ring glinting in the morning sunlight. He shot a hard stare my way. "But for now, we are not talking to the press. We are keeping this in house. Got it?"

My throat tightened. I'd convinced myself Coach had brought us together to see how we were holding up. Instead, he was worried about the press. The game. Our *record?*

Talk of Friday sent me free falling into a deep, dark hole of thoughts when Coach called me out. "Ben, you hear me?" he nodded my way.

"Huh?" The eyes of my teammates bore into me from behind and beside me, surrounding me almost, pressing down. Everyone was waiting for my input. I nodded quickly. "Yeah."

Coach's gaze lingered on me before he nodded and got back to pacing. "The best thing we can do is move on. Now, there is one other thing. The powers that be have decided to push the Clearview game back a week. Clearview's schedule accommodates that, and it was awfully nice of them to agree. Personally, that's just fine with me —more practice reps for the playoffs. That said, is there anyone who needs anything?" he added as an afterthought. "Mr. Russell has informed me there are some counselors on standby, I told him I didn't think it was necessary, but..."

He didn't think it was necessary. Wasn't that nice? Glad he could speak for all of us. We'd just watched a man spill his guts on the field, his eyes rolled back in his head, moaning, everyone screaming in the background, like something out of a war movie. *Nope, things are just fine,* Coach said.

With that out of the way, Coach Campbell took this extra time with us to talk more about the next game, and soon it was like any other time the team got together. As he went on, some of the guys relaxed and started goofing around.

I thought about Jeff. How he'd been pacing around in the locker room. We weren't as tight as we used to be, and his dad had been acting stranger by the year since we began high school, and I'd started keeping my distance.

As the team broke apart, I asked Moose about Jeff. He stared at me before he shrugged, said maybe he and his dad went hunting, then got back to laughing with Chris.

It wasn't long before Moose was bragging about how many heads he'd bashed. Coach Stinnett kind of smiled, pulled the defensive guys, and told us to get focused on Clearview. The Briggs game was done. Besides, from what he'd seen, we had settled down out there before the fight, and it was clear we were getting stops, and the offense would have scored on the next drive, and we'd have been on our way.

I couldn't do it, couldn't fake it like it was just another day. So as everyone was going on about what would've happened and what was going to happen, I started for the path, all too ready to return to my bed. But Coach Campbell called me over and set his hand on my shoulder. Not for the first time that day, my stomach revolted, and I swallowed down the familiar sour bile that had kept me up most of the night.

"You okay, Hoy?" Coach asked, in a way that meant I should say yes.

I glanced off with a nod, about to tell him I was because it's what he wanted to hear. But again, I couldn't, couldn't shake the image of the blood. "That guy, the one who got stabbed..."

Coach frowned. "Hey, look at me."

I raised my head and found Coach's slate gray eyes. The skin around them was lined with creases. He was a few years younger than my dad and had only one speed, full tilt. "Look, the guy was a thug, some gangbanger." He leaned in closer, the burn of his chewing tobacco causing me to blink. "I need you for the postseason. You gotta put this behind you."

Put this behind me. *This* was hours ago. Again, I started to nod because it was what he wanted me to do, but the weight of his hand on me, pulling me down, was too much to shrug off. My throat hurt as I swallowed down whatever I'd been going to say. I glanced over to the field.

Coach sighed. "Come on, take a walk with me for a minute."

He steered me away from the bleachers, his tone softening. "Ben, I'm not saying it's easy, but we're a team, and you're a big part of that. As a captain, you're a leader. The guys look to you for direction."

The captain speech. I'd heard it before, but this morning it came off more like a threat. We started down the track along a string of maple trees, tackle dummies, abandoned pads and shirts. Coach stopped, turned, and faced me again. "And you gotta stop feeding the press. Look, you were distracted last night, before any of this stuff went down. Ben, this team needs you if we're going to make a deep run, hear? Again, the younger guys look up to you. You're our leading tackler. But not last night. It was like you weren't even there, you hear me?"

Coach Campbell had put me on varsity as a sophomore. Midway through the season, I was a starter. From there he'd helped me along—conditioning, camps, training, even when I made my decision to go to Virginia Tech over Pitt and Marshall. I knew he was all about football and his players, but now, with the town the way it was, this monument thing and last night, it felt like he was leaning on me to pick a side. Calling that guy a thug and a gangbanger. Maybe I didn't need a counselor, maybe I did. Or maybe I just needed some time to process everything, get the images out of my head. Just a day or two, at least.

But that wasn't going to happen, not as Coach looked off in the distance before he turned to spit, then wiped his mouth and faced me full on. "Where you're headed, next year? You're going to see some tough environments. So don't get caught up in last night. The guy was out there looking to cause trouble, got it?"

It was like a script, as though he was helping me with my lines. But I couldn't say whether or not Reggie was looking for trouble, and even if he was, he wasn't the only one. Either way, I'd had enough for one morning. I nodded all the same to get through it. A few pats on the back, and we returned to the bleachers.

Coach brought the team in to talk Clearview. Get focused, playoff time. The usual stuff. Then he told us to enjoy the rest of our weekend.

A shiver washed over me, chills on my arms, and the deep pit forming in my stomach had me too sick to enjoy anything. I drove home and went straight to bed.

CHAPTER 4

I slept into Sunday and kept right on going, until Parker came down to my room to throw stuff at me. When that didn't work, she jumped on the bed until I had no choice but to roll over and knock her feet out from under her. By then I was awake and forced to face the world. I took a long, hot shower and got dressed. I thought about eating, but it never happened.

Sundays usually meant meeting up with Liv at Sal's, where she waited tables. Things had been so-so between us for a while—nothing awful but nothing spectacular. Still, it was strange I hadn't heard much from her since the game, besides a quick text to ask how I was doing. At the same time, I'd sort of avoided everyone, so I told myself it was nothing.

I took the scenic route to the restaurant, over the bridge toward Upper Main Street, jolted by the sight of a couple patrol cars parked near the terrace, home of the General Elijah Abner statue—where this whole mess had begun. Unaffected by the police presence, the old general sat poised on horseback, facing south, overlooking the lower basin. The officers looked to be keeping him safe.

Ridgeton isn't a big city. A Target, a Walmart, some hotels, two small colleges, and a slew of chain restaurants. It had a quaint old town feel to it, where everyone seemed to know a family member or a neighbor or had some sort of connection down the line.

I came to a stop at the light, tapping on the wheel, when a car door shut nearby. I jerked around, expecting some Briggs guys catching me in traffic. My mind flashed to our coaches on the field, throwing punches at the guys. All that blood on the grass. I squeezed my eyes tight. Just someone getting in their car. Green light. Sweat rolled down my back. I started driving again.

By the time I got to Sal's, I was ready to go back home. I wiped my face, pulled myself together. I wasn't going to crawl into bed every time I thought back to Friday. I fought off the sinking rock in my stomach and climbed out of the truck before I could talk myself out of it.

It was dark inside the restaurant, the curtains pulled to fight off any semblance of daytime. The smell of bread reminded me I hadn't eaten in a few days. Most of the regulars were sitting around, watching ball games, and drinking beer, talking about what they used to do on the field. Olivia saw me and smiled. She finished up with an order and hurried over.

Usually, the old guys would congratulate me, offer tips and pointers on what they saw in the game. They'd smack my back and tell me to keep it up with the perfect season and all. Today they only half turned before getting back to their beers. No hero's welcome this week, I guess.

Liv came up and nudged me with a small smile. "Hey," she said as she came in for a quick kiss on the cheek. She pulled her hair back and fixed her ponytail, her eyes shifting around the room. She smelled like pizza and lip gloss, not a bad combination. It was how she always smelled when she was working. The apron thingy she kept her straws in had flour on it. Everything was the same, but not.

"Hey."

I wanted to talk to Liv about Friday, see if I was the only one struggling to make sense of things. But Liv seemed busy, distracted, almost aloof. Then again, I'd sort of holed up in the house all weekend. I should have at least called or reached out.

"Sorry I've been kind of out of it since the game."

She shook her head, eyes darting over to one of her tables. "Yeah, that wasn't a game. It was, I don't even know."

"Yeah," I managed.

I heard they postponed Friday's game," she said, changing the subject. Then, starting for the kitchen, as though to rid herself of the conversation. "So, you want your usual?"

"No, I'm good. Thanks."

An order was called, and she went to grab it. Liv moved to Virginia from Florida the summer before our junior year. Shiny brown hair, tan and pretty, I couldn't keep my eyes off her when she arrived at school. We'd smile in passing, until last year, after a game, we met up at a party. She told me she had a secret to reveal. A crush. Ever since, we'd been together in this good-but-not-great relationship where sometimes we struggled to keep things moving.

I found a seat at the window and pulled the curtains open because my chest was tight, like I was suffocating.

Liv laughed, put on a big smile, and made small talk with the regulars as she took drink orders.

Bus Clayton hobbled off of his stool, wiped off his lap, grabbed his beer, and lumbered over to my table. Wonderful.

"Ah, look. Mr. Kumbaya himself," he said as a way of hello.

"Hey, Bus."

Bus considered himself one of those *tell it like it is* types. He played O-line back in the day when the team won two state championships, and he refused to let you forget it. He was cocky as hell, even now when he could barely do more than hobble to the bar for his beer. Normally I put up with him, but I wasn't in the mood for it today, not as he settled in across from me, twirling his beer bottle around.

"Saw your little interview." He nodded toward the TV hanging over the bar.

Liv snuck a glance our way. I wiped my hands on my pants and eyed the door, wishing I was anywhere but here, sharing a table with Bus as he stroked his goatee, smirking through his fleshy cheeks. "Scheduling is a mess. I heard there won't be a make-up date. That right?"

"Think so," I said, picking up a saltshaker. "At least that's what Coach said."

He glanced out the window, chewing a toothpick. "I don't know what this world is coming to. Place was a jungle."

I slid the salt from my left hand to my right, feeling his beady eyes on me, looking for what? Agreement, confirmation, an argument? I sighed. Only a week ago I was welcome here. Now Bus was interrogating me, as though he wanted me to declare my allegiances. I shrugged.

He sat back. "You hear they arrested Gunny?"

I snatched the saltshaker and clutched it tightly. A chill ran through me. "What, a DUI or something?"

He clicked his teeth from within his deep, bushy beard. "Nope. Malicious wounding. They picked him up this morning." He glanced around, snorted, fixed his hat. "You didn't hear?"

I studied the checkered pattern of the vinyl tablecloth, attempting to hide the shock my eyes must have held. That, and the room took a spin. Gunny, up in the stands, waving the flag Friday night. I saw the blood again. Heard Reggie's gasps as he lay crumpled on the field. Gunny did that? I swallowed. "What are you saying?" I tried to get the words right. "Gunny stabbed that guy, Reggie?"

Bus stopped short of sipping his beer. "No. He defended himself, is what he did."

I hoped Jeff was doing okay, his brothers and all. Hoped they were doing better than I was. I wiped the sweat from my forehead.

Bus shifted in his seat. "*Reggie*. Listen to you. What, are you on a first name basis with some crack dealer now?" More head shaking. "Damn shame, back in my day, this would have never happened."

"Amen to that," came the grumbling from the bar. A conversation about old times ensued. Three flannel-wearing guys talking openly about how great it was when they played at Stonewall Jackson High School, as it used to be called.

I withstood the urge to remind them how our fans were hurling trash and insults on the field. They, too, had rushed onto the field looking for someone to hit. But I didn't say a thing as Bus tapped the table, then hobbled back to the bar where they talked about the good old days. It was all I could do to catch my breath.

Eventually Liv arrived at my table, a little out of breath and flushed. "You okay, Ben?" she asked.

I nodded. Still staring off at nothing.

"Okay." Her gaze lingered on me. She raised her eyebrows. "I'm ready to go now."

I left without a word of goodbye to Bus and the boys.

By Monday everyone was talking about "the war" at City Stadium. About Reggie. About Gunny. Who was right and who was wrong.

I'd finally caught my "interview" on the news. It was cringey, my voice was high and my eyes wide and wobbly. I had, after all, just witnessed a stabbing, or the immediate aftermath of a stabbing, but it was hard to watch. I shut down the laptop and hoped it would all just go away.

The local paper had no shortage of letters to the editor. Suddenly everyone was an expert on race relations and the monument and states' rights and reasons. No one offered any solutions on how to come together and try to heal from all this.

Blame was tossed around as two narratives emerged: Stonewall was nothing but racists, or Briggs was a bunch of thugs. From there it only got worse.

Thugs.
Rednecks.
Assault.
Self-Defense.
Us.
Them.

Pick a side, find a reason, shout over the opposition.

Jeff wasn't at school but showed up for practice. He looked

terrible, his face gaunt, peaked, with hollow eyes and slumped shoulders. Instead of sending him home, Coach commended his efforts, said if Jeff could make it, with his dad sitting in a jail, we all needed to pull our weight. Let's do it for Gunny.

At one point, I left the field, found a stall, and threw up my lunch. How could Coach use this as motivation for a football game? And Moose went right along with it, plugging along about how it was all bullshit. It was self-defense. The guy was going to kill him, so Gunny struck first. He'd be out by week's end.

When I returned from the locker room, the team took notice. Coach glared at me as he brought us in. He took off his hat and wiped his brow. "Look, we're going to take it easy the rest of the day, as it's been a rough weekend to say the least. First, I want to get a few things straight. It's been finalized. There will be no make-up game with Briggs. We've decided to let it go, in light of what happened."

The team groaned. I stared at Jeff. His reddish hair sticking out in the back, his splotchy beard long and scraggily. I still couldn't believe Gunny was in jail. I mean, yeah, the guy was a drunk and no stranger to the clink. He liked to talk, but I never pictured him stabbing a guy. I was still hung up on it when I noticed Coach paying close attention to me.

"Like I said on Saturday, if anyone needs to talk, let's talk." He threw his hands out as though it was silly, but he'd entertain it anyway. "Get it out now so we can move on. One last thing, too. We're dedicating this playoff run to Gunny." He let that sink in. "Jeff's family has set up a FundMe page, they're taking donations for his bail. See me or Coach Stinnett after practice if you want to help out."

I looked up. *What?* We're taking donations for Gunny's *bail?* What the hell? Everything was upside down. My stomach turned again.

Coach may have said we were taking things easy, but not by much. He was giddy about a whole extra week of practice, and we got in plenty of reps. Clearview liked to run the option, so the defense worked on taking the edge away. It wasn't happening on my end, my feet were heavy. I was slow, sluggish, like a robot, going through the motions, everything else was weighing me down. *Taking donations?*

The bile sat at the back of my throat. Weren't there rules about that sort of thing? Conflict of interest or something? Would we be considered witnesses? Was anyone going to ask what Gunny was doing on the field in the first place?

After a disastrous practice, I was glad to be back in the locker room, only wanting to pack up my things and get home. Moose and a few of the linemen were talking trash, still hung up on Briggs and how we would have come back and beat their asses. I tried to hurry and pack up my things without being obvious, but all I could think about was crashing in the safety of my bed, when Moose called out.

"Ain't that right, superstar? We was ready to get our licks in on them."

I popped my head up. Moose had taken to calling me superstar ever since the Virginia Tech thing. But never in front of the team like that. Brantley, the quarterback, watched with a dumb smile on his face. I glanced at Logan and Eric, two of the six Black kids on our team, changing out. Eric had his headphones on, bobbing. They were cool, but when Moose started popping off, they usually made a quick retreat.

Moose looked around before he called out again. "Said, ain't that right, Ben?"

His cheeks were flushed like they always got after practice, but his deep-set brown eyes were sharpened and narrowed on me.

I shrugged, shut my locker, then set my arm through a strap on my book bag as I started for the door. I caught Ryan Buckley's eyes. He wasn't smiling, but watching, like he was waiting on my reaction. I threw my hands out. "I don't know, Moose. Probably time we moved on, like Coach said, right? Besides, we weren't looking too good out there."

"Yeah okay," Moose scoffed, looking around, playing it up for his audience. "Not we. You. *You* weren't looking too good out there."

For all his faults, Moose had never called me out in front of the team like that. We were captains, if we had something to say, we did it in private. We stayed unified. Up until now. I wanted nothing to do with this.

I closed my eyes, exhaled, and again turned for the door. I was two steps out when the door swung open, and Moose's heavy strides caught up behind me. "Some captain you're being right now."

I spun around. "Look, man, I just want to get home."

Moose pointed back to the door, to the dented lockers, rust creeping up from the floor as the place hadn't been renovated since my dad went to this school. "There are times you gotta lead, Ben. That's why the team voted you as a captain. You got no problems with it when you're accepting scholarships and raking in all the media attention."

That one got me. I spun around. "What does that have to do with this?"

He shrugged, happy to have landed the jab. "I mean, the team needs you. And if you're not up for it..."

I gripped my shoulder straps to steady my hands. "If I'm not up for it, what? Are you a coach now?"

I tried to hold his eyes, but my head dropped. I needed some time to find out what happened, try to cope with what I'd seen. But they wanted me on the field, being the captain, winning games. Dedicating the season to Gunny. It felt wrong. "Moose. A guy got stabbed on that field."

"Yeah, and luckily Gunny acted first or it would've been him laid out on the field. From what I'm hearing, the dude had a gun on him. That's the part they aren't putting in the papers." He tapped his forehead. "You gotta think for yourself, Ben. You're not getting the whole story."

He moved in closer, using his size to make a point. He was a few inches taller than me, wider. Up close, his freckles were buried beneath the flush in his skin. His black hair was spiked and glistening.

I took a sharp breath and fell back a step. Maybe I was being overly sensitive. I'd known Jeff since grade school. I held my hands up. "I just need to sort some things out, okay? I'm fine. I'll be fine on the field. Damn, you know that."

"Yeah, okay. But not just the field. We need you to be with *us*."

Us. Them. Back in the locker room, it had felt like the walls were closing in on me. Now, the hallway was squeezing me. I just wanted to get home. It was easier to nod. I shrugged. "I'm trying."

"Good to know, Ben." He turned for the door. "At least think how Jeff feels, that is if you're able to think about anyone else at all."

CHAPTER 5

On Tuesday morning, I rolled over, blinked, but couldn't escape the grayish swamp of consciousness clouding over the room. Upstairs, everything was still and quiet because Mom was at work and Parker was at school. I turned the other way and went back to sleep.

I stayed that way until I was jolted awake by the bang of the front door being slammed upstairs. Next came the thud of Parker's book bag hitting the floor, followed by her marching down the hall. I swear, the girl weighed ninety pounds but stomped around like a rhinoceros. I placed my feet on the floor, my legs feeling like noodles beneath my weight as I got out of bed, my mind in a fog as I got dressed and hiked the stairs. I found a place on the couch, where I sat and wondered why I'd bothered.

The TV stayed off, a shiny blank as I had no desire to turn on the news or check my phone. I was fine with doing nothing.

Parker came down the hallway and stopped short. "It's alive," she said, but without much in it.

I rubbed my eyes. "Don't you have debate stuff?"

"Yeah, in a bit. You're taking me." She plopped down on the other end of the couch, tucked her hair behind her ears.

When the afternoon sun hit her face, I could make out the small scar on the bridge of her nose. When we were little, I used to spin her around and around and she'd laugh and squeal until Dad banged into the room and told us to knock it off. One night we didn't knock it off, and she slipped from my hands and hit the coffee table. Three stitches, and I thought Dad was going to strangle me. But it was

Parker who stepped in and said it wasn't my fault, even though it was. You couldn't see the scar anymore if you didn't know where to look, but I still felt terrible about it.

"I heard about Gunny," she said, glancing off.

I nodded. I hadn't thought much about Parker and her friends, what they made of all this. She didn't play sports but did debate and school council and all the other stuff as she was sharp beyond her years. I told her about Coach, the FundMe page, what happened with Moose. Once I started, it all sort of came gushing out. I guess I'd needed someone to talk to.

She sat up straight. "FundMe? For his bail? Are you freaking kidding me? I'll bet every redneck in this town has what, two bucks to pitch in?"

I smiled at her, not for the first time realizing how she was the brave one in the family.

She wrinkled her nose at me. "What?"

"Nothing, it's just, sometimes I wonder where you came from." A quick kick to my leg. "Ouch." Did I mention my sister had a violent streak?

"Same place as you. It's crazy, a guy was stabbed, and here you speak out against it and people act like *you're* the one talking crazy."

"So I guess I don't have to wonder what they're saying at Stonewall Middle?"

Her gaze fell and she shook her head. Told me all I needed to know there.

I dropped Parker off at her friend's house, then went for a drive. I made my way out toward the mountains, the road winding as I came up on Big Island, realizing I was headed for my dad's house. My chest tightened as I came around the bend, the James River glittering in the late afternoon sun. It wasn't like I wanted to visit him—it was never fun. I guess part of me felt compelled to talk to him in person, explain what I'd seen. Or maybe I just needed to get away from Ridgeton.

Over the past few years, as my dad's health continued to decline and he continued to do absolutely nothing about it besides complain, the visits became more like work. They took stamina, patience—a load I wasn't sure I could carry anymore.

It had been two months since I'd seen him. The thought of sitting in his house—shut in and dark, filled with enough cigarette fog to set off a smoke detector, as he sat and watched TV while I waited on the couch and counted the minutes until I could leave—it was something I had to prepare myself to endure.

Past the old church I hung a left, where only a few houses sat submerged in the hills. I pulled up the rutted gravel driveway unannounced, then sent him a text because he didn't like surprises. I knocked and waited because he always kept the door locked. Eventually I heard him shuffling through the kitchen, the way an elderly man would, before he fiddled with the deadbolt.

My dad used to be a big guy, six-two, two-fifty or so, with hands like concrete blocks. But more recently, he looked small to me. He'd stopped eating and took more pills. He'd lost weight, and his skin sort of hung off his frame. His cheeks were sunken, and his shoulders sloped. I knew part of it was that I'd caught up with him in height and I basically lived in the weight room, but it was something else too. A smallness that lived in his eyes.

He peeked out, saw me, then opened the door. "Ben. Hey."

"Hey, Dad."

He gave me a once over, blankly, then opened the door wider. "Here. Come on in."

I slid inside. It took a minute for my eyes and lungs to adjust to the smoke. Dad used to laugh about how great it was to live alone and not have my mom nagging him all the time. But he didn't say that too much anymore.

The house was a mess. Nothing had a place, everything was strewn over furniture and spilling out of the shelves. DVDs and magazines, cartons of cigarettes, cough medicine, prescription pill bottles, lottery tickets, empty two-liters on the brick fireplace.

I cleared off a spot on the wrap-around couch, trying not to look as uncomfortable as I felt. Dad sighed as he fell into place in his lazy chair. Smoke plumed from a forgotten cigarette in the ashtray on the small table at his right elbow. I couldn't imagine anywhere more depressing.

He'd paused whatever old movie he was watching on the TV, and it felt like I was interrupting him. I set my chin on my chest, trying to get my nose into my hoodie as a filter from all the nauseating smoke. If Dad noticed, he didn't say anything, and kept right on smoking.

I rubbed my hands on my lap, eyed the deer head on the wall, scanned the old rifles hung for decoration. Dad said we had family who'd fought for the confederate side. He said it was an honor. He said no one took the time to learn history anymore—it was why they wanted to rename streets and parks and erase the past. Like we were supposed to forget where we'd come from. They didn't understand.

I'd never thought much about it until all the monuments talk.

He hacked for a minute, then sipped his soda. I waited for him to launch into the whole Gunny thing and everything else that was going on with the football team. Instead, he leaned back in his chair with a grunt, picked up the remote and the lighter, and grabbed a new cigarette even as the other one was still burning away. "How's school?"

I shrugged. "Didn't go."

He stopped short with the lighter. I wasn't about to tell him that whenever I tried to sleep, Friday night crept back into my dreams. I saw myself back at City Stadium. There was no game. I was alone on the field, with no one to chase, no one to tackle. Only the monument stood at the fifty, protruding from the blood-soaked grass, honoring the confederate dead.

Dad studied me.

I picked up one of his hunting magazines and flipped through the pages. "I just needed a day off, figured I'd check in with you."

He lit his smoke, took a drag, and then got back to staring at me. I figured he'd say, "Wait until you're in the real world, no days off then," or something like that. At least go on a lecture about school, football practice, how I shouldn't skip, but maybe we were past those things—things like Parenting.

"How's Parker?" he asked.

Flipped another page. "She's good." I shifted. Whatever the reason I came here, it wasn't to talk about Parker. Dad didn't know the first thing about Parker, and it annoyed me when he acted like he did—when he went all tough-guy daddy about what she wore, or who she was friends with, how she ran her mouth—when he just sat out here and did nothing.

"How are things with you?" I said, trying to move on. "Back still bothering you?"

"Yeah, never quits," he said before launching into a cough. He finally noticed that other cigarette and dabbed it out.

He'd messed his back up two years ago at work. I figured he'd have surgery by now, or at least try. Instead, he did this.

"Maybe you should try yoga."

Dad nodded, exhaled a blast of smoke into the room. "Funny. You're a funny kid."

He fell back into the western on television. This is what we did. He gambled, small time, on college football, NFL games. He flipped through the hunting magazines—like he was ever going to climb into a tree stand again. Like he was ever going to do anything but sit there and watch his enormous TV.

It was hard not to stay angry with him for leaving the way he did —even if the last thing I wanted was him back home with Parker and me. Harder still trying to come up with something to say to him. He'd worked at Vera Tech for years. They ran network cables for large companies. I'd been with him plenty of times, climbing into the ceilings, running cables.

He always wanted me to learn a trade. "Better than college," he liked to say. He thought college was for rich kids. But now that I had a full ride to Virginia Tech, I knew he was torn between his pride and principles. He wore a VT hat and told all his bookie friends to watch out when I got there. The thought of him betting on those games made me sick.

He hit a button on the remote. On the screen, a cowboy had barricaded himself behind an overturned wagon, taking on the law. The sheriff demanded he come out of hiding. The cowboy spit on the ground and said he'd be damned.

I thought about how I was hiding, from all sorts of things, recently. My school, my friends. People I'd known all my life. I shivered, thinking I was becoming like Dad, hiding from life.

"There's some pizza on the counter," he said without taking his eyes off the TV.

I wasn't hungry but needed to escape the noxious smoke. In the kitchen I found a stale Sam's Club pizza, the cheese nearly translucent. Even from the other room the TV was loud, with the shootout and all—pretty sure the cowboy was going down.

"So, you heard about Gunny?" I called from the kitchen, debating on a slice of stale pizza. My stomach twisted at the sight of the rubbery cheese.

Dad paused the movie right on our hero cowboy—his teeth gritted as he blasted his way out with a rifle. Dad grunted.

After the other night, it was clear where he stood, but I couldn't help myself, I needed a reason to stand up to him. "I mean, Coach said they set up a FundMe page for his bail. They made him sound like a hero or something."

Dad shook his head. He rattled the ice in his cup, then sipped his soda. The ice rattling took me back. Swish, rattle, sip. That same red plastic pizza cup. He'd done that since I was a baby.

"Sounds like he was getting jumped, from what I read," Dad said finally.

"Well," I said, then checked my voice as I stepped back into the living room. I didn't want to come on too strong. "I mean, Gunny did rush the field with a knife. It wasn't like he was out there just minding his business." I returned to my place on the couch.

Dad shifted his eyes my way, now willing to take the bait. "Well, the guy he stabbed—if Gunny was in fact the guy who stabbed him—he was no angel, either."

"How do you know?" I blurted out, then, backtracking, "Have they said anything about the guy?"

Dad shrugged. "Come on, Ben."

I was still tripped up on the getting jumped thing. I knew for a fact Gunny was not *getting jumped*. No one out there was *getting jumped*. If there was anything I was sure of at this point, it was that Friday night had been a free for all. Not that I was surprised with Dad taking this stance. In a way, I was only getting what I'd wanted.

But Dad wasn't finished. "Then that dumbass was on the news. The superintendent. The one with the bowtie. He called you out, you know?"

He had my attention now. My stomach dropped, and I scooted to the edge of my seat. "Called me out? What do you mean?"

Dad shook his head, rattled his cup of Dew. "You're telling me you haven't seen it?" Mercifully, he stubbed out the cigarette. "He said you had it right. There shouldn't be two sides. That change begins now, after this, or it will continue. Where'd you get that stuff from, anyway?"

"Nowhere. I mean…" I cleared my throat, glanced at the window. Between the smoke and this surprise he sprang on me, I needed some fresh air. "Wait. Dr. Jamerson said that?"

He scoffed. "*Doctor*. Right. And no, he didn't say it, you did. That change stuff. He was talking how the schools are still segregated. Stirring up the past and riling folks up with all his radical, self-righteous talking points. Wants to start a call to action or some nonsense. This is what they do to get what they want. Every damn time."

I sat back and blinked, trying to sift through all the muck he was spewing to figure out his point. "What?"

"Ask me, they're just trying to finish off what they started. What, they didn't get enough of you on Friday? I'd tell him where to stick it if I were you. He's only using you for an agenda. That's what they're doing. I wouldn't be surprised if the whole thing was staged."

That was laughable. But I'd primed the pump for his thoughts and now I was getting them in heaps. I guess I'd goaded him with the hope he'd have something different for once, maybe he'd stumble upon a gem and offer some advice on how to deal with what I'd seen the other night, because ignoring it wasn't working out too well. But in the end, all I got was the usual huffing and puffing. It was all I could do to nod through the rest of his conspiracies and rambling without listening.

Dad continued through his whole "world is a dumpster fire" routine, touching on the president, rigged elections, and even managing to lump in a spiel about gun rights, for a while longer, until we settled back into an aggressive silence. After he got back to the movie, I stayed as long as I could manage, still mulling over what the superintendent had in mind. Maybe I'd check out the news when I got home.

After a while, I stood and asked if he needed a run to the store, considering he hardly drove anymore. He said Gary and some of the guys had made a run for him. I waited a beat, my nose in my shirt, wondering what else there was to say. Seemed like goodbye was it.

I was thankful for the fresh air as I stepped out to the truck. Behind the steering wheel, I stared at my father's small house, relishing the sunlight fighting through all the trees.

An agenda. What did that even mean? I thought we could all use an agenda or something right now. And I couldn't help the swell of pride that found my chest that Dr. Jamerson was "using" me. Not for an agenda, but maybe...an example? For the first time since Friday night, I felt something besides the life-sucking dread that had been sitting on my shoulders.

CHAPTER 6

Moose wasted no time at school on Wednesday. He found me before first period and asked where I'd been, what was up with me, why I was acting so strange. I told him I'd been out to visit my dad and that got him to let up, but then it was more of the captain and leadership stuff.

"Well, I went out to Jeff's last night. His mom has lost it. She was crying and everything, his little brother still asking about what happened. Jeff kind of zoned out. I'm worried about him, man. If they lock up Gunny like this..." He shook his head. "Bullshit, man."

Jeff's folks didn't have much money. His mom didn't work, and Gunny wasn't exactly known for holding down a nine to five. Gunny went days into weeks sometimes without working at all. And when he was working—when he could wake up, get some side work fixing up decks and painting houses—he spent the money down at Sal's drinking beer.

The bell rang, and I turned to leave and gather my thoughts when Moose wiped his face and leaned in. He lowered his voice. "And you need to talk to Parker."

"What?" I whipped to attention, my chest going tight. "What's she got to do with any of this?"

Moose rolled his eyes. "She started a petition to change the name of Stonewall Middle."

I closed my eyes. Of course she'd done that. We needed to have a talk. But for now, with Moose eyeballing me, I only wanted to be alone, away from school.

"I know how she is, but you gotta talk to her."

My stomach was in knots. "Look, just..." I waved him off and started down the hall.

Moose called after me. "We gotta do something, Ben. It's up to us. We're captains."

He's right about that, I thought as I walked away, walked straight outside and to my truck and drove home.

I hopped on the computer and found the interview—the one Dad was talking about. Dr. Jamerson, with his trademark bowtie, sat poised behind a desk, fingers clasped as he spoke to a reporter about the need for unity in our town. A lot of it was the usual PR stuff, clichés and all that, but then came the part where he talked about how I had it right. There shouldn't be two sides. My skin puckered.

"Change isn't easy," Dr. Jamerson said, "but sometimes it takes moments like these, moments of shame and tragedy, for us to start anew."

I was already nodding my head.

MOM CAME RIGHT out with it at dinner. "I'm worried about you, Ben." She glanced at Parker. "Your sister and I think you need to talk to someone."

I looked up from my plate...all the way to the ceiling, took a breath. "Like counseling?"

She turned a knob on the oven, fixed her own plate.

Parker was uncharacteristically quiet.

Mom sat and spread her napkin over her lap, shrugging it off. "It's nothing to be ashamed of, Ben. This is very traumatic."

No doubt about that, but I wasn't ready to talk about it. Or maybe I was, why I took the whole trip out to Dad's place. I couldn't say for sure, but the thought of "seeing someone" made me want to puke. Instead, I tried to change subjects. "So what's going on with you, Parker? How's school?" I shot her my fakest smile.

Parker twisted her napkin. "Huh, oh, not much."

Busted. Parker loved nothing more than to discuss all the things she was doing at school, so when she studied her plate like it had all the answers, even Mom knew something was up.

I cocked my head. "Oh come on, there has to be something. What about, I don't know, any petitions to speak of lately?"

Mom turned to Parker, who set her fork down and wrinkled her nose. Her cheeks flushed as she shot me a glare before turning to Mom. Her shoulders went up as she exhaled loudly. "Well, I think this is a great time to start thinking about a name change."

Mom's eyes went big. "Parker Hoy, what are you up to?"

I smirked, using muscles in my face I hadn't used in days.

Parker shot me a glare before closing her eyes. Another sigh. She looked at Mom. "I'm simply bringing attention to the fact that we have a school named after a confederate general in 2024." She shrugged. "Maybe that should be rectified. But we were talking about Ben, remember?"

Mom's gaze remained fixed on Parker. "I'll get back to you, miss." Then she was back on me. "Ben, what's this about skipping school?"

My smile vanished. So much for that.

I shrugged.

Mom's eyes darted from me to Parker, then back to me again. But it wasn't so funny anymore. Her face was lined and heavy. She was working eight- or ten-hour shifts and dealing with my situation. And while she still looked better than Dad—like ten years younger, at least —sometimes, after a long shift, worrying about everything, well, it was clearly taking a toll on her.

"I'm fine," I said, repeating the mantra, although all three of us knew it wasn't true. I didn't feel like getting out of bed most days. I'd even skipped football practice—unimaginable last year. No, not fine.

"You're sleeping all day," Parker pointed out, nodding to my hardly touched plate. "Not eating. Normally you'd be on thirds by now."

I turned to my little sister. "Thanks, *Mom*, but I said I'm fine, okay?"

Mom pushed around her food. "I feel like you could use a change."

"What does that mean?"

Mom got back to her plate. Dinner went silent.

WHETHER I COULD USE a change or not, Mom didn't demand that I get up the next morning, so I didn't. I was still lying in bed when my phone buzzed with an unfamiliar number.

Spam. I ignored the call. Then it buzzed again. I ignored it. When it buzzed a third time, I took the call. "What!"

"Ben Hoy?"

The voice in my ear was deep and distinguished. Not spam. I sat up too quickly, causing the room to take a spin. Lately it felt like my head was full of mud, and now, as Dr. Jamerson introduced himself on the other end, the mud thickened to concrete. He was plenty patient as he plowed through the small talk while I tried to figure out if this was real life or another one of my washout dreams.

"Mr. Hoy, I've been wanting to speak to you regarding the incident last week at City Stadium."

I rubbed my eyes, got to my feet. Bad idea. I plopped back down. "Okay."

"In person, if that suits you." He chuckled.

A small bloom of panic found my chest. *Call to action. Agenda.* My father's words resurfaced as I opened my mouth, but no sound came.

"Let me be clear, Mr. Hoy. What transpired on Friday night was tragic, make no mistake. But as you said on the news—something that has stuck with me, by the way–is that we have a chance to make some changes."

It should have made me weary, him using those words against me. But oddly enough, as I forced myself up onto my feet and stood in the middle of my messy room, I found my footing as the superintendent said those words to me. It was like the dread I'd been hauling around on my back gave way to something more hopeful. The worry was still there, coming in waves down my neck to my heavy legs, but it was more like pregame nerves.

I thought about how Coach wanted me to put it behind me, how Moose said I wasn't being a leader. Then I saw the blood and the tear gas, heard the screams and the hatred on the field that night. Leading wasn't always easy. I started pacing. Two steps and I spun around. "Okay."

"Okay," he repeated. "Are you free tomorrow?"

Wow. The superintendent was moving fast. I nodded, kept pacing, cleared my throat, and told him I was free. I could meet him in the morning.

As soon as we ended the call, I stared at the wall, trying to make sense of things. Could this help? Was there really something I could do? Maybe not fix things, but...play a part in getting there?

I couldn't say. So I made my bed. I did laundry and cleaned the kitchen—mopped the floor and everything. I spent the day doing yardwork, housework, anything to keep myself busy.

Mom walked in from work, looked around, and asked, "Do I need to take your temperature?"

I told her about the call, talking fast, mumbling, half expecting her to make me sit down and explain it like she usually did when she was confused.

Instead, she wrapped me up in a hug and said, "Maybe this is the change you need."

Parker breezed through the door as we were hugging. She dropped her book bag. "What's going on?"

We told her about the call, and she joined the hug.

Again, it was only a talk with the superintendent. No big deal. But it *was* a big deal. It was the first time I thought about that night and wasn't sick to my stomach.

I didn't sleep much that night, but it wasn't like the other nights. I didn't sweat through my sheets. Instead, I imagined all the things I might say. What he might say. The next morning, I woke up to the alarm and dressed nicer than normal. A button-down shirt instead of a tee. Mom had breakfast ready. I made a plate.

"You look nice, Ben."

I scrunched up my face at her, stuffed half a piece of toast in my mouth before I made it to the table. I laughed at my nerves. I was uneasy, scared, anxious all at once. And still I couldn't talk myself out of going, even when I turned to Mom and asked her what I'd been wondering all night. "What am I doing?"

She took my shoulders. "You're standing up for your beliefs."

Not really, I wasn't. But after everything I'd read, heard, and seen, I wanted to do my best to make sure this didn't happen again. I had to try. And this was a start.

Still, I wasn't stupid enough to think we could get together and sing some songs and fix the town, but what was the alternative? Do nothing? Fight and kill each other? Stay divided until the end? We had to do something.

Mom called the school to approve my absence. She slid me a twenty for gas, pressed a kiss on my cheek. She fixed my collar. "Will you be back for dinner?" Before I could answer, she wiped at her eyes and said, "I'm proud of you, Ben." She sniffled, nodding like she had when I was named all-conference. "So, what about practice?"

"I don't know." My voice was shaky. I cleared my throat. "Right now, I don't even want to be on the field."

The rest didn't need to be said. I'd been playing football since I was six years old, and now I couldn't stand the thought of being on the field. More counseling ammo. And I knew what Mom was thinking. What about my scholarship? Virginia Tech. What would happen if I didn't go to practice, the games? I mean, I already had it, right? But could they take it back? I was wondering the same thing.

And yet, it felt like she was pushing me to do this—whatever I was doing.

Twenty minutes later, I pulled into BD Briggs and found a visitor parking spot like Dr. Jamerson had instructed.

Stepping out of the truck, it was immediately clear I was no longer at Stonewall High. While Stonewall wasn't exactly new, Briggs had been around for ages. The enormous oaks lining the walkway were taller, thicker, with matching brick courtyards on either side. Large columns claimed the entrance to the auditorium, where I spotted Dr. Jamerson waving me over.

I caught some lingering stares as I made my way toward him. A film of sweat hit my head, and I pulled at my tight collar. With measured steps, I did my best to keep my head down and get where I was going.

Taking the stairs, I found Mr. Ferguson, the principal from the game the other night, standing next to the superintendent.

"Mr. Hoy. Thank you for coming," Dr. Jamerson said, coming forward, his hand out. We shook, his grip was firm but not like he was trying to prove anything. He nodded to the principal. "This is Principal Ferguson."

We shook hands too, and after all the nodding and shaking, we looked out toward the curb as students came off the buses. Mostly Black kids, some with headphones, others laughing and clowning around, but I felt everyone taking notice of us. I was thankful when the bell rang and things cleared out, leaving us standing there quietly with the birds chirping and the chilly morning breeze stealing clusters of brown leaves from the massive oaks.

It didn't make me feel better that these two professionals seemed short on words. After a moment, Dr. Jamerson kicked things off. "So, as I said on the phone, your statement on the news, it was quite powerful."

Mr. Ferguson smiled at me.

It felt like a good time to clear things up. "Yeah, um, about what I said. I meant it, at least I guess I did at the moment, but...I don't remember it completely." I looked from one man to the other. "I was sort of stunned, you know? So, whatever this big plan is, I'm not exactly a spokesman or anything. If that's what you're looking for." I stammered to an end, and the two men exchanged looks.

Dr. Jamerson grinned. "I see. Yes, well, you may not remember, but we sure do. And believe it or not, these kids, well, this town, people are looking for leadership at a time like this."

There it was again, the leadership thing. I sighed, gazing out to my truck.

But before I could protest, the superintendent continued. "Mr. Ferguson and I believe your collective peers, and hopefully their parents, will listen to you. You and Devin."

My eyes snapped to him. "Devin?"

Again, they traded looks, small smiles, like this was exactly what they were expecting. Dr. Jamerson nodded, clasped his hands. "Yes, I think both of you are searching for answers. I think it's what we're all searching for today. Hell, tomorrow too."

I raised an eyebrow.

He didn't seem concerned about language. He smiled and gestured to the large doors at the entrance. "Shall we?"

I was still stuck on the Devin thing as Dr. Jamerson held the door. Thinking about how he'd stood across the field on Friday night. My chest went tight, and my legs locked up. I hesitated, wondering if it was in my better interest to get back in the truck and try to make it to school in time to be counted present, go to practice and be a captain. Try to get my life back to my life, get ready for the playoffs. Put this whole thing behind me.

Dr. Jamerson waited patiently. Maybe he saw my struggle, knew I didn't want to put it behind me, to stuff it away and hope it never came back. Just like I didn't want to keep going along with the "sides." Gunny was defending himself. Reggie was a thug. Maybe I wanted to know why everyone was out for blood on Friday. Because nothing had been the same since that night on the field, and this feeling wasn't going away until I tried to do something about it.

So I didn't leave. I followed the two men inside, walking behind the superintendent and slightly in front of the principal, still hearing those words: *you and Devin.*

Inside, the school was old but clean, the tiles worn dull from scrubbing and traffic. Old analog clocks were fastened to the walls. Cherrywood cabinets lined the lobby, and I caught a whiff of the polish used to give them their shine. We came around the bend, past the lockers to the offices, and there he was: Devin Calloway.

He sat hunched over, with his elbows on his knees, on a bench inside the office. When he glanced our way, he jumped to his feet, almost bristling as he pocketed his phone.

I stopped in my tracks.

Mr. Ferguson smiled. "No need for alarm, Ben."

No need for alarm. My thoughts zoomed back to the football field, the chants, the charge of violence in the air. The fans rushing the field. The blood. Devin across the field.

I nodded toward the glass. "So what exactly is going on? Why is he here?"

Dr. Jamerson looked at Mr. Ferguson, whose chest expanded with his deep breath. "Well, Ben. Dr. Jamerson and I have an idea."

"An idea?" My throat became like sandpaper as I started to piece this whole thing together. I saw my dad's disgust, felt Moose's anger, heard Jeff's voice, shredded and hurt. *You and Devin.* No, no, no. Suddenly I felt stupid for driving into town, for entertaining this at all. For not getting in my truck a few minutes ago and letting this whole thing go.

Devin's gaze stayed locked on me. He wore a tight-fitting hoodie and somehow seemed even bigger without pads.

I squared my shoulders, jutting out my chin. I turned to Dr. Jamerson. "Why does it feel like I've been set up?"

"Set up? Huh, well, I suppose you could say both you boys have been set up. Set up to do something big. Sometimes we don't know what we're capable of doing until the moment arrives."

I held my eyes from rolling and wondered where he copped that little nugget.

Call to action.

I looked back the way we'd come. What had I expected, coming here? Suddenly, I thought about Jeff, his dad sitting in jail while I'd come to Briggs to what, talk?

My dad's words shot through my head.

Agenda.

I shook my head. As much as I wanted to help, I wasn't ready for this. There was still time to save myself. I glanced back. "No, I think maybe I..."

Dr. Jamerson stepped toward me. He took my arm. Not forcefully, but enough. "Now hold on, okay."

Mr. Ferguson glanced to the superintendent's hand on my arm. "He's welcome to go if he wants. But Ben, I think you should stay and hear us out. It's why you came, right?"

Mr. Ferguson gazed down the hall toward Devin, who stood waiting for something to happen. "I'll go talk to Mr. Calloway."

I looked down to my scuffed dress shoes on the polished floor. Hear them out. It seemed I got to hear everyone's grievances these days. At Sal's, at school, on the field. What about *my* grievances, my fears and anger? Anger at these two men. At our town and the world in general.

Then, with another quick glance down the hall, I let all that go. I was only angry they'd taken our game from us on the field Friday night.

Dr. Jamerson cleared his throat, nudging me from my thoughts. "Let's take a walk, Ben."

CHAPTER 7

As I followed the superintendent, I stole peeks into the classrooms, once again noticing the mostly Black and Brown faces, some White kids, but a little bit of everything. At Stonewall it was more of a white canvas, dotted with a few Black kids in each class, maybe Latino kids thrown in the mix. It was weird, because only a few miles separated us.

Dr. Jamerson, perhaps sensing my frustrations, rubbed his hands together. "How are you holding up, Mr. Hoy?"

I glanced over my shoulder. "Well, I'm not really sure at the moment."

He nodded with a smile, as though this was fully acceptable and expected. I wasn't feeling very accepted at the moment though, as we continued along, Dr. Jamerson's loafers clicking across the floor as he pointed out the highlights of our tour—the trophy case, the auditorium lobby where Congressman John Lewis spoke a few years ago. The ceilings were higher, and the ornate crown molding gave the place a stately feel. The brick was worn smooth from years of use. It really was a beautiful building.

"You know, this was an all-white school up until 1970. Virginia was not all that eager to desegregate."

"So, where did the Black kids go to school?"

"Oh, down at Williams, it's a middle school now."

He seemed at ease with everything, as though this were some sort of normal conversation. He nodded hello to the occasional custodian or teacher in passing, lecturing me between greetings. "It's where I went. My class was the last one at Williams High. We have a reunion every now and then. Seems to get smaller and smaller every year." He laughed into a wheeze.

I took another sidelong glance at him. His impeccable jacket, the customary bowtie, pants down to shined leather shoes. His gray hair slicked, thin at the top.

We approached the library, and he stopped abruptly. "I'd like you and Devin to meet, Ben."

I smiled through clenched teeth. "We've met."

"Ah, that's right. Signing day. That was a big event around here, wasn't it?"

Big event wasn't the half of it. Every nearby news outlet, even some from Richmond and as far as Virginia Beach came out to cover the story. Technically, it wasn't even signing day, but we'd both committed early, so they set us up on a stage and made it an event as Devin and I shook hands and pressed our shiny hats down on our heads. Both of us were staying in state, going to remain rivals next year, and the year after that. A lot was made of it, lumping us together like that, when honestly, we hardly said a word to each other that day.

Now, under the scrutiny of Dr. Jamerson's pleasant but formidable chestnut gaze, I studied his face. His cheeks were pocked. He had a scar just above his left eye.

I gave up the staring contest and sighed. "So what is the plan exactly? Devin and I talk to our teams? We tell everyone to get along and this all goes away?"

Dr. Jamerson blinked. His smile vanished with a sigh. "Words only get us so far, Mr. Hoy."

Just like that and all the sugarcoating was gone. The strain in his eyes told me he was getting too old for new scars on his face. He glanced toward the library, then motioned for me to enter. I felt I owed him that much, for dropping the Mr. Rogers act if nothing else.

The library was more of the same. Walls lined with books, separated by arched windows with billowing floor-length curtains. Even one of those ladders that slid along for access to the top shelves.

Dr. Jamerson led me to a table near a window. It was mostly empty, being so early. A study group huddled toward the back, giggling and sneaking peeks at phones like they had no idea the school superintendent was in the room. He clasped his hands. "I think you and Devin could reach out; people would listen to the two of you."

My chair squeaked as I leaned back in disbelief. *This* was the plan? I fought not to roll my eyes. Dad was big on looking someone straight on, shaking hands and being a man and all that. I tried to hide my skepticism, but Dr. Jamerson saw through it.

"No, I know, this is not easy, what I'm proposing."

"More like impossible." I was tired of the games and wanted to move things along. "Not only will people not listen, at least not on my end, but I become a pariah. I won't be welcome anywhere."

He nodded. "I want to do a press conference. Have you and Devin Calloway appeal to the citizens of our town. The fans, the adults, maybe talk some sense into everyone. If they won't do it for us, maybe they'll listen to the two of you. They sure turned out for your last thing, the football game. I was hoping we could turn Friday's tragedy into a positive, a discussion, get it all out in the open. Let's use this to build."

I guess I knew it was coming. My gaze fell to the desk. "So, didn't you hear what I said? I'd never be able to return."

"You're welcome to come here." Hands still clasped, he actually grinned.

I tossed my head back to the arched ceiling that needed paint. I thought how scary it would be up there, on the scaffolding with buckets of paint and a roller.

Dr. Jameson waited me out.

I dropped my head. "What you're asking? I can't just leave. I can't…"

I stopped talking, because I did know what he was asking. I also knew Moose and Jeff, Bus and those regulars at Sal's weren't about to climb aboard some little peace train. People like Gunny weren't going to *discuss* this stuff. Weren't going to *build* anything. And how would it look, Devin and me up there, pleading? Were we supposed to hold hands? I'd never be able to show my face again.

Dr. Jamerson didn't miss a beat. "See, Ben, we've come to some sort of place in our society where I need the students, kids if you will, to teach the adults how to behave. What I witnessed on Friday night was a breakdown of civility. But I saw something else too. I saw two players who refused to be pulled into the ugliness. Am I right?"

On second thought, give me the ceiling. It would be a nice place to work, up on the scaffolding, painting in the silent library. Nothing felt real in here. Everything was tucked away, quietly hidden from the real world.

When my gaze came down, I found Dr. Jamerson's confident eyes waiting for me again, as I knew they would be. I quickly looked away.

That night at the stadium, while everything was happening, I'd thought that moment was some kind of secret Devin and I shared as we'd found one another across the field. But now I wasn't so sure. This man sitting in front of me had seen it. Coach Campbell, Moose, maybe they'd seen it too. Maybe that's why they'd been on my case, like they needed me to state my loyalties.

I looked around, took a breath, and considered my scholarship. Sure, I agreed with what the superintendent was saying—and I suppose in a perfect world, I wanted the same thing. But he also needed to hear the truth, and so I took a breath and broke it to him. "Look, it sounds great and all, but it would never work. People aren't going to change their minds. Not the ones I know, anyway."

Dr. Jamerson sat back, regarded the grand library with all the knowledge and history, the weight and musty scent of the written word. When his eyes found me, the mask was off once again. I saw a man who'd seen many things, things you didn't understand simply from reading books. Things a lot worse than what I saw Friday night. "Ben, we need to bring attention to the problem. Will it work? I can't say. But we have to face it. If not you and Devin, then who? Parker and Max?"

Something ruptured inside of me at the sound of Parker's name. My head popped up. I didn't know who Max was, but I never wanted Parker to see anything like I'd seen on Friday. I shifted in my chair and focused on breathing. I told myself he was only trying to recruit me. I'd been there before. With Parker in mind, I chuckled. "You know, speaking of my little sister—she's the one you need." I bit at my thumbnail, then forced myself to stop. "She's started a petition to rename Stonewall Middle."

Dr. Jamerson smiled, nodded his head a few times. "Is that so?"

Wow. I looked away, wondering why I'd let that fly. I couldn't let this guy try to befriend me, then use me for some political movement. "Look, Mr.—Dr. Jamerson, this all sounds good to talk about. Really. But I'm still trying to...I don't know, *process* all this. I mean, my coach wants us to get past it. And not even that, I...my teammate, Jeff. We used to be close. It was his dad that... He's the one in jail. If I do some press conference, I can't go back." I shut my mouth before I said too much. This guy was smooth and easy to talk to, and I'd been dying to talk to someone.

Dr. Jamerson sat back in his chair, rolled his hand with flourish. "Well, again, transferring here is on the table. We can make that happen."

My laugh echoed up to that high ceiling. When I realized the superintendent was serious, my jaw dropped. I closed it and looked away. "You've got to be kidding."

More hand clasping on his end. "I know it won't be easy for you. And the other thing I'm asking of you..."

I nearly fell out of my seat. He really wasn't joking. "Look, I'd love to help, but..."

He came forward, unclasped his hands, and set his palms on the desk. "Okay, I won't push. Give it some thought. If things don't work out, I'm extending an invitation for you to attend BD Briggs High School."

This time the laughter got caught in my throat. "I'll keep that in mind."

The librarian looked over to us, not happy with all the noise. Then again, what could she do? It was the superintendent.

Dr. Jamerson shrugged, as though what he'd asked was perfectly acceptable. "Your mother says you haven't been attending class. I understand. I'm offering you a fresh start."

He wasn't letting this go. "Dr. Jamerson. What about football? Wait, *my mom?*"

Another nod. He stroked his silvery goatee. "Well, you've already got your scholarship."

"We have *regionals*. States. Yeah, Briggs' season might be toast, but we still have games to play. And when did you talk to *my mom?*"

"I'm merely extending an offer. An idea." He leaned forward in his chair. "Come on, we should get back."

We stood, but the superintendent didn't take a step for the door. "Tell me this, Ben. Do you really think any school would pull a scholarship because a recruit stood up and did the right thing? Tried to make a change in his town?"

I rolled my eyes. I'd tried not to be rude, but I had my limits. "Well, Doctor, my scholarship has everything to do with football, so yeah, maybe."

He shook his head. "I don't think so, Ben."

Having gotten in the last word, he started for the door, leaving me to sigh and wonder. Suddenly Mom's advice made more sense. The change I needed. She was in on this all along. I'd come back to that later. Right now my heart was thumping around like it was fourth and one and we needed a stop. Devin Calloway. Me.

How did this happen?

When we arrived back to the office, there he was, DC, sitting with the principal, his backpack beside him. They were smiling, having a casual conversation. It made me even angrier, seeing them all chummy like that.

I tensed up as we walked in. DC and the principal got to their feet. Dr. Jamerson made the introductions.

"Devin, I'd like you to meet Ben Hoy."

Devin's smile faded. His arms were cut with muscle and his chest like a shield. His eyes never blinked as he set out his hand. I took it. We squeezed, neither of us backing down, neither of us looking away.

He had the beginnings of dreadlocks going on, about an inch long all the way around. Must've been new, I didn't remember his hair like that from our big announcement last year. We stepped back and waited for the superintendent and principal to expand on this great plan of theirs.

They didn't. They let us stand there and gawk at each other. I searched Devin's eyes, a light brown, nearly golden in the light. I looked for any signs of the hatred and violence I'd seen on Friday night but didn't find it. Only two ponds of calm waters. A certain kind of strength I envied.

And it was then, as we were locked in on each other, a game day glare, when Devin blinked first. He cocked his head with a smile. "You know we would have won that game, right?"

I opened my mouth to reply but all that came out was a laugh. And then it was like the whole room defused. Everything got lighter. Devin shook his head, and the two older men moved in.

Principal Ferguson gave us both a pat on the back. "Okay, let's get to work."

CHAPTER 8

Leaving Briggs, I ended up downtown, where I parked at the terrace and took the steps, unbuttoning my shirt. In the distance, our river glittered in the midday sun, and as I stood in the shadow of the man on horseback, I had history on my mind. I thought about our town's history, our country's history, and even a little bit of my own history.

When I was little, I used to climb the statue and stand with General Abner, so regal and proud in the late day sun. The stoic, chiseled face of the old general faced south. My dad and grandfather spoke of how gallantly the South had fought. I always took their words as the gospel, never even had to read the plaque. Honestly, though, it had been years since I'd thought about the statue until recently.

The sun was out but the wind brought a chill with it. It felt good on my face, and for the first time in a while it felt nice to be out of bed, without any obligations—except the crazy one Dr. Jamerson had just proposed.

There was some leftover debris from a recent rally. The rallies were every weekend now. Either monument supporters or protestors or both. I thought back to the game, the rage in the stadium that night. I wondered if there was still blood on the field or if it was just something you could mow away.

After Mr. Ferguson went over the details, Devin and I had talked for fifteen minutes or so. I was surprised at his willingness to do the press conference. He thought we could appeal to our sides and try to heal. I told him how Dr. Jamerson had invited me to Briggs, and he smiled, like it wasn't the craziest thing he'd ever heard.

I dropped my head, pulled on my hair as I thought about our short conversation. I'd said I wasn't so sure about the press conference. I needed to sleep on it. Devin said he understood. I needed to be clear, so I told him there was no way I was going to Briggs. He said he figured. We exchanged numbers and didn't get much further than that.

Doing this was social suicide for me. There was no explaining it to Coach or Liv or Moose or, especially, my dad...or anyone else I knew. It would change everything. I'd lose my friends and possibly my scholarship. I'd be giving up on the teammates I'd known since little league. I'd be walking away from what I'd worked for my whole life. Everyone would hate me for it. And yet here I was, about to do it anyway.

I sat off in the shadow of the great monument. Everything kept going back to the post-game interview. My words about change. The words I couldn't take back and were destined to haunt me. Now I had a decision to make.

A family shuffled down the steps, looked up at the monument, and then to the scenic river below. I tried to imagine the statue gone. In a museum. The river would still be there. The town wouldn't change. Another glance up at the general. How were we still fighting this battle?

Dr. Jamerson had already reached out to the TV stations, and they were onboard. The press conference was scheduled for Wednesday. Some time to think on it but not enough. What in the world would I say? Dr. Jamerson was all about stepping up and doing difficult things at difficult times. And as much as I wanted to scoff at that, it was what drew me in, kept me from saying no.

I liked the idea of trying to actually *do* something instead of staying in my corner and keeping quiet. As it stood, everyone blamed everyone else. No one wanted to change their point of view, opinion, stance, and least of all their minds. The superintendent was right. People were acting like children.

With a sigh, I got to my feet, took one last look at the statue, then hiked to the truck and drove around town. As I passed the string of fast-food places, getting closer to home, the press conference seemed to gain weight, pressing on my back until it was crushing me. It seemed less like a good idea and more like a very stupid move.

Sure, Jeff and I hardly hung out. Gunny had been getting worse over the years until I found him unbearable anymore. That said, Jeff and I went back to grade school.

Grade school. Middle school. High school. There had always been this kind of unspoken pride at how we were able to hold our own with the other schools in basketball and football. You could feel it in the hallways after a win, at the pep rallies. And most certainly at the games.

All the former players, the older guys around town, found ways to praise us. When we beat Briggs in basketball one year, the old guys went on and on about old Larry Bird. How if a White kid made a play, he was smart, studied the game. If he got dunked on it was because Briggs was athletic, could simply jump higher. It was always there, this unsaid difference, this tension sitting between the words, between breaths, living in every joke and story passed around.

That was probably the worst part about being *chosen* by Dr. Jamerson. It's not like I was innocent. Sure, I'd never attacked anyone because of how they looked or what color they were, just like I'd never told racist jokes. But all my friends had, and I couldn't remember ever stopping them. Maybe that wasn't as bad, but it wasn't good, either.

All those years. All those practices and games. Turning my back on my team was not something I could just wake up and do. If I did this presser, Coach would lose his shit. Moose and Jeff would never speak to me again. Right before the playoffs.

Driving along, I came up with a plan. I wouldn't do it unless I could convince Coach to support it. It was the least I could do, what I was supposed to be doing—uniting people. I tried to envision the Briggs Coach and Coach Campbell, sitting down like Devin and me, pleading with the good citizens of our town to behave and try to fix things. I was caught up in that scenario when I pulled down our street and saw Coach Campbell's F-150 swallowing up our tiny little driveway.

I nearly ran off the road before I recovered, cursing under my breath as I pulled the truck to the curb. It was going on four, and the tug-of-war in my head came crashing to an end as all my hope, courage, and strength quickly lost out to the fear, guilt, and betrayal pumping through my blood, depriving me of oxygen as I sucked down empty breaths.

Then again, this was my chance to talk to him. I wiped the back of my neck. Maybe we could work it out here and now, although it felt like he'd shown up to bully me, parking in the driveway like he owned it.

I slid out of the truck. Coach spat, adjusted his hat, and squinted in the sun.

"Where you been?" he said, glossing over my button-down shirt. His tone was curt and to the point, commanding, like when we allowed a team we should have smothered to hang around.

"Took a drive." I looked off, determined not to buckle. Normally, I would have stammered and stuttered, kicked my feet and struggled to come up with a reasonable excuse. But this wasn't normally. A new emotion was taking hold: anger. I wanted his support, but the tough guy routine was getting old. Someone had been stabbed on the field. There had been a riot at our stadium, and it felt like our whole town was ready for more. Why couldn't we at least address that for a second?

He glared at me, waiting me out. But I didn't have to answer him. Mom knew where I was, and that was all that mattered.

When it was clear I wasn't saying anything else, he spat again and nodded, as though this were a perfectly good excuse. "We got practice in twenty minutes, thought I'd give you a ride. Go get changed."

A ride. No, thanks. I shook my head and stuffed my keys in my pocket. "Coach, I need to talk to you about something."

"All right, get in," he said, a hand on the door handle.

"I had a talk with Dr. Jamerson. That's uh, that's where I've been."

He jerked his hand from the door like it had shocked him and closed the space between us in a few quick steps. "Excuse me?"

"The school superintendent."

Another step toward me. "Yeah, I know who he is." He set his jaw. His chest moved as he breathed in a few nasally breaths. "Look, Ben, I know last week shook you up some, but we gotta let that stuff go, son. We got five extra practices to get things done. We put this behind us, and we have a good chance to make a run. It's what we've been working toward all season. Since last year."

Since your whole life. He might as well have said it. But I was numb to it now. None of it was getting through to me. Not since I'd seen the blood, Reggie's body sprawled out on the field. Now football, and everything else, took a backseat to my thoughts. All this stuff Coach was saying? How it was like some gift with all the extra practice time? It wasn't hitting on much.

I wiped my brow. "Coach, I really think we should talk about the other night."

His face twitched. Coach was a one-way discussion kind of guy. He spoke, we listened, and that was all. He wasn't here to be a guidance counselor. Tough love and discipline, stepping up and being a man. I was sick of his bullshit.

Standing in my yard, it occurred to me I was going to have this same talk twice tonight, maybe three times including Liv. And even more striking was how suddenly it hit, how fast it came, how sure I felt about what I was doing as I stood before him, kicking leaves around in my front yard. I was going to do the press conference.

Perhaps he saw it on my face, but he took off his hat, wiped his head with his forearm. "Ben, come on, let's—"

I wasn't going to let him drive this time. Not to practice, not this conversation. I needed to say what I had to say. "Anyway, Dr. Jamerson wants me and Devin, Calloway, he wants us to address the media."

If I'd punched him in the face, he would have taken it better. He staggered back, left his hat in his hand as it fell to his side. "I don't really care what he wants."

I shrugged, cleared my throat to hide the nerves in my voice.

He tugged the hat back on and pushed off the truck toward me. I wasn't prepared for the power in his voice. "Damn it. What is he doing calling my players, is what I'd like to know."

I swallowed down the urge to back away, to run off. I did my best to speak steady and sure and look him in the eyes. "I'd like your support. The team's support. I could talk to them, I think we could—"

He scoffed. "I'll be damned." He spun around, inches from my face. "Any of my players go near the media, they're off the team. Is that clear?"

I cleared my throat. "Well, I just think—"

"You *think*. You're not supposed to be thinking about anything but Clearview. Where's your head, Ben? Going over there, hanging out with them like that." He shook his head.

I waited to see if he was going to finish the thought, but he only stared off, face flushed a deep red, breathing through his nose. He was defensive-breakdown-mad. He was Friday-night-mad.

I caught my breath. While I'd known it was a hard sell, I wasn't expecting so much anger, which he directed at me, personally. Again, I tried to keep my voice calm. "Coach, I think—I mean, it might help with things, you know, get it out in the open."

He walked away. "You too, Ben. I mean it. You do this, you're off the team. I even hear that you're talking with *Doctor* Jamerson, any of 'em, and you don't bother coming back, you hear? You go to the media, same. We're a team, son, I thought you knew that."

"Coach, I do know that. But Devin and I could appeal to the town, try to help. Do *something*, you know?"

He started around the truck and stopped, pointing at me like he did the refs when he was good and heated. "Devin Calloway, huh? You know, next thing you two will be holding hands, waving rainbow flags, and chanting Black Lives Matter. I've never in my life..."

Wow. I dropped my head, cleared my throat. "No, I mean... Coach, I'm trying to sort this out. Someone got stabbed at a football game."

"You're damned right. And your teammate's dad is sitting in a jail cell right now, and you're off with a bunch of—"

I jerked my head up, and he caught himself, removed his hat again. His hair was thin and matted to the side so he looked nearly bald. He looked older, scared, but mostly he looked weak.

He quickly reset the hat on his head and took a breath. "You're off with Briggs and that racist superintendent. What the hell is wrong with you, Ben? You got Parker running around like an activist, and you're hanging out at Briggs. What would your dad make of all this? You told him yet?"

Coach bringing Parker's name into things only sealed it for me. I glared at him, my face heating up. And yeah, he'd come undone like I'd never seen before, but if he mentioned Parker again, it was me who'd be undoing him.

He stared me down, mistaking my silence for submission as he turned for the truck. "I didn't think so."

He opened the door. The truck dinged. It was nice, fully loaded. Leather seats and everything. Coach shook his head, turned to me once again, maybe a last-ditch effort as he lowered his voice. "Look, Ben, okay yeah, last Friday night was a lot. But I need you on this team. I need you with *us*, not them. You gotta think about what's next, son."

What's next was exactly what I was thinking about. What about next year? Or the next game with Briggs? What was next for our town? Where did we go from here, after having a brawl on the field where fans were trying to stab—no, not trying, actually stabbing—the other fans? Kill the other side? Maybe someone would bring a gun next time. Did we just wait for more bloodshed on the grass, more questions we'd ignore?

Coach wiped his face. "I know you mean well, but it's a bad idea, okay?"

That blood, shimmering in the lights. The screams, the sirens, the police on the field. The sounds of the bleachers clearing. A week later and it wouldn't go away.

"Okay?"

I couldn't snap out of it. I tried once again, thinking he would support me. I pled with this man who'd taught me the game. "Coach, this is important to me."

The anger flashed back to his face. "Your team should be your priority. You do this, you're gone, got it? Is that part clear?"

I started to nod, but the scholarship stopped me. And I swear he knew what I was thinking.

"You're not done, yet. You think that Tech thing is a done deal? Let me tell you something, you go through with this, and I will personally do everything I can to undo that deal, hear me?"

I cocked my head. "Are you serious?"

He sniffed, got in the truck, and looked me over. "Damn right."

So, this was it. In the middle of the afternoon, as the team was taking the field for practice, Coach was parked in my own driveway, making threats. I thought about football. How much I loved it, playing under the lights for the whole town. And still, maybe it was stubbornness, or anger at him for dragging Parker's name into this, although I hoped it was something bigger, but I turned away from him. The next decision came to me as fast as the first. I might be transferring to BD Briggs. "Well, I guess we're done, Coach," I said, then stormed off toward the house.

"Ben," he called out as I got to my door. Then once more before the truck started and he backed out of the driveway. The tires crunching on the loose asphalt.

And still, it wasn't easy. Part of me, the little leaguer with the big dreams of football glory, wanted to run out there and hop in that truck, get to the field and hit someone. But I didn't, and when I moved to shut the door, I found his face as he shook his head. One last guilt trip for the road.

"Ben, you think about what you're doing. You got a whole team you're letting down."

He was right. I would need to face the team. But if anyone was being let down it was us, the players. We'd been let down by everyone at the stadium that night who thought it was okay to jump the gate, storm the field, and take the game away from us.

And if that cost me my scholarship, I guess I didn't want it in the first place.

CHAPTER 9

I was already in bed, the curtains pulled against the stubborn evening sun, when my phone buzzed. Even as I'd known Dad would call, it didn't make it any easier. I wiped my face, told myself I'd dealt with Coach earlier, why not do this today too? Get it over with.

"Hey, Dad."

"I just spoke to Coach Campbell. Want to tell me what you think you're doing?"

Upstairs, Mom was cooking some sort of meat from the smell of things. Earlier, I'd told her and Parker everything about the press conference, even about Dr. Jamerson's crazy proposal to go to BD Briggs. Again, Mom wasn't shocked, as she'd already spoken to Dr. Jamerson. When I'd called her out on it, she said it was my decision to make and that she'd stand behind me. Parker launched into a hug and told me I was amazing.

I wasn't feeling so amazing as a wave of chills rolled up my neck. I did my best to keep my voice from betraying me. "I figured he'd call you."

Some lung hacking on Dad's end. "Just going to throw it all away."

I slammed the phone down on the comforter, punched and punched and punched the bed. Dad talking about throwing things away. He'd moved out when I was ten and Parker was six. I still remembered the day clearly, how I'd told myself it was no big deal because he spent so much time on the road anyway. Still, Mom didn't leave my side for a month. Nowadays, every once in a while, he figured he'd pause the westerns and call in some parenting. But this was different, him telling *me* what *I* was throwing away.

The phone lay on the bed, unaffected by my muted violence. I considered ending the call, but it was best to get all this over with now. I picked it up and tried my best to remain calm. "Dad."

"No, Ben. Don't *Dad* me. I thought I made this clear when you came over. And then you went straight home and quit on your team? You're a captain, Ben. That means something, thought you knew that. Besides, Jeff is your friend."

"This isn't about football. Or about Jeff. I tried explaining that to Coach, but he wouldn't listen to me. Neither will you."

"I can't say I blame him. This is not how you were raised. Why are you trying to get attention with this?"

"*Wow*. You can't be serious."

"Watch your tone."

The last thing in the world I wanted was attention, but it seemed like no one else cared one way or another about what had happened. I took another deep breath, held it in for a few seconds, and exhaled. I did some more pillow punching and then got back to Dad.

"I'm not trying to get attention. Dr. Jamerson asked me and Devin to come out, to appeal to both sides. We need unity—"

"Of all the stuff I've heard. Come on, Ben. You're being indoctrinated. Why are you stirring things up?"

"Dad. It's already been stirred up. I watched a guy bleed out on the football field. I thought," my throat caught, and I squeezed my eyes shut, "you know, I thought you might be proud of me for doing the right thing."

"For abandoning the team? Everything you've worked for? Hell no, I'm not proud."

I squeezed my eyes again until I saw sparks. It was crazy how when I'd been out to see him, he hardly had anything to say, but now, on the phone, he was all worked up, Mr. Righteous. And then it dawned on me. "Am I embarrassing you, Dad? Is that it?"

"Watch it. You hear me?"

Watch it. Right. Like he would ever get out of his recliner, leave the house, and drive down the mountain to do anything. He didn't even come to my games.

Somehow, through the sparks and pillow punching, I managed to keep my voice level. "Dad, I'm not after attention. Not for myself at least. But on Friday I was playing a football game and the bleachers cleared. Has anyone stopped blaming people long enough to think about that? How we'll remember that night, the fight, the ambulance, all of it—I will at least—for the rest of our lives? I'm trying to—Devin and me both—*we're* trying to, well, I'm not sure yet. But we need help. We need your help. We need parents to look at each other and listen."

Nothing on his end. Then, the flick of a lighter. Dad getting high. A quick hit, cough, then some wheezing. "You're throwing so much away, Ben," he managed between coughs. "You've worked so hard. You could lose that scholarship."

Everything I'd just said meant nothing. "I could've been killed, Dad."

More wheezing. A man who'd decided to hide in the woods and die wasn't going to listen to reason. So I decided not to take his words to heart—or mind them at all. I told him I loved him and ended the call.

Upstairs, I found Mom and Park at the table. Mom pointed to the crock pot. I scooped out a bowl and took my place with them. I stared at the steam rising from the stew. Mom warmed some bread. Maybe they'd heard me talking to Dad, but for once Parker didn't bombard me with information or questions. It was quiet, a much-needed sort of quiet.

"I don't know what to do," I said after a while.

Mom slathered some butter on her bread, thinking before she spoke. "Well, there's no easy answer." She shook her head. "I wish I had better advice for you. I wish you didn't have to go through this, Ben."

"Dad's pissed."

Parker, who wouldn't even take calls from Dad, rolled her eyes. "Pfft."

Mom set her knife down. "Yeah, of course he is." She bit into her bread, probably to keep from saying anything else.

Mom was always careful not to trash Dad around us, but he did a good enough job of trashing himself. My dad, for all the "take responsibility" talk, never seemed to heed his own advice. He was pissed at everything. Mom. Me. Parker. The government. The president. The galactic powers that had forged against him. The world was one big conspiracy.

I stirred my stew. "Coach said he might have my scholarship revoked if I talk to the media."

Two nearly identical faces went atomic with rage. Mom threw down her spoon. "He said *what*?"

Parker made that scrunched up squinting face she was working so hard to stop making in debates.

I rubbed my eyes. "Mom, please."

"Oh no," Mom said, leaping up. I swear, Mom could work ten hours straight and she'd still get up and pace when she was pissed. She had no chill. She whirled around, searching for something in the kitchen. "He can't do that. I'd like to see him try. I'll call up Watson right now."

Watson was sort of like my ambassador to Tech. My go-to guy on all things college. I didn't want Watson to know *anything* about any of this.

"Mom, please. I'm trying to figure out what I'm going to do."

She threw herself back in her chair, fuming. She took five or ten deep breaths before she could talk. "Like I said, I'll support you either way. But I'm not sure I can ever talk to Coach Campbell again. I might smack him, Ben. I'm not lying."

Parker laughed. "Who does he think he is?"

It wasn't hard to imagine my five-foot-three mom marching down on the field and letting Coach Campbell have it.

"You won't have to worry about it," I muttered. "The team'll never take me back anyway. Or the school." I shrugged. "Dr. Jamerson said I could always go to Briggs."

I was half-joking, but Parker lit up. "You should totally go to Briggs."

Mom and I looked at Parker.

She shrugged. "What?"

I laughed. "I'm not going to Briggs."

Parker bit her lip. She looked at Mom, then to me as though she had news she didn't want to break. "Ben, like you said though...if you do the press thing..."

She didn't have to finish. If I did the press conference, I could never go back to Stonewall. Actually, after the blow up with Coach today, even if I stuck it out, went back and told him I was through with Dr. Jamerson and wanted to play, well, who knew what he'd already told the team. It had probably spread through the school by now. Maybe the town. Not sure the fellas would take too kindly to that.

Mom shook her head. "I can't exactly homeschool you."

"Yeah, probably not." I shot her a smirk. "But Parker could."

Parker raised a brow. "I don't know. We'd have a lot to catch up on."

Mom looked up, her eyes sharp. "And what do you mean, 'probably not'? What are you trying to say?"

I shrugged, laughing for the first time in days. "I mean, with work and all."

"Yeah, okay."

It felt good as we laughed at the table. The tension in my jaw, from clenching my teeth on the phone call with Dad, seemed to give way as Parker did her impression of me—which was basically a caveman. Mom followed with her impression of Parker—which was a high-pitched know-it-all. I only sat back, smiling, wishing we could stay right here at the table for a while. Like maybe a year.

The laughter fizzled. Mom focused on me and shook her head. "You know, I never thought it would be this." I opened my mouth to speak but she was lost in thought. "I miscarried once before you were born. So when you came into this world, big and healthy, my goals were clear cut. Easy. Protect you. Keep you safe. That was my number one job."

Parker picked up her bowl and started for the sink. "Here we go."

Mom ignored her, setting down her spoon. Her eyes were glazed over, lost in the memory. I noticed the bags beneath them, the exhaustion she tried to keep hidden away from us. She smiled through it all. "I was always after you, wear a helmet, don't jump off the bed, be careful in the woods. I never, I don't know..." She sniffled, her eyes going shiny. "I never thought it would be hatred that came chasing after you. I thought it would be a different kind of evil, you know? A stranger in a car. Bad guys lurking in the park. You don't think it will be your neighbors. Your own town eating itself, eating everyone in its path."

I swallowed down the lump in my throat. She looked so weak right then, so weary of it all. Who knew what she'd been hearing around town? I'd only thought about what I'd seen or heard, not what Mom was hearing, seeing, worrying about all the time.

But it was no secret. The whole town had witnessed what happened on the field. Sides had been chosen, and somehow Devin and I had been lost in the battlefield before the two sides clashed. The chanting. A stupid statue had caused this? I had my doubts.

I was sick of everyone telling me what they thought. I wanted to do what I knew was right. I guess that's why I looked at Mom and said, "I'm not going to let Dad or Coach scare me out of the press conference. I want to do it now, more than ever."

Parker squealed.

Mom closed her eyes and looked down, perhaps she was saying a silent prayer. When she looked up, she was stronger, still tired, but now with determination as she took a breath and wiped her eyes. She pulled her hair back and smiled. "Okay then, do it."

I craved the cavernous dark of my room, where it soothed out the tightness in my jaw, loosened the wiry stiffness in my neck and the crushing weight on my chest. But I wasn't done with the day. I still had to talk to Liv. The way things were blowing up, she was bound to hear all about it soon enough, and I wanted her to get it straight from me. Plus, I owed it to her to tell her about the press conference face to face.

Mom and Parker pretended not to watch from the window as I backed out of the driveway, until I smiled and waved and shook my head at them as they waved back like dorks.

I pulled into Sal's, wondering what old Bus would have to say as I parked the truck and collected myself. It seemed like this moment had been coming for a while now.

Family Friday's at Sal's meant kids ate free. As I sat in the car, the warmth giving way to the night's chill, part of me still thought this would end up okay, people would calm down and come to their senses. Maybe next year, when I was playing big time football, I'd come back to town and kids would look up to me, knowing I did the right thing. Changing things wasn't easy. At least that's what I believed.

It would have been easier not to go in, not to do this at all. But as I climbed out of the truck, I thought, *I've already lost my team, my coach, my dad, and maybe even my school. Might as well finish it off right.*

With the game postponed, the restaurant was slammed. Entering, I stood amongst the families huddled and waiting for a table. Most of the men wore coveralls, faded and filthy as they'd come from work, while the women with them had loose, frizzy ponytails and bounced babies on their laps as they thumbed through their phones. The older kids fought over the video games that had been there since I could remember. It seemed every parent there looked washed out tired or plain pissed off with the way things were going in their lives. Seemed no one knew what to do with themselves without a high school football game to take their mind off things. Including me.

A few of the older kids gave me head nods and smiles just as Liv scooted through carrying a tray of drinks. With a slight frown, she shot me a look, gone in an instant as she set the drinks at a table. I was trying to think of what to say to her when my good friend, Bus, knifed through a group of women at the salad bar.

"You shouldn't be here," he grumbled. I mistook his meaning at first, and almost took a step back when he cuffed me on the shoulder. "You boys should be kicking some tail tonight," he added. "Got cheerleaders waiting tables. It's Friday night, doesn't make sense."

I exhaled, took a look around. "Yeah, well."

I left it at that. The crooked grin on his face told me he was five or six beers in, easy, as he smacked me on the back. The woman beside us turned to better follow our conversation, while the guy with her tugged at his greasy hat. Every time I came here, I was forced to see my future if I stayed. Working at the factory all day and coming to Sal's to drink. Not judging, but it wasn't for me. I wanted to get out of here and do other things. And I *really* didn't want to do what I was about to do right now.

I nodded at Bus, and he leaned against a post, in no hurry to get anywhere, a toothpick rolling around in his mouth. "I hope ya'll get things right. I want to see you boys bring it all home this year. Especially after last week." With that he came off the pole and leaned in closer, so his shoulder brushed up against mine. His breath stunk of tobacco and Budweiser. "We're meeting up at the monument tonight. Got some things going down. Since you're free, you should come check it out."

It was already hot with all the people crowded in the restaurant, but my face went rashy. Before I could ask what he meant, Liv came over in a rush. "Ben." Her voice was soft, but she didn't lean in for a quick hug like she normally did.

Still, I jumped at the chance to escape Bus Clayton, even though I wondered what exactly was "going down" at the monument.

Liv looked around. "What are you doing here?"

"Oh, I just needed to talk to you." I'd never needed a reason before to come see her. Things were changing too fast in my life. I was struggling to keep up.

She frowned. "I'm kind of busy here."

Wow. I wasn't sure what to say to that. I took a breath. The people waiting made no effort to conceal their interest. I glanced back. "Can we step outside, just for a minute?"

"Okay," she said. Then, turning to the family, in her sweet bubbly voice, "We're cleaning up a booth now. Should be just a few minutes."

The lady scowled. Coveralls said it was fine, just fine.

Outside, the air was cool after being in the stuffy restaurant. Liv picked at something on her shirt. I jammed my hands in my pockets.

"Hey, so, I wanted to tell you before you saw it, but I'm going to be on the news tomorrow."

Her wide brown eyes cut to me. Her eyes had always done me in. How they could be fiery and bright in the morning, or dark and cozy in the evening. But now her eyes were scanning me, searching me, they were as unfamiliar as a stranger's.

"Okay?" she said, meaning, *go on*.

"Well, it's this thing. Like a news conference. Me and Devin—"

She wrinkled her brow. "Who's Devin?"

"Plays linebacker for Briggs, the one going to UVA next year."

Her expression dulled as she watched me silently, waiting for me to explain all of this to her.

"Anyway, Dr. Jamerson and Mr. Ferguson, the principal, thought that—"

"The principal at Briggs?" She said it like she had hair in her mouth. Spat it.

"Well, yeah. We want to try to help. It's actually got nothing to do with Gunny, not directly. I spoke to the superintendent. He called me, really."

She gazed out to the street. I could tell I'd lost her. I could tell by the way she'd said Briggs. How she crossed her arms and looked at me. "Why *you*, though? I mean, what exactly are you supposed to do?

Go over there and hold hands? They attacked ya'll on the football field. What about Gunny?"

A table of four watched from the windows. I shuffled around, kicking at loose asphalt. It had been easier standing up to Coach, or even my dad, this felt like I was tumbling downhill. I'd wanted to do this a bit more gracefully. A car chugged into the lot, the dim lights sweeping over us. "Liv, Gunny was the one with the knife. Our side was just as—"

Her arms flew out. "What are you saying? I mean, is *this* what you came to tell me?"

Her voice broke, and I looked away, wondering all over again why it only made sense to me. "Yeah, I mean." I took a breath, bracing for impact. "I don't want to argue with you about it. I wanted you to know, that's all."

Liv's mouth hung open. She closed it. The door swung open, and two men came out, lighting up smokes. We waited for them to walk to their truck, laughing and talking about nothing.

Liv glanced back at the door, then she turned to me. "I don't know what happened to you the other night, but you're making a huge mistake. Okay? Huge."

"I'm only trying—"

"I can't believe you." Her voice broke again, harsh, lashing me with an anger I didn't know she possessed. "This was *days* ago, and now you're doing some press conference with *them*? Seriously? What did Coach say, Ben?"

I looked at my feet.

"Yeah, that's what I thought." She was getting angrier by the second. She exhaled through her nose as she glanced at the door. "I'm not sure what to make of this right now."

"Liv. This doesn't mean..." *I want to quit us.* I could've said it, but I didn't. "I just, I—"

"Oh and what? You want me to go along with this?" She smacked her sides with her hands. "Act like nothing's happened at school? You know what people are going to say if you do this? If you do this to Jeff?"

It was hard to take her seriously there. Liv was never exactly close with Jeff. She'd always said he was weird, a bit off, strange. Now she was worried about what I was doing to him? I let it go. "Well, that's the thing, I'm trying to get some of our guys involved. I just think if we all—"

The door swung open again. A woman led two kids by their wrists, dragging them to the car. The kids' faces were smeared orange, one had a sucker in his mouth and the other was crying over it. Liv's boss poked his head out, saw her, and hooked a thumb toward the restaurant. "Liv, you got some tables."

Liv went back in character, setting her waitress smile on her face. The smile that brought in the tips. The one she aimed at the men with cigarettes in their mouths. And it was with that smile, her eyes narrowing just enough for me to see, that she left me outside. "*Goodbye,* Ben."

And that's how we left it.

Leaving Sal's, I drove downtown, wondering what had happened and what it meant for Liv and me. Remembering Bus's invitation, I hung a left and turned down toward the monument, where a cluster of pickup trucks and Jeeps were parked on the curb.

Got some things going down.

My heart hammered away in my ears as a quick sweat broke out on my brow. I counted ten, twelve trucks, maybe some more around the side. I worked to control my runaway breathing as thoughts of knives and blood flooded my brain. Everyone I knew had rifles on their wall or hanging in their truck. Things could get worse than a stabbing on the football field. Way worse.

I drove another block before I pulled over. My curiosity won out against the panic, and I opened the door and started up the block, then crept down a few steps toward the monument. I stuffed my hands into the front pocket of my hoodie, leaning into the chilly night as I surveyed the small crowd. Someone was lighting candles at the base of the statue while the others huddled around with American flags, yellow flags, a few confederate flags with the poles resting on their shoulders.

It had a ceremonial feel to it, one I would have felt better about had some of the attendees not had ARs strung over their chests. Others had pistols on their hips. My pace slowed on the steps.

A man dressed nicer than most of the others took his place at the base and spoke about rights. He wore a polo shirt, jeans, and boots, and his accent was just a little out of place as he railed about what was happening in our town. Something about an agenda. About intellectuals. About crooked elections and individual rights. About Gunny.

I pulled my hoody tight around my neck, a chill sweeping over me as the men nodded in unison.

Innocence. Self Defense. Schools. Briggs. How the country was going down the tubes and it was up to them to save it. Gunny was a hero, plain and simple. All of them nodded.

Up the block I spotted a single sheriff's cruiser, idling with the parking lights on.

Seemed like the superintendent wasn't the only one making plans. I rubbed my hands together to get some feeling in my fingers. My feet were numb, and it had nothing to do with the cold.

Dr. Jamerson wanted me to reach out to the community tomorrow. To these people. But from what I could see, they were already set with what they wanted and how to go about getting it. They were armed and organized, seemingly ready for war. And tomorrow, when they saw me up there with Devin, with the principal, I would place myself directly in their sights.

CHAPTER 10

I was really getting to know the walls in my bedroom. I spent another weekend in my room, went through the motions at football practice on Monday, and then skipped both school and practice on Tuesday. I couldn't say if I was avoiding Coach Campbell, Liv, or just the world in general, but I woke up Wednesday morning—the day of the big press conference—to a barrage of text messages. Four from Liv, letting me know my things were in a box on her porch.

My stomach sank. I started to text her back but couldn't string together the right words. For all our differences, Liv and I'd had some really good times. I'd known we weren't going to last forever, but I never saw it ending like this.

But there was no time to get hung up on that, at least not now. I had another text, from Devin Calloway.

> meet me at McDonald's, the one near the library - D

The dull ache in my chest turned jittery as I thought about the men with guns and flags. The press conference took center stage in my head. Was I really going through with this? I slid out of bed and glanced at the text one more time. Seemed like there was no going back now.

Upstairs, Mom was scrubbing the kitchen sink. The sun streamed through the windows, glossing over the counters. At night, the kitchen looked all right, but the sun seemed to highlight every stain and notch, all the scratches and wear. Everything was yellow or brown where it was supposed to be white. The cracks seemed to deepen into the walls, the plaster peeling in places over our heads. Everything was worn from age, but Mom did her best to manage.

I went for the cereal, and she smiled. She rinsed her hands and hurried into the other room only to return with a button-down shirt and tie. "I ironed your shirt last night. Does this one even fit you anymore?"

Only one way to find out. I went to put it on when Parker strolled in and took it from me. "No, eat first, or else you'll make a mess of yourself."

Mom smirked. I rolled my eyes at Parker, but before I could tell her off, Mom took my face in her hands and kissed my cheek. She smelled of comet and fresh laundry. "I'm proud of you, sweetheart. I know this isn't easy, okay?"

The way Mom was smiling, how Parker was joking, holding my shirt as her eyes shined with pride, it hit me hard how they were the only ones who understood. The only two people in my corner right then.

I dropped my shoulders. "Okay, okay. Both of you stop. Let's eat."

Mom backed off. "One last thing. I want you to know that when you're older, you will look back and know you did the right thing. That's what's important. Okay, I'm done, I promise. Maybe."

"Thanks, Mom."

I didn't tell either of them about what I'd seen last night at the monument—the guys with guns and flags. I didn't bring up the whole thing with Bus or even Liv at Sal's. They were too happy, too proud of me. I didn't want to ruin it.

Instead, I listened to Parker's silly jokes and Mom's corny inspirational speeches even after she promised to stop. I slurped down cereal and reminded myself I was doing the right thing. At least I hoped I was doing the right thing.

The McDonald's near the library sat in a semi-circle of rent-to-own businesses, dollar stores, a bank turned smoke shop, and at least three payday loan places. I parked the truck, smoothed down my shirt, and took in my surroundings as I strode through the parking lot toward the doors.

Devin Calloway sat in a booth near the back. Two empty wrappers sat on a tray off to the side. His elbow rested on a legal pad, but his attention was on his laptop screen. He was typing like a maniac.

I hardly recognized the all-district linebacker, the glare of the screen captured in his black-framed glasses. I was wondering if the glasses were prescription or fashion when his head popped up. I nodded and he nodded back. Then he was typing again.

I slid into the seat across from him, waiting for something to happen. I noticed a collared shirt beneath his hoodie, as he seemed content to ignore me while he continued to clack away on his keyboard. His fingers zipped along, sometimes pausing before he backspaced, then his fingers were dancing again. It went like this for two or three minutes, until I gazed out the window to the lot, hoping I'd locked the truck. I checked my phone. I guessed we had some time, but the silence was killing me.

"Homework?" I asked.

He shook his head. His eyes scanned left to right over the screen before he pressed a button. Then he sat back and clasped his hands behind his head. "You ever heard of Alexander Hamilton Stephens?"

I looked around. "What? Well, I mean I've heard of Hamilton."

He shook his head quickly. "No, no." He chuckled. His hands came down and he picked at something on the table, like we had all morning. "*Stephens*. He was the vice president of the Confederate States of America."

For some reason I thought about Coach the other day. "Okay, and..."

He grinned at me, glanced out the window. "So, this dude. He made a speech about how slavery was the cornerstone for the confederate states." Devin glanced down to the laptop. "He said, and I quote, 'The negro is fitted for that condition which he occupies in our system.' And he also said... Where is it? Ah, this one, 'Our new Government is founded upon exactly the opposite ideas; its foundations are laid, its cornerstone rests, upon the great truth that the negro is not equal to the white man; that slavery, subordination to the superior race, is his natural and moral condition.'"

I was expecting a lot of things today. I knew things would get uncomfortable, that it wouldn't be easy, talking about race and culture. But I had no idea what to make of *this*, as Devin grinned at me until I shifted.

He sat back. "I mean, damn, right? Tell us how you really feel, Alex."

"So, is this about our press conference?" I said, then cleared my throat.

Devin laughed. "No, but that would be interesting, right?" He nodded at the laptop again. "This is for a paper I'm writing refuting claims that the Civil War was about states' rights. How? When this guy, the veep himself, calls slavery the *cornerstone* of the confederacy. I mean, busted, right?"

I looked around. "I guess."

Before I could finish the thought, Devin picked up the legal pad. "*This,* is what I'm working on for today."

Last night, and a few times over the weekend, Parker had mentioned jotting down my thoughts, what I wanted to say. I'd waved her off, no need to have some prepared speech. Now I wished I'd listened to her, and while I wasn't about to admit it quite yet, I got the feeling Devin was a lot smarter than I was. More educated at least. Definitely more prepared. Where football had been everything for most of my life, Devin clearly had other interests as well.

My cereal long forgotten, a whiff of breakfast hit my stomach like a punch. Be it nerves or hunger, I sat up and pulled out my wallet to check my cashflow. Seven bucks, I was in business. But before I could get up, he slid a biscuit my way.

"Sausage, egg, and cheese."

"Oh, cool. Thanks." I grabbed the biscuit. "I don't have a speech written."

He looked up with a smirk. "A bit more on Hamilton. He did a few months' time for, you know, warring against his own country. When he was pardoned, he went on to serve in the U.S. House of Representatives. He was governor of Georgia. His bust sits in the capitol building." He tapped the table for emphasis. "Like, right now, as we speak."

I wanted to respond, but nothing came to mind. Finally, I sighed. "I don't know, it's..." I unwrapped the biscuit, went to take a bite but stopped. I figured it was time to ask something I'd been wondering. "Do you feel like your life will improve if the Elijah Abner monument comes down?"

Devin sat back, removed his glasses, the smirk blooming into a full on smile. "You know, I've read a lot about ol' boy. Elijah Abner only owned five slaves. It said that in a book I read. *Only* owned five slaves." Devin cocked his head. "Isn't that nice?"

He wiped the glasses on his hoodie and frowned "General Lee wasn't a fan. Called him the 'bad old man' or something like that. Anyway, after the war, Elijah ran off to Mexico where he wrote his memoirs. When he was pardoned—they all got pardoned, by the way—he returned to Virginia as a crabby old man." He rolled his wrist, waved his hand with flourish. "The rest is *history*..."

His words dripped with sarcasm. Again, I knew better than to mix it up with Devin on this. Still, I opened my mouth to speak but wasn't sure where to go. He watched me, still smiling. When I shut my mouth, he continued, tapping his chin with his index finger.

"So, you ask, will my life improve if they remove the statue of this great man of the cause from our town square? Well, I can't say, but I'm going to venture a guess that it might be refreshing to take a stroll downtown and not have to look at a public monument dedicated to a man who fought for certain peoples' rights to own other human beings—ones who looked like I do." He shook his head, got back to his computer. "But that's crazy talk. I could be wrong."

With a nod, I went for my biscuit. I tried not to think about what Moose would make of me sitting here with Devin Calloway, talking slavery and causes. I took a bite, but I was determined not to concede everything. "So what, we remove all the statues, the history, then what, start over?"

He shook his head, set the glasses back on. "No. We don't, *start over*. Removing a monument dedicated to a general who fought *against* this country isn't erasing history. That history will always be here, trust me on that."

Knowing I would never win a philosophical debate with Devin, I took a more logical route. "Okay, but you know this town. They'll never go for it. And how does it end? The game, what happened and everything. I'm just..." I thought back to what I'd seen at the monument last Friday, whatever they were planning. "People aren't going down without a fight." I leaned forward. "I get what you're saying, I do. Or, I'm trying to, but at the same time, how do we..." I shook my head, stuttering and stammering to a clumsy end.

Devin shut the computer. "Hey, I know, I get it. You're trying, though. Otherwise, I wouldn't even... I'm not naïve enough to think we can change our town or our country in one day. But what else do we have? I'm guessing most of your friends want to fight to keep those monuments standing, right? Think they're losing something. Just like everyone *I* know is ready to fight to see them come down. What we saw at the stadium was the absolute worst in people. So that leaves us, you and me, to sit here and come up with a way to change—or try to change—minds, perceptions, traditions. Do I know it will work? Hell no."

I set myself back in the seat. "Damn, man. We had one more year to get through this, and then we were out of here. Oh, and after today? Well, I might be off my team, out of a school. I could lose my scholarship."

He gave that some thought. "I don't know what to say about that.

Our season is done. But I can't imagine them pulling your scholarship, not for this."

I looked up. "That's the thing, though. What seems right, at least to us, feels like a threat to some people."

Devin smiled. "You remember last time we were on the news? I mean, not the last time. But our little early signing day?"

I wiped my face, nodding. The conference center up the road was deemed a neutral site for two hometown heroes, as they called us. Mom, Park, my dad, and Coach were there. Only, when it happened, and Devin's friends and family took one side of the room, mine on the other, it wasn't the best look for our town.

"Remember that one reporter wrote something about it?" Devin tilted his head. "It was the first time I thought about it, like, really. How we were the same, right? Both of us from this little town, same age and all, same position, but we might as well have been across the country from each other."

"The sides."

His smile fell. "Huh?" Devin looked at me head on, his brown eyes intense and searching. He had a tiny scar on the bridge of his nose.

I shrugged. "The sides. Your side and my side."

He nodded, as though realizing something. "Yeah. I don't think we even spoke to each other. I mean, separate but equal and all."

I sat back and looked out the window at some people milling around outside the library. Some looked rough, with trash bags and shopping carts. My part of town was rough too, but in a different way.

Separate but equal.

"Hey, so I always wanted to ask. Why Virginia? Is it because you knew you couldn't get on the field at Tech, with me going there?"

His eyes widened with his smile. "Yeah, okay. You should be thanking me. But no, I'm going pre-law, and according to the U-BLSA—"

"Whoa. The *what*?"

He wiped the lid of his laptop. "Yes?"

"You sort of lost me back there."

"Sorry, so yeah, the Undergrad Black Law Students Association."

"Ah, okay, yeah. Cool."

I planned on going to Tech and playing ball. General Studies type deal. Devin was going to law school. Dude had options. Okay then.

He flipped up the lid and logged in, started typing again like something just came to mind.

I figured we needed to talk about what was coming up. "So what's the plan? We get up there and ask people to be nice?"

"That's exactly what I'm going to do."

I pushed around a balled up wrapper. I couldn't tell if Devin was kidding or not. He wasn't like I thought he'd be, which I couldn't quite define in my own head. He was easy to talk to but then again not at all. He was complicated, smart, and most of all confident. Within one breakfast he'd made me think about things I'd never given any thought. Now, I figured since we were talking, I'd ask something I'd been wondering. "So what would happen if I came to Briggs?"

He glanced off to the side, grinning as he fiddled with his hair, twisting, as though pulling on it so it would grow faster. "So, you *are* coming?"

I quit pushing around the wrapper. "No. I mean, I don't know what's going to happen. My coach is done with me, same for my friends, probably." I stopped, because it sounded like a pity party.

His eyes changed from playful to thoughtful, his mouth closed like he hadn't expected what I'd said. He thought on it for a moment. "Okay, well, I won't lie to you then. In the past couple of days, I've been called a sellout, a punk, an Uncle Tom, and been told I'm acting White. You name it. My coach told me to think long and hard about what I wanted to say today."

"Sounds familiar."

Devin raised an eyebrow. "Oh, so you got called an Uncle Tom?"

"No, not what I..." I noticed his smirk and stopped. "It's just been, everyone thinks I'm a quitter. Quitting on my team."

"Right, with the playoffs and all."

"Yeah, you wouldn't know anything about that, though."

His eyes widened, then a full smile broke out. "Oh, okay. I see how it is. We certainly weren't having any trouble whipping ya'll though, right?"

I shook it off. "Hey, I wanted to ask, about the guy, Reggie? How's he doing?"

Devin let out a sigh. "It's tough to say. Day to day and all. Stable, but not good."

We sat in silence, both of us replaying Friday night all over again in our heads. I wiped my face, sitting up some. "So, I mean, honestly. We go out there and hold hands? Ask people to get along? That stuff never works."

Devin thought about that for a second. "Well, we probably shouldn't hold hands. I mean, I just met you. But no, I get it, man. Mr. Ferguson and Dr. Jamerson, they're asking a lot of us, and while I can't speak for you, it feels like I've been given an opportunity to speak my mind. I can't go through life wondering why I didn't take it."

He tapped his laptop. "I'm doing this either way. I got this little speech prepared, and I'm going up there, and if my team or family or friends can't deal with it, whatever. I'm tired of blaming people."

"Do you blame Gunny?"

"Gunny? Is that the guy who stabbed Reg?"

I nodded.

"Who else *would* I blame?"

"So you *are* blaming people."

He stared at me until I looked away. Lately, it felt like all I did was parrot things I heard. Things from either side. I quoted Dr. Jamerson. Moose. My dad. Coach. Parker. And now, as Devin and I were all set to plead peace to our town, I couldn't say why I wanted to ask Devin if Reggie was a gangbanger or a thug, when really, what difference did it make?

Devin, across the table from me, set both his hands on his head and sighed. "Look, part of me is glad I'm getting out of here, leaving town this summer. Then again, I have a little brother, and I want him to know we tried to fix it. To change things."

"Max?"

He glanced up, surprised. "Yeah."

"Dr. Jamerson, when he was talking to me, used him and my little sister to guilt me into this."

He nodded. "Parker?"

"Yep."

It was crazy how we had the exact same thoughts, only filtered through our own experiences. Our own sides of the table or field. I wanted to change things for Parker. Devin for Max. So here we were. And while I'd never seen the monument as a symbol of oppression or hatred, Devin saw it specifically as that. His thoughts seemed to arrange themselves in stream with his words. The way he spoke what he was thinking reminded me of the way he played football—strong, precise, well executed. Lawyer. Yeah, I was seeing it now.

I plucked at the wrapper on the tray, talking more to myself than Devin. "How did we get here?"

Devin stared out the window again, shaking his head. He wiped his face, then stared at me for ten, twenty seconds. "I told them to call you."

The room spun. "Wait, what? You mean, Jamerson?"

Devin nodded. "Dr. Jamerson, yeah. I said they should reach out to you. I thought you might come. I told him we needed you."

"Needed me?" My father's words hit me. *Agenda.* "Why?"

Devin shrugged. "Because you're White. Because you obviously care, more than anyone else on your team, or at Stonewall, really. Look at it this way, if it's just a bunch of kids from Briggs," he said with a shrug, "nobody cares."

"Wait, because I'm White? Isn't that like, reverse racism or something?"

He laughed. "Yeah, sure." He shifted. "Look, Ben, I'm only being real. If it's just me and Dr. Jamerson up there with his bowtie, people are going to see it and say, there they go again, those Black folks causing trouble." He gestured between us. "But if we go up there together, maybe they'll listen. Some of them."

"Nobody I know."

Four Black guys walked in, saw us, and started for our table. Big guys. Football guys, I could tell by how they moved. Especially the tallest, a dark-skinned guy with the makings of a mustache. I recognized him as the quarterback. He led the way, his eyes all over me.

"What's up, Dev?"

Devin's smile vanished. He tensed, then quickly recovered with a nod to the guy.

The tall guy glanced at me again then turned to Devin. "This your boy? Ya'll doing some community service today?"

It only then occurred to me that Devin was catching heat for this too.

Devin sighed. "Going to try. What about yourself? What are you going to do today?"

The quarterback glared at me. "You know we would have kept stomping ya'll, right?"

I shot him my finest smile, refusing to give him the satisfaction. At the same time, I waited for Devin to say something, to back me up. He was the one who invited me over here in the first place.

But Devin got back to his laptop as the quarterback set his jaw and nodded. "Yeah, you know." He turned to Devin. "All right, Dev, I'll let you and..."

"Ben," I supplied, hoping I didn't look as nervous as I felt.

"Yeah, I'll let you get to it."

A few smirks and uneasy stares as they passed through, but if I was worried about what it might be like to go to Briggs, this little encounter told me maybe it wouldn't be so bad.

When they were gone, Devin started packing up. Almost like he was trying to make a casual retreat. "You drove, right?"

"Yeah."

"Cool, let's get over to the school."

Things were cramped in the truck with the two of us, as we were nearly shoulder to shoulder. Usually, it was only Liv riding with me. Thinking how that would probably never happen again set me back. At Sal's last night. The texts she'd sent. How she had a box of my things for me to pick up. How I still hadn't responded.

If she could see me now.

Devin rubbed his hands together. "You ready?"

I wasn't ready, I was distracted, confused, wondering what I was doing or what was going to happen. I nodded to his backpack on the floorboard between his legs. "I didn't write anything."

"It's cool. Like what Mr. Ferguson was saying, I was going to," he bent down and checked his bag, "I was going to ask people—grown people—to help us make it through this difficult time. I hate that term though, 'difficult time'. I hate clichés almost as much as I hate stereotypes."

I thought about his starter dreads, about him typing away on that laptop. How honestly, I hadn't thought Devin would be this sharp or well prepared, so...ready for this moment. I sure wasn't.

We stopped at a light, and Devin continued hashing over what he wanted to say. "...I mean, a lot of the parents, their whole life has been a difficult time..."

I told myself I was impressed with Devin Calloway—how he spoke, carried himself, prepared—because he was a football player, not because he was Black. Before I could decide whether or not I was lying to myself, the light turned green, and he was talking to me.

"So, we were talking about the scholarship, about you coming to Briggs. You were named all-district last year, right?"

I looked over to him and smiled. "Like you don't know."

He laughed. "We'll see next year, got my eye on you."

"Why, so you can learn something?"

Devin covered his mouth. "Okay, okay. Ben Hoy is coming out of his shell."

I laughed as he pointed to a side entrance, and I pulled into the parking lot. He motioned where to park.

Once I turned off the engine, I looked at him and shrugged. "Honestly, I don't even know what I'm doing here, really."

Devin's smile dropped. "You're doing what I'm doing."

"Yeah? What's that?"

He grabbed his bag, opened the door, and turned back to me. "Trying to be part of the solution. Now come on."

CHAPTER 11

We hiked around the tennis courts toward the side of the gym. Through the double doors we cut across the basketball court where a pickup game was going on. Devin pretended not to hear the ball stop bouncing, as everyone quit what they were doing to stare at us.

We came out at the lobby, to the trophy cases I recognized from my visit. Black faces lined the walls. A couple larger ones under a banner that read, *Briggs Doing it Big* with photos of athletes in the pro ranks or in suits, a headshot of a girl who looked to be an actress or model. Dr. Jamerson himself.

We were almost at the offices when Mr. Ferguson motioned for us to hurry. "Come on, this way, hurry along now."

Devin smiled at me. But Mr. Ferguson wasn't smiling as he ushered us past a sobbing student in the hallway, a nicely dressed lady trying to console her. Mr. Ferguson whisked us into an office and shut the door. He unbuttoned his jacket and nearly fell into his seat.

I glanced back toward the hallway.

Devin spoke for both of us. "What's going on?"

Mr. Ferguson studied his desk. He removed his glasses before he looked up and took us in. "Well, things have taken a turn. Reggie Watts passed away this morning."

Devin's shoulders slumped. His head fell as he let out a long, deflated sigh.

"I thought he was stable?" I said, my voice like an accusation.

Mr. Ferguson wiped his brow. "Yeah, I did too." Then, as though he just noticed I was in the room, he looked over to me. "Well, um,

Ben, thanks for coming. This, this is going to make things a bit more somber, to say the least."

Beside me, Devin found a seat and sunk low in the chair, his chin down, staring at his hands. "Damn."

Dead. So that was it. We'd watched him get killed, basically. For some reason my thoughts raced to Gunny and the more serious charges coming for him.

A quick knock at the door and a lady poked her head in. "Charles, News Six is ready. Do you want me to...?" She glanced at Devin and me.

Mr. Ferguson looked from Devin to me, as though to see if I was still up for this, whatever we were doing. "Mr. Hoy? Mr. Calloway?"

They waited for us, like this entire little plan was hinging on our decision, and for a split second, I thought it might be the perfect escape for me. Then I thought about those words Devin had written, how passionate he'd been about change. I turned to him, and he nodded. I shrugged. "Yeah, I mean, we're...yeah. Might as well go on with it."

Mr. Ferguson's mouth went tight. He nodded gravely, still watching Devin as he spoke to the lady at the door. "Tell them we're ready."

We left the offices and headed down the hallway. I was dizzy with shock, the weight of Reggie's death swallowing my thoughts. Stares followed us closely, and I felt like an idiot, overdressed, stiff, in my button-down shirt. There I was, the whitest White guy in the world in my scuffed dress shoes and wrinkled khakis. Thankfully, I'd left the tie at home.

Devin, in his hoodie and jeans, looked natural, comfortable even, when I knew he was reeling. The news of Reggie's death had landed a harsh blow to his spirits, and now, with the cameras and the crying, this press conference had gone from serious to life or death.

I didn't know what Reggie's death meant for our town. Football. The monument. But I imagined things would only get more explosive. How would I ever return to Stonewall after this? And

Briggs, judging by the cold stares coming my way, didn't seem much better.

We took our seats to the left of the podium. But Devin and I weren't hometown heroes this time. We weren't choosing hats on a table, between Pitt and VT for me, Virginia and North Carolina for him. There were no softball questions coming, no lighthearted ribbing and jokes about who would beat out who for a starting spot, as we grinned and cheesed and gunned for the camera, our stiff new hats with crisp bills sitting before us, smiling for our friends and family.

Separate but equal.

Someone was dead. And we were supposed to change things. Be the solution, as he'd put it.

Dr. Jamerson gave me a curt nod as we sat before the cramped auxiliary room. Three mikes stood at the podium, a tangle of thick cords snaking across the floor, taped down near the railing. A couple of cameras, blinding lights, smart phones all over the place. My eyes adjusted, and I made out the faces in the crowd, people still squeezing in, the two armed officers flanking the doors making room. It was bigger than I'd thought it would be. Especially now, with Reggie Watts dead.

I focused on the back wall. The doors kept opening and shutting as students continued to file in. I jumped when someone coughed. Security, with their stiff necks and buzz cuts, lent authority to the situation. More guards in the back, by way of coaches and teachers, standing by to be sure it was all in order.

Dr. Jamerson fixed his tie and nodded to another well-dressed person. They shook hands. About five minutes of solemn greetings as more students arrived with hard faces and sharp eyes, some clutching book bags, others clutching each other, while I couldn't shake the vision of that girl crying in the hallway.

The superintendent eyed his watch. "Should we get started?"

More nods. Another light flashed and Dr. Jamerson cleared his throat and dove right in. "Welcome, everyone. First, I'd like to offer my condolences to the Watts family. This comes as a bit of a surprise. I visited with Reggie two nights ago, and I was hoping for the best. This tragic occurrence marks a sad day for our community." He paused.

A series of camera flashes hit us, and I pictured myself in the paper.

Dr. Jamerson powered through. "Reggie attended Briggs not too long ago, and while I never met him personally before the other night at the hospital, many here today remember his bright smile, his friendly personality, and his many jokes."

A sudden wail in the audience took me by surprise. I squirmed but tried to do it carefully, gently. Devin hardly blinked as Dr. Jamerson glanced down to his notes. "Reggie's loss highlights what we're doing today. The events on the field Friday night were reprehensible—all around—and prove we have work to do in our community."

Dr. Jamerson's kind and soothing voice seemed to warm the room. It was clear he'd done this sort of thing before, tended to gaping wounds, lending a spark of hope to tragedy. He went on like that for a while, and I sat, stiffly, sweating, all too aware of the cameras, my face, the position of my legs as I gazed ahead, up, down, anywhere but at the faces in the crowd.

Mr. Ferguson took the mike next. More of the same, only he seemed more shaken up, less polished. At this point more kids were showing up. More teachers and admins, clutching cups of coffee and openly weeping. It was standing room only, and the room was hot. I wiped my forehead when I thought no one was looking.

"Now, as we stand here, these two brave men, both linebackers for their respective teams—one from Briggs, one from Stonewall—"

A collective sneering fell over the room at the mention of my school, until Mr. Ferguson shook his head. "No, no. Today is for healing. And what these young men are doing by coming forward today is no easy task. I want you to listen, to hear their pleas and follow their lead. I want the adults, parents especially, to take heed from our children. To start behaving like adults. Enough is enough. Black, White, Brown, we need to work this out. We need to open the dialogue. Now more than ever."

I thought about my dad on his recliner, scoffing as he stubbed another cigarette into his ashtray, coughing, cursing, shaking his head as the principal spoke, veering into cheesiness but doing his best to bring us together. His voice, so deep and cutting, it moved through the crowd, and finally, as he turned things over to us, I couldn't imagine what I must have looked like up there: embarrassed, frightened, uncomfortable at best. Then it was happening, as Devin was summoned to the podium.

He rose to his feet, sniffled, and quickly wiped his face. Some words of encouragement came from the crowd, and suddenly, I was thrust beside him.

With the cameras pinning us down, capturing us for the world to see, Devin turned to me with a slight nod before he set ahead and addressed the mikes, his classmates, the world at large, or so it seemed.

"Well, first off, I'd like to offer my deepest sympathies to the Watts family. Reggie was always cool to me. Sometimes he'd show up at practice and help out. Coach said he was a pretty good ball player back in the day."

I blinked rapidly. Devin hadn't mentioned *knowing* Reggie. Then again, we'd basically met an hour ago. Also surprising was how well Devin carried himself in front of his classmates, even as he was shaken by the news of Reggie's death. Pre-law. Again, I saw it. Collected and calm, he carefully unfolded his prepared statement. With a quick swipe at his brow, he took a breath and glanced over his words.

"Every year, for a month or less, we're taught about the Civil Rights movement. We're told of the brave efforts and the noble sacrifices of those who made it possible for someone like us to attend this school. We learn of the battles fought by Rosa Parks, Ruby Bridges, the fights at lunch counters, Selma. Dr. King's dream.

Desegregation. And well, I guess it's nice to be able to go eat in a restaurant, to be afforded some opportunities my grandparents never had. But I, for one, have loftier goals..."

This was not what I was expecting, which was an appeal to the town, to let us play football peacefully, to honor Reggie. My throat constricted as Devin stopped to some mild applause. I was a little taken aback. Again, I tried and failed to look comfortable, because I wasn't. Wasn't even close to comfortable.

A round of amens and Devin looked off, let his words sink in, then got back to his notes. "What I saw Friday night was not civil, it was not desegregated. And it was not a dream but a nightmare. It was hatred. It was ugly and violent and went beyond any semblance of rivalry."

More murmurs came from the crowd. I locked my right hand on my left wrist in front of me. My throat went dry as I wondered for the thousandth time what I was doing here, if they would ask me to speak. It was bad enough I had nothing prepared, but now my mind was completely void of thought.

"Lately, I've been thinking about my little brother, who was sitting in those stands when the bleachers emptied and our town stormed the field to punch and kick and attack each other, attack *us*. And then, there was Reggie. On the ground, blood leaving his body. It was something I'll never forget."

His composure waned. His chin quivered and he muttered under his breath, dabbing at his eyes. When he spoke again, his voice broke. "What I wanted to know when it was happening, and now, more than anything, is, why?"

After a long pause, Devin found the camera and stared into the lens. "Why? Is it really about some statue dedicated to a lost cause? Or is it something else? Are people afraid to share equal footing with those who look like me?" He let that hang there. Then he shrugged without making any effort to wipe the tears streaming down his face. He choked, cleared his throat, and tried again. "Or was it simply because of football? Was it too much to ask of people to watch a high school football game without leaving their seats to throw a punch? To stab someone. To kill someone? Why?"

By then Devin Calloway had completely unraveled, crying freely and without shame. Mr. Ferguson set a hand on his back. I stared at my shoes. Some noise came from crowd. When I looked up, I saw the football players, the ones from this morning, watching me with blank faces and little movement.

Mr. Ferguson asked if I wanted to share anything.

I stood before the crowd. It was hot. The faces waited for me to follow Devin, to answer the question he left hanging over us. They were both daring and demanding I speak up or speak out. And it was like the game all over again, looking to the Briggs side, an entire side of the stadium rooting against me. I thought about where I lived, the things I'd heard people say when no one was watching.

About Briggs.

About sides.

About politics and hatred.

A million and one thoughts flashed through my head. I plucked out a few of them and tried to find my voice.

"Until Friday night, my whole life was football. I wanted to hit the hardest and make every play. I wanted to be the best, even better than Devin."

No one laughed. It wasn't the time for lighthearted jokes. I was sweating as I looked over to Devin, then glanced down to my knuckles. I thought about Parker watching me and found the strength to keep going. I wiped my forehead on my sleeve.

"Hopefully, Devin and I will meet on the football field again. But Friday, at City Stadium, when the game was taken from us, or before that even, when I felt what was happening—because you could feel it before kickoff—I didn't want to play. I was ashamed. Ashamed of what people were saying. I was ashamed it had gone on for this long, gone this far, gotten to the point that people thought it was okay to shout those kinds of things from the stands.

"But…I'm also ashamed of myself. For every time I laughed when someone said something terrible. I don't know, I just…"

I took a second. The room was so quiet I could hear my heart thudding away in my ears. Again, I fought through the shakiness in my breath, still thinking about all the times I'd been with friends and they'd told a Black joke, or the guys down at Sal's, what they said about White women who dated Black guys. I thought about Gunny and the things he'd said. How our fans brought a confederate flag to a football game. What kind of message was that? How many times had I done absolutely nothing? *Every* time. And I couldn't change that. But I could start now.

And yet, as I turned to the left slightly, thinking how easy it would be to walk, to step out the door and leave the way I came, I caught Devin's eyes.

He nodded. "You got it, Ben."

I squeezed my eyes shut, forcing myself to say what I needed to say without blubbering. Judging by the mood in the room, I would get zero sympathy. Unlike Devin, I wasn't at home, this wasn't my school. Yet everyone hung on the silence, even the football players in the back. I figured I might as well say what I'd been thinking about since Friday night.

"I'm seventeen, and now I've watched someone get killed. Not in a war or an accident, but at a football game. All I wanted to do was play a sport. But it's like everything I've been taught leading up to this was a lie. A story. A means to an end. And I'm sick of it. I'm ready to make my own way, starting with this, right here." I tapped the podium. "I'm done with all that. I'm done with all the hate. The quiet hate, the loud hate. The fear and the rules. Rules *we* never made."

I looked down, away from the cameras. And then, for reasons I'll never fully understand, I took a breath and made a declaration. "After speaking with Dr. Jamerson…I've decided that I'm transferring to BD Briggs, because I'm ready to change opinions, and I'd like to start with my own."

There was no gasp in the crowd. No standing ovation. I made my declaration and backed away suddenly, awkwardly, as it felt like I'd said too much already. Thankfully, Dr. Jamerson swooped in and shook my hand. He looked me in the eye as he cuffed my shoulder.

Devin's hand found my other shoulder. "Welcome to Briggs."

The superintendent nudged me back to my seat, which was good as my knees were about to buckle by the time we sat down to take questions. I was out of breath, sweating, my jaw locked in place as reporters bombarded Mr. Ferguson and Dr. Jamerson.

One asked Devin if he considered me a friend, and Devin grinned and shrugged. He said, "Sure, anyone willing to help is a friend."

The questions continued. They began with a rematch between Stonewall and Briggs of all things, before turning to what they were after—all the racial tension in the counties. Devin was asked if he had any White friends, me if I had any Black friends. I did my best and answered honestly. Devin was still recovering but powered through it, and by the time we walked out of the room, he was going to class, and I was going another way.

Outside, I took a few deep breaths and tried to come to terms with what I was feeling. I wasn't numb. I wasn't a zombie. It actually felt like I'd accomplished something. I'd stood up for what was right, and that was enough to keep me going.

I had no idea what would be waiting for me when I got home.

CHAPTER 12

I was in the parking lot when I realized my phone was buzzing. Six missed calls, a few numbers I didn't recognize. I returned Mom's call, and she picked up on the first ring.

"Sweetie, are you okay?" She breathed hard, like she'd been running.

I grabbed the back of my neck. "Yeah, I'm fine."

Four news trucks sat parked along the curb. A fifth, a box truck, was backing into the auditorium loading dock.

"Okay, good."

"Did you see it?" I asked.

"Yes, I...yes, I did. Are you on your way home?"

Besides being out of breath, Mom's voice was higher, strange. Something was up. "Mom, what's going on?"

"I'll tell you when you get here. Just, be careful, Benjamin, okay?"

Benjamin. That told me all I needed to know. "Okay, but you're kind of freaking me out."

"It's fine. Just get home."

I ended the call and saw I had new text messages. The first one was from Moose.

> Don't ever come back. Ever

I FLIPPED through the local stations on the way back, settling on a talk show. It went to commercial break, then national news. The election. Some reality TV show scandal. Then came the local news.

Devin Calloway and Ben Hoy, opposing linebackers from Friday evening's brawl at City Stadium in Ridgeton, pled their cases with a heartfelt call for peace at a press conference at B.D. Briggs High School this afternoon. This coming on the heels of the news that Reggie Watts, Friday night's stabbing victim, succumbed to his injuries. Full story tonight, only on News6.

It still didn't seem real. Since the game, my life seemed more like something I was watching rather than living. My name on the radio didn't feel like my own. I'd watched Reggie Watts bleeding out on the football field, and now he was dead. Gunny was in jail. I'd just declared on live television that I was going to BD Briggs.

For some reason, I drove past the monument. The sun rained down on me as it reached its peak, flinging light on the trees on the hill, across the river. Another buzz and I checked my phone. A number I didn't recognize. But the message was clear enough.

> You're dead to me.

I should have expected it, but that didn't make it any easier. It didn't help stop my hands from shaking on the steering wheel. It didn't catch my breath as I glanced down to the terrace in passing, where the general stood, soaking up the shiny midday sun.

Homemade signs had been set at his feet. *Protect our Heritage.* I stopped in the road. For years I'd dreamed of playing varsity. From elementary school, middle, all those slogs through practices in high school. I'd never given thought to anything outside of what happened to us, outside those walls, off the field. Now that bubble had been popped, and everything I knew, or thought I knew, was gone. My phone buzzed again.

Time to go home.

I wasn't even out of the truck when Mom bolted from the house, her eyes wild, frantic. She brought me in for a hug. "Are you okay? Where have you been?" Another hug, she clutched me tighter. "Are you okay?" she repeated.

"Mom. I'm fine. What's going on?"

She set a hand on her forehead, her eyes darting around as she tried and failed to smile. Only then did I put it together–the texts on my phone, the fear on her face as she tugged on my arm and started for the door. Seeing her struggling to keep her composure, the way she kept checking over her shoulder to the street.

I stopped and faced her. "What? What is it? Did someone threaten you?"

Her hands trembled. I'd never seen her like this.

"Mom, please tell me what's going on."

"I'll tell you in a minute." She pulled her jacket tight, as though she were freezing and couldn't get warm. Then she reached out for me. "Get in the house."

I did as she said, following her up the porch before my tiny mom basically shoved me inside. "Mom, seriously. I'm not worried about them." But then I thought of her, going to work, coming home late. "Will you talk to me?"

She locked the door, deadbolt too, then took my hand and led me down the hallway, away from the windows. "I don't think it's anything. I got a call earlier. A prank."

My feet went cold. "What call? Mom." I looked around. "Mom, I got some texts. Where's Park?"

"She's at school, Ben. It's not even one o'clock." Her voice shook. She kept reaching for me, touching my arm. "Someone saw you on the news, said you shouldn't be there. They said some awful things."

"Who? Like what?"

The *thunk* of a car door outside got my attention. I scrambled past Mom to find a policeman ambling toward the house. This was crazy. "Mom, did you call the cops?"

She nodded furiously. "Yes, I want this reported."

I recognized the officer approaching. I'd seen him working the games or around town. He was an older guy, maybe in his forties, still rocking the high and tight haircut, but it was graying some. He paused, spoke into his radio, then started for the house, fixing his belt as he approached.

Mom unlocked the door. The officer set his sunglasses on his forehead and nodded with a smile.

Mom took a breath and tried to force a smile on her face. "Thank you for coming out." She opened the door wider, taking an exaggerated look at his badge. "Officer Lewis."

"Call me Dave." He nodded to me as he slid into the house.

Mom fiddled with the curtains. I couldn't sit. My shirt was untucked, and it felt like the walls were closing in, watching Mom act like this. After the press this morning, and now a cop at our house, I was worried about Parker. It was starting to be too much.

Mom offered Officer Dave tea or water, but he declined and went back to eyeing the shelves, taking inventory of the books, the messy dining room table still holding this morning's dishes. Pictures. Eventually he turned to me.

"So, Ben."

"Yeah." I cleared my throat, wiped my palms on my hips. "I mean, yes, sir." I glanced at Mom, wondering why he was starting with me. And I still wanted to know the details about this "prank" phone call that had her ready to join the witness protection program.

"Caught some of the news conference today. Heard it on the radio," he said, a little smirk on his face.

"Oh." I looked to Mom, who kept eyeing the picture window like armed assassins were lurking in the bushes.

With a grunt, the officer sat and crossed his legs. His polyester pants rode up to reveal a blue sock gripping tightly onto the flesh of his pasty white leg. It looked painful.

"So I'm going to run a few things by you, Mrs. Hoy. Speak bluntly, if you don't mind." He spoke to Mom but stared at me. "Have a seat, Ben."

He gestured to our couch as though he were at home. Mom nodded. I lowered myself to the edge of the couch.

Dave tilted his head back, set a hand on his knee. "I wouldn't get too worked up about all this, probably just... I don't think there's much to this threat. People are emotional right now, but it should subside, especially with the playoffs coming up, you know?"

The hairs on the back of my neck rose to attention. It was surreal —Reggie's death, the press conference, now a cop in the house. His thick badge, the officialness of the patch on his sleeve, the gun, holstered but ready—it was hard to focus on anything.

Mom was recovering though, as she cleared her throat and cocked her head. "I'm sorry, but a death threat is a death threat, and I think it should be taken seriously." She looked poised to strike.

Dave nodded. "No. Yes, ma'am. Of course. Of course it should." He gave me a small smile, as though to say, *Women. Ain't they cute?*

He shifted, switched legs. "It's just that, and I hope you don't mind me saying this, because we do take these matters seriously, but" —he uncrossed his legs, leaned forward—"Ben, this whole thing, I'm sure you're shaken up with it." He glanced at Mom. "And I want you to know, you have our full protection under the law. But between us, words have meaning. Actions have consequences, and—"

I turned away from Officer Dave. "When did this happen? The death threat?"

The officer scowled.

Mom's jaw was set, eyes narrowed like she was ready to strangle him. "Earlier. Right after the press conference."

Officer Dave shifted to face me head on. "Now hold on, here. Ben, listen to me. You need to be careful, keep a low profile. No more press conferences, that's all I'm saying. We'll keep an eye out the best we can." He glanced at his watch. "And shouldn't you be at school?"

Mom huffed. "With all due respect, officer, I didn't call you here to discuss the press conference. Are you insinuating *we* are to blame for this? Because it sounds like you're saying because Ben went on that news conference—"

Officer Dave held up a hand. "Now, I'm only stating the obvious. It was an emotional scene Friday, you boys went into a hostile environment, I'm only glad everyone came out okay."

"Well, Reggie Watts didn't," I said.

He glared at me for half a second before he regained his professionalism, only not completely. "Let me tell you something about Reggie Watts. He'd been arrested more than a few times. Do your research. It's public record. Anyway, it goes to my point." He sighed, his face ruddy and gross. "I think we should all just take a breath and—"

"I can't believe this," I mumbled.

Mom cleared her throat, obviously struggling to remain civil. She shot Officer Dave a polite smile, her hands glued to her hips as she nodded to the door. "Well, thanks for coming out. You've done plenty to put our concerns at ease."

Officer Dave obliged, rising slowly, eyebrows arched at Mom like he was expecting her to admonish me. Mom walked over to the door.

He took the hint, tipped his hat like the good old boy he was. "Anyway, we'll keep a cruiser on patrol. But things should simmer down. As long as..." He turned to me, then back to Mom. "We just gotta let things die down."

I opened my mouth to say something else, but it was clear it would do no good. The officer stepped out. I got to my feet as the door squeaked and slapped shut. Officer Dave pulled his sunglasses over his eyes and set off for the car, his radio squawking. He looked left then right, then moseyed to his cruiser.

I looked at Mom. "He's acting like this was my fault."

"Well, he's always been a dumbass," Mom said, entirely serious.

And for the first time that day, I laughed.

Mom spent the next hour storming the house with nervous energy. She flung herself into cleaning, marching from one room to the other, vacuuming, folding clothes, scrubbing things like she wanted to rip them apart. I tried not to think about practice, the text from Moose, the split with Liv, all the new threats I'd received, was still receiving, Reggie's death.

I was all set to crawl in bed when Mom peeked into my room. A mix of tears and desperation to go with the dash of humor on her face. "The middle school called. Seems Parker got into a fight."

I closed my eyes. "Sounds about right."

CHAPTER 13

Mom locked the front door, double checked it, and we hustled to the car. Stonewall Middle sat less than two miles from Stonewall High. We made good time. Mom pulled in with screeching tires, banged over the three or four speed bumps, and came to a grinding stop at the curb.

"Stay in the car," she said.

I shook my head and opened the door.

We found Park in the office, sitting on a bench. She looked tiny with her legs pulled up and her chin tucked between her knees. My steps slowed seeing her puffy eyes. Parker never cried. In the fifth grade, she wrecked her bike and dragged it home where she threw it in the yard and gave it a kick. Hours later she told Mom her wrist hurt. She'd broken her arm in two places.

Mom rushed in the office. "Baby, what happened?"

Parker wiped her eyes with her sleeve. "Nothing, just..." She looked past Mom and saw me. Her eyes widened. "Hey, Ben."

It crushed me, the way she put on a brave face. And it only made it worse that whatever happened probably had something to do with today. Maybe she was defending me.

I came in and hugged her tight. An office door opened, and Principal Marshall, who'd been around since my time, stepped out to greet us. "Mrs. Hoy." He looked at me, no smile. "Ben."

"What is going on? What happened to my daughter?" Mom demanded.

"Please, step into my office." He gestured to his door.

It was clear I wasn't invited. Fine by me, never liked the guy anyway. I sat down next to Parker, who was no longer sniffling but sitting up straight.

"What happened?"

"It's nothing. Stupid people."

"Park."

She shifted in her seat, shaking her head. Strands of blonde hair fell over her face, down her arms. "I can take care of myself, Ben." Then, with a breath, her voice lowered. "I heard about Reggie."

"Yeah," I said, wiping my palms on my lap. "So, this fight..."

"Rodney Milby," she blurted out. "He's a stupid hick. He called you a name—something despicable—and I didn't appreciate it. There, now you know."

"And so you...?"

Park's hair flew from her face, revealing a set of ice blue eyes. "I punched him in the face, okay?"

"Parker. What in the..." I turned my head, trying to hide my smile. Not that it was funny. It wasn't.

Parker was still staring at me. "Trust me. He deserved it."

"Well, now you're probably going to get suspended."

She shrugged, lifted both her legs, and studied her feet. "Maybe I can switch schools too."

I rocked forward, looked back at her. "You heard that part too?"

She rolled her eyes. "It's all people are talking about. Anyway, I was thinking you could talk to Dr. Jamerson?"

"What? No."

"Why not? I make straight A's. Any school would be lucky to have me."

"Not to mention your modesty."

She laughed.

The principal's door opened, and Mom stormed out of the office. "Come on, let's go."

Parker glanced at me, then Mom. "What happened?"

"We'll discuss it at home."

Parker followed Mom. I got to my feet and turned back, where I found Mr. Marshall watching from the door to his office. I shot him a smile and waved. He didn't wave back.

In the end, Park got nailed with a two-day suspension. It would have been more, as it was explained to Mom, but Parker was a star student without a blemish to her record. Mom fumed, huffing about an appeal with the school board as we left the office. Rodney Milby had obviously instigated the incident and her daughter was only defending herself.

Listening to Mom's griping on the way home, Parker probably thought she was off the hook. Back to her old self again, she scooted up between the front seats, hounding me about Dr. Jamerson.

But Mom had her scrubbing the bathroom as soon as we got in the house.

We didn't mention the "prank" call.

My phone stayed busy. The next morning, I received a call from Principal Howard at Stonewall High. He asked how I was doing. When I told him I wasn't doing too hot, he asked if there was anything he could do, which, I wasn't sure how to answer, because it seemed like he should've been making this call days ago. Finally, he got to the point. He saw me on the news and he wanted to meet with me in person.

I figured he was going to try and talk me into staying, to assure me everything was safe. And a small part of me still hoped that was true, that maybe some students, even players, at Stonewall had seen me on TV and decided to speak out. Even after the threatening texts and the awkward visit with Officer Dave, I wanted to believe things weren't too far gone. That besides a few idiots out there, most people only wanted to figure this out. We could have an assembly, air out our grievances and talk about rectifying things. It's what Devin and I were trying to do anyway. So I agreed to meet with the principal during lunch, just the two of us.

Parker didn't share my high hopes. She thought I was out of my mind. But my hope was stubborn, and it clung to me all morning. Strengthened by the familiar sights and smells that greeted me as I climbed the steps and walked into Stonewall High, what I'd done hit me like a punch. For a second, I wanted to follow the murmur of conversations into the cafeteria, take my seat, and be done with it. Then I remembered all the stuff Coach had said about not coming back, the texts from my old friends. My seat at the table was long gone already.

I didn't have time to dwell on it. As soon as I entered the front office, Mr. Howard popped out, motioning for me to come into his office. I glanced at the secretary pretending not to watch us, a few kids out in the hallway pointing and whispering. Maybe Parker was right.

Mr. Howard gestured to a chair as he came around his desk. "Have a seat, Ben."

His face was tight, his gaze level. This wasn't the *my-door-is-always-open* guy I was used to seeing in the hallways. I was no longer the football superstar but a pariah. Whatever I'd hoped this meeting was going to be flushed out of my system when I noticed the box on the floor containing the contents of my locker.

Mr. Howard must have seen the news conference. If I had any second thoughts about going to Briggs, it was clear by this icy reception there was no going back.

I took a deep breath and held it in my lungs, counting it down like Mom suggested. Dad had called last night—we'd spoken three days in a row, a new record—to tell me all over again how what I was doing was reckless, dangerous, and flat out stupid. He said I was throwing my life away. It seemed to be the consensus around Scott County.

Mr. Howard sat down. He actually rolled his neck before settling in with a cold stare. "So, I've been contacted by Dr. Jamerson as well as Mr. Ferguson."

I'd been in Mr. Howard's office a few times, slap-on-the-wrist stuff. Last year, Moose and I hung a banner that read *Beat the*

Flunkies before the game with Plunkington High. But that was nothing, he'd been half laughing when he told us to take it down. Boys will be boys and all. Not today. His face was hard as stone as he picked up a pen, flipped it around in his hand. "You're really going through with this?"

I nodded. "It feels like it's the right thing to do."

His chair whined as he leaned back. He seemed to be considering his words, restraining himself. "The right thing to do," he repeated, mocking me, before he came forward and cocked his head with a bitter laugh. "Well, I shouldn't have to tell you how much of a distraction this has been around here." He tapped on his desk. "Especially to your teammates."

I shifted in my seat. Sure, the box was a clear sign, but still, I wasn't expecting things to go off the rails so quickly. My shoulders drooped, but then I caught myself. I employed another one of Mom's suggestions—thinking about what I wanted to say before I spoke.

"Mr. Howard. A person died on the football field. Some of us are trying to process what happened, sort this out."

He dropped the pen on the desk, fixed a button on his cuff, glancing off. "Look, Ben. I know this was a difficult time. That said, Jeff Giles' father is sitting in a jail cell."

"For murder."

His gaze flicked up to me as his mouth parted, like he could not believe I had the audacity to say such a thing. But I did. I was tired of Reggie Watts' death being treated as an inconvenience.

I forced myself to sit straight and look him in the eye.

His face reddened and his head jerked back with a sharp laugh. "There's a lot of circumstantial evidence. In fact, the team could be called into trial as witnesses."

His jab landed. I tried not to flinch, but I hadn't thought about that. Our team, taking the stand, reliving that night in front of a jury, a judge, Gunny, the town. Mr. Howard watched me take that much in.

I ran a hand through my hair. "Look, Mr. Howard, I want to get past this, really, I do. But I also want to try to prevent it from ever happening again. If this is what it takes to change things," I shrugged, "I'm fine with being a *distraction*."

Mr. Howard set his jaw before he recovered with a nod. "I see. It's a great sentiment. Really. I think your intentions are noble, Ben. Your heart is in the right place. But..." He flopped his hands out on his desk. "This world is complicated. Especially now. To be honest, I don't know how you kids can keep up anymore. All this...social unrest. It's sad, what things have come to."

"I don't know about that. I'm only trying to do what I believe is right," I repeated, glancing at the box, hoping we were coming to an end. "All this, it should be out in the open."

He ignored me completely. "Let me cut to it. I've spoken to your coach. He's under the impression you might make amends with your teammates, perhaps issue an apology, then possibly return to the field tomorrow night."

I lunged out of my seat. "Coach wants *me* to apologize? For what?"

"Have a seat, Ben." Mr. Howard grimaced.

I stayed on my feet, looking around his drabby office, the faded pictures. Old people in brown suits, his family, him with the former superintendent. The guy was a dinosaur. I wasn't about to listen to whatever else he had to say. "Why would I apologize? I've—my family has received a death threat. Why aren't you sending me to guidance? Almost the entire school witnessed a death. How come there aren't any grief counselors here?"

"You know, Ben, when I was younger, my father used to tell me to suck it up. The world is harsh, and—"

Nope. I shook my head in disbelief and grabbed the box. "This is crazy."

"I'm not excusing you, Mr. Hoy."

Mr. Howard stood, and there we were with only his desk between us.

I gripped the box. "You know, Mr. Howard, you're right. The

world *is* harsh. But you *chose* to be a principal. Maybe it's you who needs to suck it up, start doing the right thing. Maybe you should start doing your job."

There was nothing more to discuss. Clutching my things, I marched out of the office.

"Mr. Hoy," he called again as I kicked his door shut and strode down the hallway.

I called Devin that night, because I didn't know who else to call. Other than Mom and Park I had nobody to talk to about what had happened. Besides, Devin was the only person I knew who completely understood. He'd been there too.

He picked up on the first ring. "Ben."

"Hey, man, you getting death threats?"

He laughed. "Right to the point, huh?"

"Sorry, it's been a day."

"Yeah. And I've gotten three. Death threats, that is."

"What's going on, man?"

"I don't know."

I told him about Officer Dave, how he was acting like it was my fault. Then all the stuff Mr. Howard had said at school. Devin didn't sound at all surprised about any of it. I was still going on about my day when I realized he hadn't said a word or hardly made a sound at all.

"Hey, did you even hear what I said? What this cop said to my mom?"

"Ben?"

"Yeah?" I said, running a hand through my hair, pacing. "What?"

"I don't know how to tell you this, but..."

"Tell me what?"

Devin only chuckled. "Get used to it, okay?"

"Used to what?" I asked, a little annoyed that he was still laughing. My face flushed. "Why are you laughing?"

"I know, sorry. It's just...welcome to the cookout, bro."

"What cookout?"

Then he really lost it. "Nothing, it's an expression. But you've left Stonewall. You're going to Briggs. To them you're siding with us. How did you think that was going to work out?"

I fell onto my bed, still thinking about Mr. Howard. I understood what Devin was saying, and yet, I wanted to argue the point. Tell him he was wrong. It wasn't because Briggs was a Black school. It was because I quit the team. It was because Officer Dave was old and lazy and didn't feel like coming out to a death threat call. It was because Mr. Howard... It was because...

"Hey, Ben, though, seriously. It takes guts to do what you're doing."

"Thanks. But you too, though."

"Hey. Did you see Stacey Pendleton, the news lady? I think we should seriously consider an exclusive interview."

"Yeah, I think you're right."

After that we were laughing, talking about football. Devin was hoping Clearview would pull off the upset, saying I should too, now that I was going to Briggs. I told him it was too soon. I couldn't just pull against my team like that. Things got quiet. Until we started talking Stacey again.

"Hate to tell you this, but you got no chance," I said.

"Man, Keesha would kill me anyway."

"Is that your girl? What does she think about all this?"

"Well, she thinks a lot about this. It's sort of complicated. So, who's your girl, the cheerleader?"

"Yeah, well. No." I tried to explain about Liv, how she thought I was throwing everything away, how part of me felt like she was right.

"I can't tell you what to do. I'm still trying to figure that out myself. But I'm glad you've come this far. And from what you said to the press, and after the game, I think you know why you're here."

We ended the call, and I sat back, thinking how the day had sucked like no other. Then again, I was smiling. It was nice to be able to talk to someone who challenged me, made me think, and best of all, made me want to do better.

But my smile dropped as I thought about what I had to do now, which was start over, at a new school, without football, and tell myself that it was going to help, somehow, although I couldn't see how at the moment. Everyone was dug in, set in their beliefs. How would me switching schools ever change that?

Too late now. I'd made my decision.

CHAPTER 14

Liv texted me on Friday afternoon.

> You haven't picked up your stuff

From the way we'd left things the other night, I'd known we were done. Still, it seemed so final. *My stuff.* Just like school, my old life in boxes. It was around five, and I pictured her in the car, outside the stadium. The cheerleaders had to be there early, and this was the last regular season game.

I typed out three different replies and then deleted them. I wasn't sure what to say, and I was about to put the phone down and figure out if I wanted to listen to the game or not when my phone buzzed again. I sighed. I was so sick of explaining myself. Before I knew it, I was calling her.

She picked up on the first ring. "I seriously can't believe you're doing this."

Rubbing my forehead, I took a breath. "Liv. I just want to help."

"Yeah, you're doing a wonderful job. So, what, you're going back on the news? More handholding? Ben, Jeff's dad is probably going to be charged with murder."

How many times could I explain it? "Because he *murdered* someone, Liv. We saw it happen."

"It was self-defense."

A bitter laugh scraped my throat. "No. It wasn't. It was a stabbing."

"Are you serious, Ben? Whose side are you on? You've known Jeff for what, five or six years? He's your teammate."

"And where does that end? What does our playing football together mean in court? In real life?"

"I'll tell you what it means, it means you have your friend's back. You stand up for what is right."

My voice broke. "That's what I'm trying to do, Liv."

"Yeah. I have to go. I'll leave your box on my porch. Please don't come see me at work Sunday. It's probably not safe for you anyway."

A flash of Mom. The death threat. "What is *that* supposed to mean?"

"Nothing." She let out a sigh. Then, her voice went softer. "I'm still trying to look out for you, even if you need to get your priorities straight. Goodbye."

That evening, I lay on my bed with my laptop and browsed through my socials. Bad move. I was being called all sorts of names and most of them weren't good. Scrolling along, I came across a link for the Giles family FundMe page. All kinds of groups were popping up—militia groups, southern heritage groups, new confederacy. Some boosters wanted Stonewall to wear *Stand for Elijah* stickers on their helmets.

And the comments. It started with the *Free Gunny* stuff, but then evolved into weird stuff about conspiracy theories. Some guy with a confederate flag avatar said Gunny should have used his shotgun. This comment was liked twenty-seven times. Crazy. I let that sink in. A comment about gunning down people at a football game was liked twenty-seven times.

A few RIP Reggie comments quickly turned into taunts, which became threats, which slid down a slimy path of humanity where people thought Reggie got what he deserved. Others took it further, saying he should have been strung from a tree. Then, when I thought I couldn't be shocked anymore, someone posted an old creased black and white picture of a smiling crowd gathered around a mutilated body, still with a noose around the neck. The caption read, w*hat they should've done.*

I deleted my account.

My mind spun. My body was restless. I flopped onto my back, but sleep wasn't going to save me this time. I needed to move. I tied up my shoes and hit the trails faster than usual, barreling into the woods, plowing through my thoughts about monuments and history and the vicious things people were saying.

Somewhere I'd heard it called treasonous, naming a school after a Confederate general. But my dad had always preached the *Heritage-Not-Hate* stuff for as long as I could remember. How they were our ancestors, and we should be proud of our past. And it had worked for me until a week ago. Now I remembered what Devin had said about what it meant to him, walking past these statues every day. Men who fought to keep his ancestors in chains. What he'd said about their shadows. My ancestors had come to America seeking a better life. Devin's were *forced* to come here and were still fighting a battle almost everyone I knew was trying to ignore.

The run helped. It felt good to move, and I chugged along all the way to Briggs—my new school—nearly five miles total. But I wasn't done, I hit the track and circled around five or six times until my legs gave out and I had to stop. I climbed the bleachers, gazing out to the strange field. In the distance, I heard the crowd over at City Stadium, where my old team was about to kick off.

The track was maroon instead of blue. The goalposts were white, not yellow and splotched with rust, sagging some in the middle. The field itself was mostly dirt in the center, but with the huge trees breaking into dazzling oranges and yellows, lending shade to the south end, it was a nice view from the stands. The sun dropped into the horizon. Some people walked the track.

I fiddled around on my phone, reading about our news conference, when the squeak of the gate caught my attention as a tall, slender girl entered the track. She wore a thin fitted hoodie, yoga pants. She stretched for a minute before breaking into a run with long, effortless strides that made it look like she was floating.

No longer moving, a chill swept over me as dusk settled in. I watched the girl run for half a lap until I decided it was best not to stare. Instead, I put my earbuds in and tuned into the Stonewall game.

Things were set to kickoff across town. If I took one earbud out, I could hear the band in real time, the crowd in a roar as old Griff Spitz, the radio announcer at WERN, went on about how a big win would be a great way to bounce back from all the "distractions" of late.

Old Griff had been calling games for the Stonewall Rebels for years. And the guy had no problem speculating as to my absence. Between stats, he mentioned how his sources had told him I was suspended for violating policy—not that I'd transferred schools. He did his best to make it sound like I'd flunked a drug test or something.

Coach Campbell had been hush on the situation, but not Griff. He went on and on about my news conference, even hinted around that I was an agitator, trying to stir up trouble. The way Griff saw it, the team didn't need any distractions as they made their push to the playoffs. This team had goals. And even great players could hamper those goals if we weren't unified.

No team was bigger than one player.

I laughed openly in the empty bleacher section. The guy had been spouting off clichés since my dad laced them up, why stop now?

I stared out to the empty field as the captains marched out for the toss. I could almost transport myself there, on the field, as the energy of gameday was still in my bones even if it wasn't in my heart. I rocked back and forth, thinking about Moose and I locked at the elbow in unity as we trotted out to midfield. I could hear it, smell it, feel it.

I was so into it I didn't notice down at the track the girl had stopped running.

She cocked her head and cupped her hands around her mouth as she called up to me. "You okay up there?"

I removed one earbud as Griff was working himself into a tizzy.

Kickoff. Boom. The crowd went wild, a slight delay from the crowd in the distance to the one in my other ear. I fumbled around, took the other one out. "Oh, um. Huh?" What a genius.

The girl shook her head. Even from the bleachers she had a smile that had me smiling back. I stood, started clanging my way down the bleachers, hoping not to trip. "Oh, yeah. I'm just. I'm…"

I stepped off the last bleacher, onto the track, and wiped my forehead, still sweating from my run but now cold from sitting.

She pulled her hair back and fixed her ponytail. She had smooth brown skin and hardly seemed out of breath from her own workout. She had gorgeous eyes, hazel with a hint of amber, although something seemed familiar about them when she squinted at me. "Ben, right?"

I nodded.

She nodded, then stuck out her hand. "I'm Zakia. Ferguson."

I looked around, thought about it for a second.

She laughed, closed her eyes, and nodded. "Yes, as in Mr. Ferguson's daughter. We've actually met before. A while back at a swim meet."

"Yeah? Oh wait, yes. I remember." I'd been dragged to a swim thing for one of Liv's friends. Zakia had killed it. Tall, strong, fluid motions, and not to be a creep, but she had a body that was hard to forget. "Right. You won states last year, yeah?"

She nodded again, one eyebrow cocked with surprise. Some color in her cheeks. "Yeah."

She eyed the earbuds. "Are you…are you listening to the game?" She nodded over my shoulder in the general direction of Stonewall, then shot me a smirk. "I mean, I won't pretend I don't know what's going on, with…that."

"Yeah." I looked at my phone. Now it was my turn to blush. "I just…old habits and all."

Zakia nodded, stepping back. "Well, I'll let you..."

I pocketed the earbuds and laughed. "It's okay, I really, I don't need to hear this."

She looked at me for a second, then gestured toward the track. "Walk?"

"Sure."

We started around the track. Around the first bend, Zakia glanced at me. "So, how are you holding up?"

My steps slowed. I was about to go through the motions, say everything was good, but then, I wasn't in the mood. I didn't have the energy. Besides, she'd kind of said she knew already. "I don't know. I thought I was okay, but..." The crowd in the distance roared again. I took a breath. Nodded in that direction. "It's strange, not being on the field tonight."

"I'll bet it is."

"Were you at the game last week?"

Zakia shook her head. She swung her arms out at her sides before she clasped her hands together. "No. I don't. I don't go to the games."

"Not a football fan?"

"It's not that, it's... I mean, swim, clubs, studying. I sort of need a break after a while, you know?"

That made sense. But then she looked at me with those glittering eyes and small smile, the last of the sunshine at her back. "And some of us, we're sort of, we're boycotting anything to do with Stonewall High, no offense."

I'd been staring off into the distance. Now I took her in. "Really?"

She nodded. "Yeah, I mean, it's not much, but... Why would I want to support a school, or city—a society—that thinks it's okay to honor confederate soldiers?"

"Yeah, I hear you. But...I'm just so sick of it, thinking about race and all."

"Well, again, no offense, but it's easier for some to ignore than others."

Okay, so Zakia wasn't one to hold back. I glanced over to her as we came upon the north end zone.

She put her hands in her hoodie pocket and looked back at me. "So, what are you doing down here? Getting to know your new school?"

"So you know about that too?"

She ducked her head and smiled at me. She really was gorgeous. "Well, my dad *is* the principal and all."

"So, are you like the ambassador?"

"Nope. Sorry, I've got too much on my plate," she said, starting off. "I'm going to run now."

I called after her. "But you'd make a great ambassador."

"I don't think so," she said with a laugh, talking over her shoulder. "Why don't you try to keep up?"

"Oh, um, okay," I said, my lungs burning and my legs like rubber. Another breath, and I took off after her.

CHAPTER 15

I drove down Fifth Street, Parker in the passenger seat, her face glued to the window as she took in the endless line of cars parked along the curb. I had to circle back around and get the truck situated before we hiked down the sidewalk in the general direction of the music. It wasn't quite Christmas-parade packed, but close.

Reggie's funeral service had taken place at eleven that morning, and the news reported a couple hundred people in attendance, including the mayor and some city council members. I didn't go because I hadn't wanted to be a distraction—to use Mr. Howard's term. Besides, I hadn't known Reggie, so I was fine hanging with Park and doing nothing until Devin texted about the gathering downtown.

Now here we were, hiking down to Church Street at three in the afternoon, fighting off the chill as Parker zipped up her fleece and bounced along in stride. While I was a bit uncomfortable, Parker seemed completely at ease. That, and she was just happy to be out of the house as Mom had worked her to the bone all week. Either way, she'd demanded to come with me.

At first, I'd said no, I wasn't so sure about it. Lately, crowds put me on edge, and I had no idea what to expect, showing up here. But my little sister could be quite convincing—and annoying—when she wanted something badly enough.

We spotted Devin near the Freedom Monument. He broke away from what I assumed was his family and approached with a smile. "Hey, thanks for coming out."

Parker didn't wait for introductions. "Hi, Devin. I'm really sorry for your loss."

"Oh, well thank you."

"I'm Parker, Ben's sister."

Devin took her hand, and they shook. "Nice to meet you, thanks for coming."

I didn't have much to say. I gestured toward the crowd, rubbed the back of my neck. "Yeah, it's um, a big turnout."

The mood was upbeat but determined. It was clear by the size of the gathering that a message was being sent. I continued with my secret breathing exercises, did my best to block out the wave of dread threatening to wash over me as I looked around for signs of confrontation.

The chilly air was refreshing, and while I wasn't about to tell my little sister, I was glad she'd come with me. Since the game, my instinct was to avoid people, being out in public, and life in general, and I found myself wincing at every little noise, my eyes darting, searching for trouble. I kept imagining worst-case scenarios.

Devin watched me closely. "You okay?"

"Yeah. Just..." Parker gave my hand a squeeze. "I'm good."

Devin nodded, as though he understood. "It's good here. We're good. Hey, come this way. Meet my pops."

Park and I followed him over to a well-dressed man with a grayish beard. He looked to be in his late fifties, holding hands with a woman who appeared to be the same age. I assumed they were Devin's grandparents, but there was something about the way the woman kept a hand on a little boy's shoulders that seemed motherly.

The man smiled as Devin gestured to us. "Ben, Parker, this is my pops. Pops, Ben and Parker Hoy."

"Hello Ben, Parker." He nodded. "So glad you could join us today."

I shook his hand. With his wool coat, suit, tie, and newsboy cap, he was dressed nicer than anyone I knew around town. He held a strong resemblance to Devin, just grayer. Devin turned to the lady and the kid.

"This is Bibi, my mom."

Bibi was maybe five feet tall, with a tiny head and dainty wrists that made it impossible to believe she'd ever given birth to someone who grew to be as massive as Devin Calloway. She took my hand with both of her own, thanking me. Everyone was thanking me, like I'd done something praiseworthy.

Devin nodded at the little guy. "And this little shrimp is Max."

The boy shrugged out of his mother's grip. "Hey."

Parker smiled at him. "Hi."

They might have been around the same age, but Park was taller.

Devin shot Max a wink. "I don't know. I think she's got you in height."

Max frowned, inching up on his toes. "No way."

Blonde, blue-eyed, and lanky, Parker stood out in the mix. But she was fearless. Never short on words, she was already chatting up Devin about her plans to switch schools as we shuffled closer to the terrace. Devin laughed, trying to keep up with her plan—she had an answer for everything—when a large man took the podium and introduced himself as Clayton Briggs.

"Hello, all. Thanks for coming out. It's a shame that our reason for meeting here today is that a young man was taken on the football field, that we're still fighting battles we've been fighting for way too long now."

It took me a minute to put the name together. "Briggs, like BD Briggs?"

Devin nodded. "His great-grandson."

I turned my attention back to the man.

Devin nudged me. "You know who BD Briggs was?"

"Well, I mean, the school, right?"

Max hopped in place for a better view.

Was I supposed to know who BD Briggs was? I knew the name because of the high school. I'd heard it all my life. I guess I knew BD Briggs was *somebody*, a name from the past I never learned about. I didn't make a habit out of reading historical markers.

Devin popped Max on the head, then gave me the quick history lesson I didn't know I needed. "BD Briggs fought with the union in the Civil War. He kept a journal detailing battles and strategy but also personal accounts in his infantry. It was a glimpse into the life of a Black soldier, what they experienced firsthand in the south. The journal was published after the war. He sold his memoirs for something like five-thousand dollars. Crazy money back then."

"Wow."

"Yeah, wow. It's some little-known history. At least around here."

I zipped up my hoodie. After another quick speech, we all started walking. It felt good to move, even if I didn't exactly know where we were headed. I kept glancing back, checking on Park as we came over the hill. Somewhere in the front section, people started singing a hymn. Low, soulful hums I could feel in my chest, massaging my heart. But I was still thinking about this BD Briggs guy.

"Okay, so how did an escaped slave—"

Devin shook his head. "No, he was born free."

"Really?"

"Oh, yeah. There was this small plantation, right outside of Ridgeton. The owner, Briggs, freed all his slaves just before BD was born."

"How do you know all this?" I felt stupid. I memorized answers for tests, reports. Devin spoke casually, like a guy who didn't have to think about the answer because he knew it. Because he enjoyed it.

He knocked his head back toward his dad. "My pops makes us read. Stuff you don't learn about in school. Likes to say, 'you never know where you're going if you don't know where you come from'. Anyway, my family owns the music store, Cal's Music, down on Main Street, but it's more like a museum dedicated to little known history. At my house, we don't have Black History Month, it's like Black History Lifetime," he said with a laugh.

Cal's Music, on the last block before the bridge. It had been there forever. I'd been there a couple of times. That made sense. "Gotcha. Okay, so how did a school get named after a Union soldier?"

Devin's grin widened. "Ah, now there's the beauty of it. See, back in the day, when it came time to name a Black high school, White people didn't care much what they wanted to call it. From what I've found, he claimed to be a poet or something. They were like, 'Okay, whatever, give the guy a school if it will keep them happy.'"

Max ran up behind Devin and smacked his shoulders, then took off to the other side of the march. Parker giggled and chased after him. A charge of worry set through me, watching the trails of her blonde hair thread through the crowd. But it was nice to see her being a kid for once, so I turned back to Devin.

"Wait, that's it? Just said he was a poet?"

"Yeah." He looked into my eyes. "Nobody cared. Just like they don't care about this." He pointed to the ground.

I wasn't sure if he meant this part of town, this celebration, or Reggie's murder.

Some of the football guys had arrived by then. The mood changed some, and a few of the older men and women, the church going types, stressed how we were there to honor Reggie and keep things peaceful. Peaceful from what, I couldn't help thinking as we began walking.

We curled around Church Street and looped down Commerce, people singing, chanting, people shaking hands and saying hello. Revelers continued to approach Devin and me and thank us for coming out, as though I was somebody. I was only beginning to feel at ease with things—Devin and I were talking about the Stonewall/Clearview game last night, which Stonewall won in a grind, 34-27, but Devin thought they were in trouble come playoffs. I was torn between defending my old team and agreeing with him—when I noticed the sawhorses and police lights.

The powerful chants sent me back a step. My limbs went heavy as I spotted the handmade signs. SELF-DEFENSE IS JUSTIFIED. Two confederate flags. Some others with symbols. A few guys were walking around with ARs strapped around their shoulders.

The air whooshed out of my lungs. My feet dragged to a halt. Devin cursed, and the whole march came to a bottleneck.

Where was Parker? I spun around wildly, bumping into people as I searched for my sister. Some of the older folks sang louder to drown out the chanting. Hymns that gave the march a surge. A push of bodies behind me pressed ahead, determined and defiant. Some of the younger guys in our group were pushing back against the chants, taunting the guys with the guns. It started to feel like things were leading up to a confrontation.

Devin and I stepped out of the way, searching for Max and Parker. My legs flopped like dead weight.

"Parker!"

We yelled after them as we trudged down the hill toward the protests. I thought about Moose's anger, Jeff's empty eyes, and wondered if they were part of the group. Why would they come to a Unity march and start trouble?

As we approached, the chants clashed with the singing, the steady hums against the barking chants. My heart raced, I cursed myself for bringing Parker into this. I wheeled around, knocking into someone. "Park!"

Devin called for Max. We started back, against the current of the procession.

"Parker." My voice broke. I cupped my hands to call out again when she and Max appeared out of nowhere.

Her cheeks were pink from the cold. "Oh my gosh, who called the hick brigade?"

I jerked her arm and clamped down to keep her close. "Keep your mouth shut."

"Ouch." She wiggled away. "Hey, stop it!"

"Park. Stay with me. I'm not kidding."

Parker shot me a glare but stayed close. The local news truck had set up on the curb, licking their chops at the chance for a story. The police set themselves between us, probably waiting for things to escalate again. Park rubbed her arm, grumbling as we approached. Her eyes widened and she stayed quiet. Cold sweat hit my neck and seeped down my collar.

It didn't seem real how quickly things had turned. I stumbled along, my jaw set, but I was struck cold at how my old teammates, friends, and adults who used to treat me like royalty because I was a good football player now looked like they wanted to spit on me. All I'd wanted was to have a discussion.

On the other side of the sawhorses stood a wall of gritted teeth, signs, battle flags. And I kept seeing Gunny's face in the crowd, even though he was locked up in the city jail. I saw what we must have looked like from the Briggs side that Friday night. And they saw me, walking with the enemy.

Max and Parker scooted farther into Devin and me.

Bus and a few of the Sal's regulars called me out. "The hell you doing, Ben?"

"You should be ashamed of yourself, boy."

I faced forward, kept my eyes straight ahead. Max didn't say a word as the four of us marched onward together. I glanced at Devin, knowing he was seeing last Friday night like I was. I set my jaw, kept my chin out, told myself not to look back. But I did. I looked right, just a peek, and I saw Jeff, glaring at me. His eyes were sharp and filled with glazed hatred. He looked like he wanted to shoot me in the head.

Parker stayed unusually quiet. I shouldn't have grabbed her and snapped like that, but I'd never forgive myself if anything happened to her. She knocked against me as I set my hand on her shoulder and we plowed ahead, our circle tightened. My body was heavy and numb as we wrapped back up to circle around.

Devin looked me over. "Keep going, Ben. Keep moving."

I did my best. But behind us, there was a scuffle, as the quarterback—the tall guy I'd met at McDonald's—and some of the football players got into it with the protestors. The few police hanging around were quick to jump in, and after some back and forth, our procession got moving again.

I managed to keep myself together for Parker's sake as we got back to the Freedom Monument—a small concrete stump to represent slave auctions—that had been erected a few years back when talk of taking down the Elijah Abner statue picked up steam. The thinking was if they built one for slavery, they should be able to keep their monument to the general. Everyone would be happy. That was the plan at least.

We were all nervous after the run-in with the counter protestors. Dr. Jamerson took the podium, and after a few quick words about what we'd just seen and walked through, he moved on. He spoke of coming together, then led us in a lengthy prayer. His tone had a relaxing effect as he spoke of hope. I looked around at all the bowed heads, finding it odd to speak of any sort of hope after what we'd just encountered, but before I could look away, he called out, "Amen," and smiled in my direction.

Devin tensed. We exchanged looks as we realized what was happening. That we—Devin and I—were the ones carrying all the weight of that hope.

Sure enough, he amened again and then held his arm out to us. "You see, we have two young men, from separate parts, from different high schools..."

The attention shifted. Every face turned on us with nods and grins.

Dr. Jamerson continued, "They've decided to break this chain of hate. This code that says *we* and *they*. Us vs. Them."

Please don't do this. Not now. This is supposed to be about Reggie.

"They're here with us today, our brightest stars, right amongst us. We should look to them when we lose hope. Because if they can come together, we should take their lead."

Do you have any idea what I'm up against, Doctor? Do you know you might not be making my life exactly easy by calling me your brightest star?

"Devin and Ben. Come on up here."

Everyone cheered, breaking into applause. Devin and I stood there, rattled to the bone as these people looked to us with desperate smiles and worried faces, placing whatever hope they had left in our cause. I swallowed, opened my mouth, shut it, as my face flushed with terror. And all I could wonder was, *How can they see anything hopeful in me, when I have no hope left in myself?*

Then I found Parker, who must have forgiven me, because she was beaming with pride, the midday sun brimming in her eyes as she gazed up to me as though I were someone worthy of such praise.

Devin seemed to stand a bit taller. He nodded at me, and we stepped forward, and with each step, I shed some of my fears and worries. Because if Parker believed I could do this, then maybe I could find the strength to hold up my end of the bargain. So I did. I followed Devin up toward the superintendent and held my head high.

While I didn't deserve this hero's welcome, all the smiles and words of encouragement, I got it all the same. Now, standing beside Devin Calloway, looking out to the crowd, at Parker, I knew I had to prove myself worthy of keeping it.

CHAPTER 16

Devin texted me early the next morning. He wanted me to meet him at the park to shoot baskets. I tossed the phone on the floor, rolled over onto my stomach, then flopped back again and gave it some thought. He was, after all, pretty much my only friend at Briggs, or anywhere else come to think of it. I got up, threw on a hoodie, and found my basketball shorts.

We met up at the court on Church Street, downtown. It was sunny and cold, and my legs were freezing. Downtown was mostly deserted on Sunday mornings, but Devin was already there, and he'd had the good sense to wear jogging pants. When he saw me coming, he folded over in laughter. "Nice legs, bro."

I looked down and laughed. "Yeah, well."

Devin had a nice shot. Smooth and fluid with good rotation on the ball. When he finally missed, I grabbed the rebound and realized it had been a while since I'd played ball.

I'd never been great at dribbling, but I banged inside and got rebounds, and had somehow found a place on our JV team sophomore year. "You play at Briggs?" I asked Devin.

"Yeah, keeps me in shape." He snatched the rebound when I missed and put it in. He dribbled out, turned around, and drilled a three. I chucked it back to him. He hit the shot again.

"Yeah, that's the only reason, huh?"

He smiled, then made another shot.

I grabbed the ball and held it. "Hey, man, can I ask you something? If everything hadn't gone down at the game the way it did, with the fight, Reggie, all that. Would you still be doing this?"

"What do you mean, *this*?"

"This," I said looking around. "All this. This thing with Dr. Jamerson. With me?"

He took a breath, clapped for the ball.

I set it on my hip.

"Yeah. We've been working on some things for a while now. But without all *this*, I don't know if we would've had the chance."

I passed him the ball.

He caught it, raised it up to shoot, but stopped. "Sometimes it takes a moment, even something tragic like death, to get people's attention."

He missed and I got the rebound.

Devin nodded at me. "You may have noticed my parents are older."

"I guess."

"So, my parents went through a lot in this town. They came up in the wake of the civil rights movement which, Virginia didn't exactly get the memo until way later. I've heard all the stories, the terrible things they went through. And I hate to think they did it for nothing."

I waited.

He wiped his face, took a breath. "What I'm trying to tell you is, my parents have sacrificed everything to give Max and me opportunities. They've taught us music, culture, arts. We went to England two years ago. *England.* We've been to Jamaica, Canada. We're going to Africa next summer."

I tossed the ball from one hand to the other. "Are you just bragging about your passport?"

Devin clapped his hands. "Give me the ball."

I chucked it at him.

He caught it, spun it in his hands, studied it closer. "Nah, man. I'm not bragging. The opposite, really. What I'm saying is, this unity thing means the world to them. And since they've given the world to me, I want to give it back to them. Make them proud of me. Make sense?"

Of course he'd have the perfect answer. He dribbled through his legs, started to shoot, then stopped again. "Look, I can tell you have doubts. You think maybe you've made a mistake. And again, I can't tell you what to do, but let me tell you this, Ben. You're the *only* one in this town willing to step outside his comfort zone." He ducked his head and smacked the basketball to emphasize the point. "The only one."

He took a few dribbles. "So maybe I should, too. I mean, ever since that game, man, it's been like we are the only two people who want to do *something*. Not fight, not break or burn things. Help. Change. Build. You feel me?"

"Yeah," I said, because I did. I remembered locking eyes with him, thinking how we were alone out there.

He missed the shot. I chased down the rebound then dribbled off my foot. Once I'd retrieved the ball, I dribbled it again, then stopped. "Oh, so uh, tell me about Zakia Ferguson."

Devin dropped his shoulders and rolled his eyes with a grin. "Here we go."

"Here we go? What's that mean?"

"It's a little too soon to fall in love. With the principal's daughter, no less. And yeah, Zakia's fine, but she's way too woke for you."

"I didn't say—what? What do you mean by that?"

Devin clapped for the ball again. "Means you got no chance, Big Ben."

THAT EVENING, Liv's car jerked to a halt outside my house. I watched from the living room window as she wiped her face, collected some things from the back seat, and marched for our front door.

She jerked to a stop as I opened the door, then recovered and set the box on the stoop and stood with her jaw set, arms crossed, her eyes narrowed at me. A slight shake of the head. "I just have to ask, was being a big-time football star not enough for you? Did you want to make sure your name stayed in the news?"

I slouched, wanting to defend myself and tell her what I'd told everyone else. But I was exhausted from explaining, defending, reasoning with people who refused to listen or take me seriously. Before I could say anything, she let her arms drop, the tears building up in her eyes. Her face was red and puffy, and I could see how much this meant to her, how much *I* had meant to her.

She thew her hands out. "So that's it. You can't even tell me why you're doing this?"

"Liv."

Her mouth clamped shut. She shook her head and rolled her eyes. "Don't. Don't talk to me like that. You've turned your back on your friends, on me, on the school, all of us."

"I'm not turning my back on anyone, Liv. I'm trying to help."

"*Help?* That's what you think you're doing?" She looked around, a wet laugh escaped her throat. "Wow. Are you delusional? One of your closest friend's dad is sitting in jail, and you're parading around with..." She shook off the thought. "What about me, Ben?"

"What do you mean? I'm right here."

It came out hollow, because it was hollow. Funny how, when the year began, I thought I could just push through the season, coast through spring, and get out of here. It was some kind of unspoken plan. Sure, I liked Liv, we had fun together. But we both knew it was nothing permanent or anything. And now, seeing her act like everyone else in town made our split all the easier to swallow.

"Ben, I just can't. I can't, if you're... Just take your things, and let's be done with this."

Our relationship in a box. Some of my shirts, my dinged-up iPod, a book, and a framed picture of the two of us that wasn't really mine, but I guess she wanted to hammer home the point.

She swung around and stormed off. My guilt won out, and I followed her out to her car.

"Hey, did you...?" I nodded back at my house, wondering what I had of hers in there, but she was already shaking her head.

"No, it's okay, I think some clothes, but you can bring it to..."

School. No, I couldn't. Not now.

Her shoulders fell. She looked up at me like she just realized something. "You're really doing this...?"

I took a breath, ran my hands through my hair. "Yeah, I don't have a choice now."

Her eyes flashed. It was like something came over her, or whatever had come over her with the tears and everything was gone. Her voice was dead. Her laugh was quick, like discarding a bad taste from her mouth. "Wow."

"Yeah."

She got in the car, rolled the window down and brushed a few strands of her dark hair from her eyes. "You know, one day, I hope this," she threw her hands up, "I hope it works out for you, I really do."

"Thanks."

Her mouth tightened. She blinked, nodded, then put the car in gear. She backed out of the driveway, and after one last glare my way, she drove off.

CHAPTER 17

On Monday morning, I entered the front lobby of BD Briggs High School, where Dr. Jamerson and Mr. Ferguson had brought me in just over a week ago. Devin caught my attention and waved. He was standing next to an attractive girl with dark brown skin and red designer glasses. As I hustled over, three things became immediately clear. One, this was Keesha. Two, she had the no-nonsense look of someone who could take care of herself and then some. Three, she made no effort to hide the scowl she had trained on me.

Devin stepped forward. "Hey, Ben." He glanced back to the girl. "I'd like you to meet Keesha. Keesha, this is Ben."

Devin's formality threw me. I was already jittery, so it didn't help that he was acting so strange. I nodded to Keesha who returned the gesture with level eyes and pursed lips.

"Hi," I said with a smile. "Nice to meet you."

"Hello," she said plainly.

Devin rocked back on his heels, gripping his backpack straps as he turned to Keesha. "So, I'm going to show Ben around. Meet you later?"

Her gaze lingered on me as she backed away. "Mmm, hmm."

I glanced at Devin, who only smiled. "That's Keesha."

"Yeah, sort of got that part."

"Come on," he said, slapping my back. "You got your schedule?"

I should have been ready for all the staring. We'd done the press thing, then the Unity thing, and it was well known everywhere that I was coming to Briggs. Some nods came Devin's way, and he worked crowd control with the greetings. This was not the Devin from the football field. He was all smiles, approachable and friendly, waving to kids, smiling, building people up. It really was a talent, how he knew everyone's name. Maybe he had a future in politics as well.

I couldn't shake the awkward meeting with his girlfriend. I glanced back toward the lobby. "So, um, Keesha. Not a fan, huh?"

"She'll be all right." Devin laughed as heads kept turning to us.

But the vibe felt more curious than negative. Maybe the news conference had helped soften the blow. A few more nods, and I even got a couple of fist bumps. I kept an eye out for Zakia, as it would be nice knowing someone here other than Devin, especially someone who looked like her.

Devin looked me up and down. "So, you ready for your first day? Nice shoes."

"What's wrong with my shoes?" I glanced down at my Sperries. "And do I have a choice to be ready or not?"

He laughed again. "Nope. This way."

I followed him past the lobby, near the drink machines where the football guys hung back, glaring at me like it was last Friday all over again.

"Sup, sup." Devin walked over to them, slapped hands with DreShaun, then Chris, then a few guys I didn't know. "Okay, gentlemen, I'm sure I don't need to introduce you to this dude, here. Ben Hoy, the all-district middle linebacker. My future in-state rival."

The quarterback rolled his eyes and clicked his teeth. "Right."

Devin was unmoved. "Okay, so Ben. This is DreShaun. Chris, Javier…"

And on and on he went. A few guys slapped my hand, but DreShaun's open glare clung to me. It was the first of many reminders that I couldn't just come in and expect everything to be all good.

The bell rang, and Devin turned to me. "Come on, I'll show you to your class."

He steered me to my English class, which of course was already in session. Devin tapped on the door as we entered. An older lady looked up and smiled. "Good morning, Devin."

Clearly, Devin was well liked by students and teachers alike. He stepped to the desk and motioned to me with a flourish. "Mrs. Johnson, I bring you Benjamin Hoy."

I shot him a look, nodded at the teacher. Zakia sat in the front row. Devin saw me staring and smirked. I set my gaze to the floor and hoped he'd let it go.

Mrs. Johnson got to her feet. "Welcome, Mr. Hoy."

I nodded.

She gestured to an empty seat near the window. It felt like I was in the fifth grade. Devin smiled at Zakia, then at me, and I was ready to kill him when Mrs. Johnson ducked her head. "Thank you, Devin."

"Oh, yeah. Okay, bye."

My face was on fire as I took a seat near the window. Without anything further, Mrs. Johnson plopped down a copy of *Things Fall Apart* and dove into a review assignment from last week. Looking at the title, I couldn't help but smile. Fitting.

I settled in, looking over the paperback. Maybe this was a mistake, taking Honors English. It was my best subject, but I was playing catch up as Zakia seemed really into the discussion, making points and bringing up questions about Nwoye. I thought about chasing her on the track last week, and I must have been thinking about it just a little too hard, because after a while, she glanced over and caught me staring. She raised a brow at me before she got back to tapping her pen on her notebook.

After class, Devin was right there to pick up where he left off. I wondered if Mr. Ferguson and Dr. Jamerson had asked him to escort me around for the first few days.

"Hi, Zakia," he sang with a smile as Zakia exited the classroom.

Zakia shook her head. "You should probably get your friend to class on time."

"Right. I'll do that. And his name is Ben."

"We've met." With that she walked off.

Devin looked at me. "I think she likes you."

I watched her walk off, never looking back, then turned to Devin. "What makes you say that?"

Devin shrugged. "Zakia doesn't talk to just anyone." He whispered. "She can be kind of bougie."

"Oh. Well, she didn't talk to me."

"Hmm." He shot me that trademark smile. "Good point."

After school, Devin invited me to lift with him. And it was almost normal, but not. Going back to little league, I'd been playing football with Moose, Jeff, and a handful of other guys through practices, camps, and conditioning. We'd worked our way up through middle school with only one goal in mind: a state championship.

Now Stonewall was undefeated. And I was here, at Briggs, in an empty weight room. I did my best to put it out of my mind. I lifted the way I always did. A few of the other guys came and went, but their season was over, and we pretty much had the place to ourselves. I tried not to look impressed when Devin benched two hundred pounds ten times like it was nothing.

He set the bar on the press. He stood and smiled. "You ready?"

He had his earbuds in, and I figured he was listening to some mumble rap or something. "What are you listening to?"

His smile doubled as he removed an earbud. "Stacey's podcast."

"The reporter? She has a podcast?"

Devin took the other earbud out. "Yeah, and we're going to be on it."

"What? When?"

"In about twenty minutes. Come on, let's go."

CHAPTER 18

"What was running through your mind when everything went down at City Stadium? How did you feel?"

Devin's eye-roll matched mine as we sat in the mostly empty studio, shoulders hunched, muscles burning, staring off through the windows while lost in the crush of bodies on that Friday night. I think he was regretting the podcast already, but I wasn't about to forgive him for dragging me into this. The week had been difficult enough—switching schools, going behind enemy lines—without this Q & A session.

I shifted in my seat. "How do you think it made me feel?"

Attractive as she was, Stacey's questions were annoying. I knew she had loftier goals than the local news, but it was like she was reading straight out of a child psychology book. But to her credit, no matter how much we complained or shifted or sighed and shook our heads, she was patient. She had no problems waiting me out.

Devin crossed his arms and sighed. "Helpless."

Stacey and I turned to Devin. He shrugged, then leaned forward in his seat. "I mean, whatever we try, peaceful approaches like marches, singing, vigils, it's the same shit. It never matters. People show up and mess it all up. Sorry."

Stacey shook her head. "No, it's fine. It's normal. And is that what happened on the field? You were angry?"

"Yeah, of course. But…"

The sound guy perked up, like a big breakthrough was coming. I think they wanted tears, emotions. Seeing how Devin and I weren't going to give it to them, Stacey knocked back her hair. "Devin. Last time we spoke, you were excited about Ben coming to Briggs. Do you still feel that way?"

I curled my toes up in my sneakers for the fiftieth time. All I wanted to do was go home, eat dinner, fall into my bed, and forget everything.

Devin stared at his hands, making a fist, then releasing it. "Yeah, I mean, Ben's a good dude. It's just..." He glanced at me, another sigh.

Stacey sensed something juicy beneath the surface and pounced. "What is it, Devin?"

Devin cut his eyes to me again, then looked away. "I mean, nothing against Ben, but it feels like everyone thinks he's the one making sacrifices, which, I get that. I do. But still, I mean, this isn't exactly easy for me. I've lost friends over this, for trying to reach out. My family is getting threats too."

I clenched my jaw. Devin had mentioned the threats, but this was the first time I'd heard him sound so defeated. I thought back to that cold greeting from his teammates that morning in McDonald's. Before I could shake it off, Stacey caught me.

She held my eyes for a moment, then got back to Devin. "These threats. Can you talk more on that?"

"Pfft." Devin shrugged, which was very un-Devin like. Usually, he knew exactly what to say or do, but now he seemed as confused as I was. "We're told it's nothing serious. People are upset. Acting out."

Stacey zeroed in on me, and I looked away. I did not want to go down this road. Thankfully, she let it go.

"I spoke with Principal Ferguson. The Ridgeton Police Department has stated there will be no unlawful gatherings at the school. Does that make you feel better?"

Devin crossed his arms. "Peachy."

I chuckled. Devin looked at me and smirked. And whatever sting I'd felt about what he'd said was gone.

Stacey flashed her gleaming white smile and tried to keep things moving. "Okay, let's shift gears. Ben, how did it go, your first day at Briggs?"

I laughed. "It was okay."

Devin shot me the side eye. "He likes Zakia."

"Dude!" I turned to Stacey. "Can you cut that?"

"Bro, you going to sit in that chair and say you don't have a thing for Zakia?" He got back to Stacey. "She's the principal's daughter too. Can you believe that?"

Stacey crossed her legs and smiled, eating up the gossip. "This true, Ben?"

Devin was grinning now.

I shook my head. "No, I'm... Whatever, man. I'm just trying to get through the day." I looked over at Devin. "Wow."

"Yeah, okay. He might have a shot too."

"I thought we were talking about..." I shook my head.

Stacey smiled at me. "Ben, you don't have a girlfriend?"

I'd almost rather go back to talking death threats. I kept my glare fixed on Devin. "Had. I came to Briggs and that sort of ended things. Don't ask me how I feel about that."

"Fair enough. But overall, you're adapting?"

I shrugged.

Devin smacked my leg. "He's adapting just fine."

Mom was in the kitchen stirring soup as I walked into the house. By habit, I set my backpack down and went for the mail on the counter. Lately, I'd been getting all sorts of mail. Some good, some official, some just trash. I had a feeling Mom had been filtering out any hate mail, because today's was mostly junk.

"How was school?" she asked, whisking me out of the way. The thick smell of beef stock made my stomach roll.

"Well, not too bad. We had some podcast thing today too."

"Oh, how was that?" She pointed to the cabinets. I was almost positive Mom had no idea what a podcast was, and I didn't feel like explaining. She reached up and grabbed three bowls.

I laughed, thinking about Devin messing with me. "It was all right. Where's Park?"

"In her room studying."

"What a nerd."

Mom nodded. "Well, I gave her a list of chores a mile long to keep her busy, so she might be avoiding me. She must not have heard you come home."

Mom set the lid on the pot of vegetable beef, my favorite, then wiped her hands. She set them on her hips and looked me head on. "You didn't tell me about what happened Saturday."

Of course I hadn't. Now that I thought about it, I could still feel Park squeezing my hand. "Oh, um, yeah, some protesters were there, nothing major."

Mom nodded toward Parker's room. "I think it shook her up some."

"Really?" I looked back to Park's room. The door was shut, the thrum of low music behind the walls.

Mom shrugged. "I'm not trying to worry you, Ben. You've got enough there. But she's not as tough as she pretends to be. "

I started for the hallway. "Should I go talk to her?"

"In a minute. Tell me about it first."

Sometimes I wondered how Mom and Dad ever came together long enough to have Park and me. When I was little, my dad hardly did anything outside of work. At home, he sat in front of the TV and tuned out reality. My mom though, working two jobs sometimes, had this spirit in her that wouldn't break. It was there when she worked late, overtime, now, as she came home from the packaging factory and put on soup. Even as her son had quit the school he'd been going to for three years. She just never gave up.

I explained what had happened at the Unity March in detail, about the guys with rifles and vests. The noose. How Parker and Max squeezed in between Devin and me. What I didn't tell her, but she was a little too good at reading me, was how a jolt of panic and nausea coursed through my system all over again when I saw them. Only this time it was worse, because Parker was with me.

Mom brought me in for a hug. She apologized for the hundredth time, like any of this was her fault. That was another thing about my mom, she took my pains as a personal affront to her motherhood. I truly believe she would stand in front of me, all five feet of her, and block an avalanche from taking me out. She would try her best, anyway.

She went back to stirring the soup when Park's door opened, and she came tromping down the hallway. "Well, how'd it go?"

I threw my hands up. "I got voted class president."

She threw her head back with a laugh. "Wow, now I know people have lost their minds."

I looked her over. I'd have to be more careful with her. She couldn't know about death threats and protests. I couldn't hide everything from my little sister, but like Mom, I'd shield her the best I could.

Stacey had suggested keeping a journal earlier, and up until then, I had thought it was stupid. Now, I wasn't so sure. It might be nice to get some of this out.

Mom clinked the spoon on the pot. "Soup is ready."

I scooped out a bowl. We all sat down. Park prattled on a mile a minute about debate stuff, whether the US Constitution was a living document. I smiled, shook my head. Sometimes it helped to have Parker just nerd out like this, so I didn't have to think about everything else.

CHAPTER 19

I awoke the next morning determined to get control of my schedule if nothing else. I arrived at Briggs as the sun was rising, where I circled the track ten or twelve times, powering through the burn in my legs as my breaths clouded the air in front of me.

The football field glimmered, the dew like broken shards of glass in the new morning light, and maybe it was the hope that came with an ordinary sunrise, but I was feeling motivated. I thought about calling up some of the younger guys from my team, Ryan and Eric, for starters. I could check in with a few of the underclassmen to pick their brains and hopefully see where they stood. This would be their town soon, their team next year. Would they be interested in helping me out or were they okay with things the way they were?

I pushed myself for two more laps, because when I was running, the blood flowing and my heart pumping, it felt like those things could really happen. It felt like a good idea. But as my steps slowed to a walk, as my mind cooled down and I walked into the unfamiliar locker room, it wasn't feeling so likely after all. Those guys were gearing up for a playoff run, and I'd abandoned them by coming to Briggs. I wasn't a leader to them, but a traitor. Why would they want anything to do with me?

English class. My hair was still wet, but at least I smelled good. I took my seat, on time, and glanced over at Zakia, wearing a pink fitted sweater and jeans. My eyes fell to her legs before I checked myself, but she'd already caught me, again. She shot me a quizzical look with what might've been a smile. Slick I was not.

Soon we were off in *Things Fall Apart,* and I was drifting as this girl named Sonya asked about similes. My focus was shot. I thought about how I'd be in philosophy class at Stonewall right now, feeling like my life was paused or on hold while I was in this weird world that didn't really exist, when Zakia nudged my arm.

"Hey. Hey, you."

I broke from my daydream to the clatter of people scooting and sliding their desks. I glanced around the room, at everyone up and moving around. Everyone but Zakia, who was smiling at me.

"Huh?"

She rolled her eyes. "I need a partner."

"Oh, okay." I wiped my mouth, tried to fix my hair.

Zakia watched me like I was a zoo animal. Then with a laugh, she scooted her desk over, and I caught a gust of coconut that woke me up quicker than the chilly air this morning. I rubbed my eyes and found her staring at me. She had her book open and ready to go. Pen and pad too. "Is this your plan? To sleep through class?"

"Well..."

She frowned. "I don't think Mrs. J would like that."

"Right. No, probably not."

She flipped some pages in her book, then shifted. She looked at the book, then set it down and closed her eyes as she sighed. "So, I like what you and Devin are doing. I think it's..." She looked away, like she was suddenly shy. Then it was gone, and she turned to me full on. "It's brave."

I picked at a hangnail. "Yeah, well, I...I'm not brave. Trust me."

"Sure you are." She picked up our worksheet packet. "Okay," she said, the smirk back in place. "Ready to write a poem?"

"Wait, what?"

Zakia rolled her eyes.

I'D SPENT my lunch period yesterday in the admin office, catching up on paperwork. Now, entering the cafeteria, I spotted Devin sitting at a table in the corner with Keesha. As I made my way over, Keesha leaned close to Devin's ear, and he popped up, bit his lip, and said something back to her.

My steps slowed, but it was too late to turn back, as I was already at the table. I took a seat across from Devin, directly in Keesha's crosshairs. "Hey, ya'll mind?"

Keesha only stared.

Devin recovered. "No, not at all. Keesha and I were just talking about—"

Javier, Chris, and DreShaun crashed down around us. DreShaun nodded at Devin. "Hey, Keesha."

"Hi, Dre," she said, her voice sweeter than I thought it capable of being.

DreShaun took me in. "So, White dude."

"Black dude," I replied without much thought.

Keesha's eyes shot daggers. Chris and Javier bristled, looking ready to slap me with their trays.

Devin chuckled. "Again. Ben, DreShaun. DreShaun. Ben. There, that's not so hard, right?"

DreShaun studied me. "Saw your boys at the Unity March the other day. You invite them?"

I made a point of meeting his eyes. Ever the quarterback, he sized me up in an instant. I looked down. "No. And not my boys."

"Ah, that's right. You're one of us now, right?"

I glanced at Devin. DreShaun was a junior. Devin had said he was all set to be a captain next year. He certainly had the confidence. It was crazy to think these were the guys on the field a couple of weeks back. The guys I'd played against for the past few years, who were there that night when everything went down. The ones Moose said those things about.

The whole table looked ready to smother me.

I kept my back straight, looked over the faces at the table, then exhaled. This wasn't the time for bravado, that had gotten us nowhere. Yet, my adrenaline spiked, flushed through my limbs. It was like taking the field all over again.

Devin spoke up. "I invited Ben to the March. He *is* one of us now. Meaning, he's going to Briggs like we are. And speaking of the Unity March, unlike you, Ben wasn't there trying to fight anyone. Seems to me he's the only one taking this seriously."

Everyone sat quietly, eyes on Devin, the current captain, the guy who was easygoing yet passionate and now in complete command of the table. Well, maybe not of Keesha, she still looked ready to come at me with her fork.

Devin nodded at me, and I shook my head. "Look, I don't speak for all of Stonewall..." I turned away, jaw clenched.

Keesha looked off.

"I mean, I guess I don't speak for any of Stonewall, being as I can't go back there. My only other option is homeschooling, but my mom isn't exactly an intellectual." My attempt at humor fell flat.

Devin glanced down, like he was thinking about something. DreShaun scoffed, still glaring at me.

Devin turned to him. "You got something to say, do it now."

DreShaun balled up his face and gave it some thought before he set his elbows on the table and leaned forward. "Yeah, I do, actually. So, this dude walks in our school and he's going to fix all our problems? Is that it?"

Keesha made a noise in her throat, as though she had much to say on it if pressed.

I set my palms on the table, ready to push off and go. I glanced at Devin again. "No, I'm not fixing anything."

I scooted my chair back. I'd eat in the gym for all the trouble. At least it was quiet, I could try to make sense out of my required reading. I grabbed my tray. "It's cool. I'll eat somewhere else."

Javier looked at DreShaun, who smiled at me. "Bye then."

I started to stand when Devin held up his hand. "Hey, last Friday, did any of ya'll see Ben throw a punch?"

I stopped, tray in my hands, somewhere between standing and sitting.

Devin looked from Javier to Chris to DreShaun, then finally to

Keesha. "Come on, let's get this out in the open. Chris, when you were throwing haymakers, did you see Ben? And don't tell me we didn't know where he was, because he was in our backfield most of the game, right?"

DreShaun pursed his lips. "Getting rolled out of his cleats."

The guys laughed, and Devin smacked the table. Trays bounced and every conversation in the cafeteria came to a halt. "I asked if any of you saw Ben throw a punch. Did you?"

No one said a word. Devin nodded. "No. You did not. I can't say the same for all of you, but Ben wasn't out there fighting. Did anyone hear Ben say anything? And you know what I mean, because we all heard what they were saying. So, did you?"

Slowly, I set myself back in the chair, wondering where this was going. The quiet cafeteria was watching now, including teachers. Gone was Devin the diplomat. He had that gameday look in his eyes, his voice holding the room. "This dude left his school. He's not here to *fix* anything but to help make change. Isn't that what we want, change?"

Blank faces all the way down the table. Arms crossed. Keesha stared into my eyes, but for the first time, her gaze had softened, and she didn't seem like a threat.

Devin continued. "Ben isn't who we need to attack, trust me. He's already under attack by those he considered friends. He's getting death threats *because* he's here. He's the one trying to open his eyes and see what no one in our town wants to see. I mean, damn, you heard him at the conference. He's not hiding anything. Neither am I. So, if you got a problem with Ben, you got a problem with me." He stood and thumped his chest so hard I could feel it in my feet. "Cause we *all* need to fix this." He looked out to the other tables, his voice breaking as he called out to the room. "You hear me? We all need to fix this. All of us."

The cafeteria fell completely silent as Devin lowered himself back to his seat. A teacher hurried over and asked if he was okay. Slowly, the cafeteria noise picked up again, gentle murmurs that got louder as lunch resumed.

I tried to hide the deep breaths in my chest as I got back to my lunch, but when I glanced up, I caught Zakia's eyes, and she shot me a quick nod and a small smile.

It was enough to get through the day.

CHAPTER 20

Devin and I walked into my house, where the aroma of Mom's famous chicken casserole put a smile on my face. We were in for a treat. Mom poked her head out from the kitchen, saw Devin, and rushed out.

"Hi. You must be Devin Calloway."

Devin bowed his head. "Yes, ma'am. It's nice to meet you."

I smirked at his manners, at Mom's manners, how formal everyone was acting. But it was Mom's idea to have Devin over for dinner, and she already had stars in her eyes. She threw her hands around the room, where I spotted vacuum tracks over the rug. A can of pledge and a rag sat on the antique cabinet in the living room. "Well, excuse the mess, I've been working all day and…"

Devin pulled the beanie off his head. "Is there anything I can do to help?"

Mom's mouth dropped. She nodded back at me with a smile. "Well, you could teach this one manners, for one. But other than that, no. Please, make yourself at home."

Parker's door flung open, and she came romping into the room. "Hey, Devin!"

"Hey, Park, how was school?" Devin asked. Mom and Parker looked at me, Parker blushing some. I couldn't resist.

"Yeah, Park, how has school been since your return?"

"Return?" Devin asked.

I scratched my chin. "Oh, she got suspended."

Devin cocked his head. I hadn't gotten around to telling him about Parker's suspension—the Unity thing hadn't seemed like the right time to mention my sister's fight.

Mom swooped in for the save. "It was a misunderstanding."

Parker nodded. "I punched a boy in the face."

Devin's eyes widened. "Oh, wow. Having to beat them off already?"

Parker glanced at Mom, who said, "Something like that."

When Mom turned away, Parker shook her head and mouthed, "No, it wasn't."

Devin turned to me for answers.

Figuring I might as well tell him, I launched into what happened, and Parker interrupted me at every other sentence to get the details right.

Devin sat back, looking us over. "Oh, um, that's..." He looked at Parker again. "Okay."

Mom offered him a soda, changing the subject. "So, Ben told me your family owns Cal's Music. That's so neat."

I smirked. Mom thought it was *neat*.

Devin nodded. "Yes, ma'am. It's been in our family for over a hundred years."

"Really? That's something."

"Yeah."

"Your parents must be very proud of all you're doing."

"They are. Very much so."

I thought about my dad, how he wasn't proud, but ashamed. I'd pretty much avoided talking about my dad with Devin. Maybe I was ashamed of him as well. But also, there wasn't much to say about it.

Devin went for his soda when he caught a glimpse of the newspaper sitting on the counter. Gunny's charges had been upgraded to manslaughter. Devin turned to Mom. "I saw they haven't scheduled his arraignment yet."

Mom and I exchanged a glance. Mom cleared her throat. "Yeah. I think they're letting things blow over."

Parker rolled her eyes.

Devin glanced at the paper again. Things got quiet. Finally, he looked up, like he was happy to have something else to say. "Well, this casserole smells delicious, Mrs. Hoy."

"Thanks, Devin. And please, call me Jen."

Parker, Devin, and I managed to polish off the casserole. Afterwards, Devin hung around to help clear the table, prompting Mom to go on another rant about how well he was raised.

Devin and I hadn't talked about school the other day, when he'd stood up for me at lunch in such a public way. Or how it had worked. While DreShaun wasn't my best buddy, he'd eased up on the taunting. Javier had taken to nodding at me in the hallways. Keesha was, well, still Keesha, but she didn't seem so open about disliking me.

I rinsed dishes, asking Parker about her big return to school, while Devin and Mom talked jazz music, of all things, when someone banged on the door.

We all froze. I looked at Mom, who tried to hide the alarm in her eyes. We were all on alert these days, as people weren't exactly stopping by with fruit baskets. I held up a hand. "I'll get it."

A tight coil constricted in my chest as I got to the door where someone was knocking like they owned the house. It couldn't mean anything good; I knew that much before I opened it and came face to face with Coach Campbell.

"Ben," he said, eyes searching over me. "How are you, son?"

Son. Like we hadn't had it out the other day in the yard. I nodded, the clinking of dishes in the kitchen reminded me how Devin was here and what Coach might say about it. Awkwardly, I stepped outside and pulled the door shut. "I'm okay."

He grimaced, then stepped back, like he'd planned on coming in for a recruiting chat. Recovering, he stuffed a hand into his pocket, and we gazed out toward his F-150, the chrome grill winking in the shine of the porchlight.

"You know, I wanted to stop by and check on you."

My faced flashed hot. I had trouble believing Coach was simply dropping in to check on me. I waited him out, ignoring the banter in the kitchen.

"How you holding up? At Briggs?"

I shrugged. "I'm okay. I mean, takes some getting used to," I said like an idiot, wondering what we were doing, what he was after.

His brow furrowed. "Yeah, I'll bet it does. Heard you were marching on Saturday?"

I forced myself to look him in the eye. What did that have to do with anything? "I... We weren't *marching*. It was a get together, for Reggie," I said, only making things worse.

Coach took a long, nasally breath as he turned and gazed down the street, in the direction of the Williams' place where a roofing crew had stripped off the shingles. I studied the back of Coach's Stonewall jacket, the cartoonish rebel mascot with smoke coming out of his ears. The old guys still griped about how the school had removed the confederate flag from the logo, leaving the bearded rebel all by himself, armed with a rifle and looking for a fight.

Coach shifted back to me. "You see we won last Friday? Undefeated. Still going to the playoffs," he said, defiantly. It was almost comical, had I not been freaking out about Devin being inside.

I tried to keep things positive. "Yeah, I saw. Happy for you."

He took a step toward me. "Are you? Well, this is it. I came here to give you one last shot at it, our championship season."

I swallowed. It was nice to be needed, but it felt like Coach was here to bully me again. I bristled, squaring up to meet his gaze. "Coach, I made my decision. I'm at Briggs."

His lips tightened. He shook his head, his cheeks reddening. "You know I can't let you do this, Ben. You understand that, right?"

So much for positive. "No offense, Coach. But I don't really think it has anything to do with you."

A flash lit up his eyes. He looked like he wanted to take a swing at me. Instead, he hocked and spit. "No, no, this is all about you, Ben. That much is clear."

I opened my mouth to argue when the front door swung open.

Coach's eyes widened. I turned to find Devin, in his stocking cap, hoody.

He nodded at Coach then looked at me. "Am I interrupting?"

"No, not at all." I shook my head. "Coach was just checking up on me."

Devin shuffled down the steps. Coach squared his shoulders up.

Devin stuck out his hand. "Coach Campbell, nice to meet you, sir. Devin Calloway."

Coach blinked then shook Devin's hand. "Oh yes, I know, son. Nice to meet you."

The three of us stood on the front stoop, in front of my house, for a few seconds. Then Coach was done. He sniffed, wiped his chin, and said, "Well, I got to get up the road. But um, Ben. I meant what I said, okay?"

"Do what you've got to do, Coach."

CHAPTER 21

By Wednesday I was able to find all my classes without help. I'd even managed to do my homework and made some headway in *Things Fall Apart*. The only strange part was lunch, where I didn't see DreShaun or Javier at our table, only Keesha and Devin. They were huddled close together and looked like they could use some alone time, so I took my tray and headed off toward Zakia.

The worst she could do was shoot me down, in front of everyone, as it felt like all eyes were glued to me as I made my way across the cafeteria. Zakia's friends saw me coming, nudging her and giggling as I came to a stop behind the empty chair at the table.

Zakia turned and looked up, a bemused smile on her face. "Oh."

"Mind if I sit?" I nodded at the chair.

With all the giggling, it felt very elementary school-ish. But it helped break the ice. Zakia's mouth opened. A slight smile as she blinked, as though she couldn't believe my nerve.

I looked around innocently. "What, I can't sit next to my study buddy?"

Zakia blinked again, but the smile grew. "I'm not your study buddy."

"But you're my partner, right?"

She turned to the person next to her, a tiny girl with a huge afro and hoop earrings. Zakia pointed to the seat I was standing behind. "This seat is taken, right? We're saving it, aren't we, Shanelle?"

Shanelle giggled.

The girl across from her smiled. Her blue braids swung as she shook her head. "I don't think so, I think your study buddy should sit down and let us get to know him better."

My cheeks went up in flames as the table erupted in laughter.

Zakia shook her head. "Fine. Sit."

I took my seat.

"I'm Alicia," the girl with the braids said, extending a hand with matching blue nail polish.

I smiled. "Hi. I'm–"

"Ben. Yeah, we know," Alicia said, tossing a smirk toward Zakia, who was also blushing but recovered with an eye roll.

She made quick introductions, going down the line. "And this is Shanelle, and April, and Jasmine. Everyone, this is Ben."

More giggling.

Zakia turned to me. "As you can see, we have an amazing welcoming committee."

"You're the one doing all the welcoming," Shanelle shot back, and everyone laughed.

I didn't know what I was doing, but it was fun. I'd thought a lot about how things ended with Liv. How we'd been so used to each other in a way that made things comfortable. Easy. And while I missed the easy parts, the comfortable moments, I think we were both ready to be on our own. And once she'd dismissed what Devin and I were trying to do, it made it that much clearer it was time to move on.

I wasn't looking for any of that now with Zakia, who looked ready to kill her friends on the spot. She tried to ignore them. "How's your week going?"

I nodded, glanced around the table where all three girls watched us without shame. "Better now, thanks."

Alicia raised her eyebrows, grinning at Zakia who did her best to keep her composure even as it was clear she was going to kill her friends later. I picked up my cheeseburger and dug in, playing it up for the audience.

This could be fun.

AFTER SCHOOL, I left my truck in the parking lot and rode with Devin to pick up Max at the music store. It was better than going home and thinking about football practice at Stonewall, or anything else I had planned.

"So, yeah. I saw you at lunch," Devin said, checking the rearview.

"Yeah?" I smiled.

"You still have no chance."

"Chance at what? Zakia is my friend. Unlike Keesha."

He laughed. "Yeah, okay, *a friend*. Right. And don't worry about Keesha. She's coming along."

He was still teasing me about the Zakia thing as he drove down Fifth Street, slowing to a crawl as we came upon a bunch of pickup trucks parked along both sides of the street. We exchanged looks.

"Hang on," Devin said, as he jerked the wheel, and we bounced down a narrow side street.

More trucks, Jeeps, SUVs, parked at angles on the curb. Some guys watched us closely, taking notice as we passed. Devin had mentioned how the gatherings at the monument had doubled in size since Gunny's charges were upgraded, and now there were talks of a big rally this weekend. It looked like they were getting an early start.

My feet ground into the floorboard. Devin's jaw clenched, his eyes darting around as he leaned forward, hunched over the steering wheel as we dipped through a yellow light. We passed another cluster of men an arm's length from the car, and I knew what he was thinking, that if the protests were already down here, edging closer to Lower Main, it wouldn't be long before they were outside the shop.

Devin banged a quick left and the car pitched forward. We jostled over the bumpy cobblestone like a roller coaster as we plunged down the narrow alley, scraping the front bumper as we came out at the lower basin, where Cal's Music sat in a row of brick buildings just before the bridge.

We slid to a stop out front. I glanced around, checking behind us, our heavy breaths the only sound in the car. Devin gripped the wheel, staring straight ahead.

"They were probably just..." My voice trailed. My thoughts went to Bus and the protestors. What were they planning? Devin's eyes never left the windshield. It unnerved me, seeing him come undone. "You okay?" I asked.

"It's only going to get worse," he said—to me, to the bridge. To no one at all.

It was exactly what I was thinking. And while this whole time I'd thought I was the only one making sacrifices by coming to Briggs, quitting football, and shedding all my old friends, the fear in Devin's eyes against all those trucks and flags—the protests inching closer to the lower end of Main Street—proved just how wrong I'd been. His life had changed too.

Devin wiped his forehead and tried to put some life in his voice. "Come on, let's go see Max."

We climbed out of the car, looking around. Devin locked up and started up the sidewalk. I followed, taking in the store I'd passed by so many times but hardly noticed.

It was a three-story brick building with large windows and gargoyle's perched on the roof. A barber shop occupied the space next door. The next block up was a different story. The old warehouse was being gutted and renovated into loft style apartments. A sleek coffee shop had taken the corner slot in anticipation of a boom. A sign announced the arrival of a pizza place across the street.

I couldn't help but notice the difference in the two blocks as we came under the green canvas awning that jutted out from the glass entranceway, "Cal's Music" stenciled in cursive on the window.

My steps slowed. "Man, I really had no idea this was your store," I called out.

Devin turned back to me, fixed his beanie. "Yeah, well, technically it's my great-grandpa's store, but my pops has run this place since I was little."

Support C-443! flyers clung to the windows on either side of the entrance, which by now everyone in town knew was the bill going before council to relocate the town's confederate monuments. I'd only seen those flyers on this end of Main Street.

A bell overhead rang as we entered. My eyes adjusted to the dim lighting and moved to the display that shined with all sorts of brass instruments, some dull from use and others gleaming and new.

"Hey, Pops," Devin called out. Inside, it was a time warp, the room narrow but long, stretching back as far as I could see. It smelled like cigars and floor wax and had the feel of an antique shop rather than a music store.

I followed Devin, taking in the drum sets, guitars, one of those big standup bass guitars. Glass countertops lined both sides, shelves of instruments spanned the walls. Framed pictures of men in suits and ties here and there, mostly Black but a few White guys too. Jazz dudes. Horns on the shelves. Worn Persian rugs on the floors.

A crash came from somewhere in the back. Devin shook his head and smiled. "Pops, you okay back there?"

Max popped his head out from a door. "Boo!"

Devin stopped. "Oh, you. I should have known."

Max saw me and smiled. "Hey, what's up, Ben?"

"Hey, Max."

Devin laughed. "Sounds like you need some help back here."

I could tell he was putting on a brave face for his little brother, same as I did with Parker.

"Well, not really." Max rolled his eyes. "Pops has me straightening up the rental section." He nodded at me. "Hey, they were talking about you two on the news again. Kendell asked if I could get your autograph?"

Devin gestured to me. "Me or Ben?"

Max laughed. "Pfft. Ben."

Devin rolled his eyes and brushed past him. "Straightening, huh?" The place was trashed. A pile of sheet-music stands, instrument cases, drumsticks scattered like giant matchsticks, guitar cases, cords, a violin missing its strings. Devin started picking things up. "Where's Pop, anyway?"

Max smirked at me. "The bank. I begged him to let me stay."

"The bank is up the street," Devin said to me, looking over the mess. His eyes lingered on the door as a figure approached.

The bell jangled as Mr. Calloway entered. He removed his hat, looking at us with a smile. "Ah, see? I knew there would be trouble."

His deep baritone carried the length of the store. He set his hat on a hook and shuffled some papers around before he made his way to the back. If he noticed the mess, he didn't seem to mind. "And how are you boys today?"

Devin glanced at his feet. I did the same.

Things got quiet until Mr. Calloway chuckled as he regarded the room and the mess. "As you can see, Max has been working today. You boys mind helping me get this cleaned up?"

We jumped in. I collected some drumsticks and placed them in a bucket. Devin got the stands in their place. Max picked up maybe two cords, but Mr. Calloway urged him to practice on the trumpet instead. Max balled up his face and mentioned how he hadn't made cuts for the basketball team as he shuffled off to the bathroom.

When he was gone, Mr. Calloway sighed. "I swear, that boy can find an excuse quicker than a breath."

Devin looked up at his dad. "He didn't make cuts?" He turned to me. "Max tried out for basketball."

Mr. Calloway grimaced. "No. I told him to keep working at it. Or at the trumpet. The boy only wants to play video games."

Devin glanced back to the door. "I'll talk to him about it."

Mr. Calloway nodded.

Devin started to pick up a guitar pick but popped his head up. "Did you see them up there? All the trucks and whatever at the monument?"

Mr. Calloway glanced at me. "Yeah, to be expected, I guess."

"It's kind of big. Bigger than it was."

Mr. Calloway straightened, keeping his voice down. "I saw."

I busied myself with some sheet music. Devin fiddled with a trumpet. He started playing a jazz number I'd heard somewhere.

And he wasn't bumbling along, he was *playing* it, perfectly. His fingers moved along with ease and grace as he closed his eyes and set his mouth to what had looked like a dull piece of brass. My jaw fell at the sound of the powerful notes.

Mr. Calloway removed his reading glasses, as though the pride in his eyes didn't need to be corrected.

Summertime, I think it was. And it was smooth as silk. The sounds found my chest, filling me with nostalgia I couldn't place as Devin flooded soul into the horn with finesse and ease. I couldn't help my smile. I had no idea.

Then it was gone, zapped from the room just as soon as Devin set the trumpet down and shrugged.

Mr. Calloway smiled at me, and I guess he saw the amazement on my face. "Oh yes, he can play," the man said with a sigh. "If only he didn't want to be out there manhandling people."

I gawked at the trumpet a moment longer, then turned to Devin. "Dude. I didn't know you could do *that*."

Devin shrugged. "*Dude*," he smirked. "I don't really play anymore."

Mr. Calloway smacked his lips. "Damn shame, too."

"Come on, Pops, don't start." Devin turned to me. "I'm looking at a full football scholarship, and he's mad I'm not playing trumpet."

"Well, it's just that, you can do both."

I glanced at the trumpet, now just another object in the room. If I could play like that, I'm not sure I'd bother with football. And I could only imagine what my dad would have to say about that, me playing jazz instead of football.

Mr. Calloway nodded to the instrument. "You could probably get a scholarship with music just as well. Your great-grandfather played the trumpet. Opened this store and taught my father how to play the trumpet, and so on. Now it's your turn, and, ah…" He waved us off in a way I wasn't sure was comical or serious. "Well, at least there's Max."

Devin chuckled. "Good luck with that."

Mr. Calloway stood, the floor squeaking with his steps. He picked up the horn. "You know, Duke Ellington toured Europe, learning all he needed to know about the world. This trumpet can take you places football can't. And you'll still have a brain cell in your head when you're older."

Devin sighed before he turned to me, a lazy grin on his face. "Only Pops would try to talk a young Black man *out* of going to college."

"No, no. Hold on now. That's not what I'm saying."

"No?" Devin looked at his feet. I got the feeling this was not the first time they'd had this same conversation.

Mr. Calloway pleaded to me. "I'm saying, well, people go to college these days and don't learn a thing. Oh, they learn how to get by, get the answers they need for an exam, but they don't... They only care about getting a degree so they can get a job, go to work, but..."

Devin shook his head, completely exasperated. "That's just it, though, Pop. What's wrong with going to college to get a job? To practice law and try to better myself? Isn't that the point?"

Both Devin and Mr. Calloway were talking with their hands now, and I was thinking about stepping outside as things were getting too personal.

"No, son, hear me out," Mr. Calloway said. "We should *want* to learn, to study the arts for what they are and not for a paycheck. We should spend our lives learning, for ourselves. We should seek knowledge to become *educated*." He tapped his temple with his finger. "We should *want* to be educated for *ourselves*, not a job or a boss."

"Yeah, well, I want to get paid. Get up out of here."

Devin and I exchanged looks.

Mr. Calloway picked up the trumpet. "These kids, they don't *learn* anything, son. They don't gain any knowledge."

Devin grinned, but I sensed something beneath his smile. Beneath everything. Something tugging at him from the inside.

Max appeared out of nowhere. "Not this again."

"Ah," Mr. Calloway said, smacking his hands together. "Show Ben what you've got."

He handed the trumpet to Max, who frowned but then brought the instrument back to life. He wasn't nearly as good as Devin, but it was good enough.

A truck roared past the store. Max stopped playing, and we looked to the windows where more trucks came growling past. Mr. Calloway got to his feet when Devin bolted for the entrance.

"Son, get back here," Mr. Calloway called after Devin. But he was already out the door.

I found him standing on the sidewalk as five or six more trucks rumbled down Main Street, confederate flags mounted on the truck beds. "What the hell are they doing?"

Whatever they were doing, things were heating up. Some honked as the drivers gunned their engines, the trucks roaring up the block, leaving Lower Main peaceful and quiet again. Devin took a breath, glanced at the store, then turned to me as though just realizing I was there. "We gotta do something."

"I thought we were," I said.

Devin shook his head. His whole body flexed as he paced, the way he did on the field sometimes before a snap, before he blitzed and wrecked whatever play the other team had in mind.

"Nah," he said, motioning up the block. "They're planning something. We have to do more. We can't just watch them—let them come through town and try to scare everyone who doesn't agree with them."

"Okay," I said, nodding, ignoring the fact that it was too late, I was already afraid. So was he, judging by the way he was breathing, eyes darting around. "But you know what? I think they're the ones who are afraid."

Devin stopped and stared at me, urging me to continue.

I shrugged. "When I was like seven or eight, my dad used to make me go hunting with him. I never really wanted to go, but I couldn't tell him that. Hunting was something he and his dad always did. Anyway, for some reason, I was terrified of getting attacked by a bear." I glanced up the street again. "My dad always said they were more afraid of me than I was of them." I shrugged. "It's the same with these guys, most of them anyway, even my dad to an extent. They're always complaining about what's going wrong with this country, or the world, how everything is going. But really, the world is moving away from their way of thinking, and it's got them scared to death. At least, that's the way I see it."

Devin cocked his head.

I threw my hands up. "What?"

"Nothing," he said. "That's the deepest thing you've said since we met."

"Yeah, follow me for more redneck hacks."

Devin was chuckling when the shop door opened and Mr. Calloway stepped outside, looking relieved to find us there. "Everything all right?"

Devin looked at me. "Yeah, we're good."

Max had his backpack on as he came outside. He glanced up the road. "They gone?"

Devin closed his eyes as though it pained him to see his little brother afraid to walk outside. "Yeah, Max. Come on, let's get you home."

CHAPTER 22

It was entirely too early to be sitting on the front row of the bleachers in the gymnasium under the glare of three different cameras on Thursday morning, as Chelsea Crawford, Virginia's hometown sweetheart, sat perched before us, armed and ready with questions.

Devin was doing better than I was, smiling broadly as we prepped. He was growing out a scraggly beard, which was driving his pops crazy, but he was pulling it off.

I'd only found out about *Good Morning Virginia* last night when I got home and Parker nearly tackled me as I walked inside. GMV was coming to Ridgeton. They'd caught wind of the story of how two opposing football players, one White, one Black, had come together to try and make a difference.

Groan.

The only good thing about this sudden interview was how I'd had little time to stress over it. And there was much to stress over, as Chelsea Crawford, who wore her hair like her smile—permanently fixed into a fake, unrelenting curl—set her sights on us.

Devin and I had joked about it earlier, right before we'd gone on. How when you first saw her, blonde, fixed up, tight dress, you thought Chelsea was hot. But once you got up close, saw the tiny cracks in her makeup when her eyes were trained on you, unblinking and crazy, that smile pressed into her face like it had been carved by a knife, well, I wasn't so sure she was human.

Now, Chelsea crossed her legs and tilted her head. "Devin, Ben, thanks for being here this morning."

I shot a sidelong glance at Devin who suppressed a grin. We were at school. Where else were we supposed to be?

Devin nodded. "Of course. No problem."

"Great. So what made you two decide to do this? To take a stand and heal your communities?"

Wow. Chelsea went straight for the cheesy. Devin shot me a *you-take-this-one* look and I cleared my throat. "Well, it wasn't exactly a long, thought-out plan. I think Devin and I were both affected by what we saw, and—"

Chelsea's head bobbed. "Yes, but there had to be some thought for you to switch schools, am I right?"

I glanced at Devin, who shot me the look again. I squirmed. "Well—"

"I mean, your former football team is undefeated and headed for the playoffs," she said, checking her notes. "That couldn't have been easy, am I right?"

Such a forceful woman, capable of ripping into the flesh of any story. She seized the talking points from a source, a guest, a victim, and charged ahead. I shot one more glance at Devin, who clearly had no plans to bail me out.

I wiped my hands on my pants. "No, it wasn't easy. It was probably the hardest decision I've ever made. But I...I feel like I'm doing something that will make my mom and sister proud. Hi, Mom. Hey, Park."

I waved and Chelsea nearly bit my hand off. She composed herself in a flash, turning her Botoxed brow on Devin. "Okay, so, Devin. You were close with Reggie Watts, how has his death affected you?"

Devin took a breath. "Well, I wouldn't say close, but his death has had a big impact on my life."

"Can you explain?"

He shrugged. "I shouldn't have to explain. A guy was murdered on a football field, during a game in which I was playing." He motioned to me. "We witnessed a guy get stabbed to death—as did our teammates. Over what, a statue?"

"Oh." Chelsea's smile faltered but remained in place. Devin's use of the word murder had her simultaneously uncomfortable and salivating. She shifted in her chair while consulting her notes. "About that, I hear there's plans for a Heritage March in a few weeks. A pro-monument rally of sorts. Any thoughts on that?"

The pickup truck convoy the other night had littered the downtown streets with flyers about it. Devin glanced at me. "I hadn't heard." Maybe it was nerves, but we both started cracking up.

"Oh. So tell me about this?" she said, changing gears, gesturing at us. "The two of you seem to be really close. What was it about that night that brought you together?"

At school the other day, Devin had played me an old song on his phone called "Ebony and Ivory." To be honest, I'd taken some offense when he talked about how White people loved this angle, but now, as he shook his head, I could only smile. It seemed the more I got to know Devin, the more I learned about myself.

Devin glanced down to his lap before he answered. "I'm hoping what happened will bring a lot of people together. Not for marches or rallies, but...as humans. I'm hoping what transpired, as well as our response, will get people's attention. Otherwise, what's going to happen? We keep doing this? Keep fighting each other? More violence, more rage. Where does it end?"

Chelsea crossed her legs again. "Ben, and you?"

I shrugged, picking up where Devin left off. "I went to Stonewall all my life, and looking back, I guess it was easy to close things off and only worry about what was happening in my own bubble. But during that game, when I looked out and saw a noose in the stands... It kind of popped that bubble. It went beyond football, beyond schools or towns or rivalries or disagreements. It went beyond human decency."

A flash of anger rose in my chest. It climbed to my throat. I tried to shut it down, but I couldn't. Once it flashed over me, it was too late.

"Someone *died* on that field. Dead. Gone. Never coming back, and now people want to *counter protest?* I mean, counter what?"

I hadn't planned on going that far. But the lights were on, and Chelsea sat there, eyes wide and unblinking, almost daring me to say it. So, I did. "Reggie Watts was murdered. I've heard all sorts of things being said about him recently. But you know what? He's not the one on trial. He's dead."

Devin turned to me.

Chelsea let the weight of my words sit in the gym until it became almost like a third guest on the show. Finally, three, four, five seconds later, she cleared her throat. "Clearly, this is emotional for you."

I wanted to wipe my face, my eyes, but those cameras were glued to us. I tried to calm myself, tame my words before I spoke again. "My whole life has been flipped over. And yeah, I'm uncomfortable. I'm experiencing things I never thought about. On top of that, my mom's getting death threats. Why? Because I don't want to cheer on someone's death? Because I don't want to look the other way and move on? Because I don't. I can't do that." My voice caught and I choked up some. "I want to try and understand why it happened. Maybe find a way to leave my hometown a better place for my little sister. Is that so wrong?"

I was about to get up and be done with this before I started crying on *Good Morning Virginia*, when Devin nudged my arm. "You asked what brought us together?" He nodded toward me. "*That*. We share the same beliefs. We refuse to believe that everything and everyone is evil. What happened on the field between us, we saw it together. We got squeezed in by the hate and watched it ignite on the field. We saw blood together. So, if you're wondering why we're close, yeah, it's that. Because of what we went through together."

Chelsea nodded, eyes blinking as she cleared her throat. "Wow. Okay, thank you, Devin, Ben, thank you for speaking to me today."

She addressed the camera, wrapping things up before the lights finally clicked off and it was like a gust of fresh air in the gym. Chelsea set the mike down and said something to her crew. She looked down, then back to us. "I just want to say, off the record, I think it's commendable what you two are doing. Good luck to you, okay? If you need me for anything, please, here's my direct line." She handed me her card.

And then she was off.

Devin clicked his teeth. "You know she's just trying to get another story."

I stared off as the crew wrapped. I was so done with the spotlight.

It just wasn't done with us.

CHAPTER 23

I found Mom at the kitchen table on Saturday morning. I poured a bowl of cereal and took a seat across from her.

She slid the paper my way. "Gunny made bail."

I set my spoon down. "What?"

Mom nodded. The dark rings under her eyes were heavier than most mornings. I knew she'd been working a lot, but with the extra stress of my situation, not to mention Perfect Parker's suspension, it all seemed to be taking its toll. I whipped my phone out and clicked on the news app.

She waved a hand over the newspaper. "He got some hotshot lawyer. National guy from out of town."

A hundred grand for bail. And yet, my feelings were at odds as I thought about Jeff having his dad around. About his family and how it must have felt. About how I'd called it murder on a live broadcast.

Still, with this Heritage March looming, the big-time lawyer, it had to be related. Apparently it was normal, though, to be out on bail while awaiting arraignment. The lawyer, Snead Perry, carried the narrative.

I read it out loud. "This is a textbook case of self-defense. I have no doubt the jury will see it as such. Is it a tragedy? Certainly, all the way around, but Reggie Watts was not the only victim on that tragic night at the stadium."

"Wow. He's comparing Gunny, the guy alive and out on bail, to the guy he killed. Yep, sure. Totally the same," Parker said, as she wandered into the kitchen. Mom had relented on my sister's grounding, and she was set to go to a friend's house for debate prep.

I shook my head and set my phone down. "So, how does this work? I mean, there were hundreds of witnesses, right?"

Mom nodded. "I don't know, sweetie. You know nobody from Stonewall is going to testify against Gunny."

Parker set her cereal bowl on the counter. "There were 'witnesses' for both sides. People will say Reggie had a knife, a gun, whatever fits. And Mom's right, people aren't exactly going to want to testify against someone like Gunny Giles."

Gunny was no stranger to courtrooms, which made the whole bail thing even more outrageous. From his multiple arrests—anything from DUI to check fraud—I remember more than one occasion when the cops had arrived at Jeff's house after Gunny came home drunk and started punching anyone in sight. But while he'd mostly been a small-town drunk, I'd heard he'd been hanging with some more serious biker types. I couldn't say, I'd quit going over to the Giles' place well before that, but it was known. Either way, I was a bit surprised he'd managed to get out of jail.

The paper caught my eye, but I managed to stay clear of sports. The last thing I wanted to do was read all the stories about Stonewall's big game with Pulaski in the opening round of the state playoffs this weekend. Again, I went to my phone, where I found more on the Heritage March, now planned for next Saturday.

Organizers were expecting upwards of a thousand people, with attendees arriving from all over the country, seeking to halt the town's plans that fell in line with what was happening all over the country—the continued "whitewashing and erasing of our history and removing of our heroes." Wow. I sent a text to Devin. He called back a few minutes later.

"You see the thing?" I asked.

"Yeah, about the march?"

"A thousand people? You think that's accurate?"

"Who knows? I just hope the town council isn't intimidated by all this mess. You know they're going to parade this Gunny clown out there for support."

"Yeah."

"Hey, what do you have planned today?"

I looked around the house. Mom was working, Parker was doing nerd stuff. "Um..."

I could almost hear his smile on the other end. "Want to see Zakia?"

An hour later, I parked near the bridge and hiked up to Cal's Music, where a small crowd was gathering on the sidewalk. My steps dragged involuntarily. Sure, I was going to Briggs, doing my best to make things right, but still, what exactly was I getting into?

I recognized Javier and DreShaun, and it was hard to miss Keesha giving me the side eye. Behind them stood Zakia. She saw me and cocked her head in surprise. Before I could wave, Devin stepped forward.

He caught me looking at Zakia and smiled. "I knew that would get you to show up."

"It's not that. I didn't have much else to do today." It sounded lame so I tried to change the subject. "So what's going on?"

Devin gave me that wide grin of his. "Right this way, snowflake."

I cocked my head. "What did you call me?"

Devin laughed, patted me on the back, and called for everyone to gather inside.

I stopped. "Hang on. How come you can call me White this-or-that but if I say something similar it's racist?"

Devin's eyes widened. He took a few steps my way, his smile fading some but still in place. He blinked a few times. "What did you want to call me?"

"No, it's not that. I mean, how come you can... You know what, never mind."

He looked around. "Okay, you're right. I'm sorry I called you snowflake."

I stared at him. "Is that just a way to call me that again?"

He smiled. "Maybe."

I shook my head. "Okay, whatever."

He threw his arm around me, and we followed everyone inside. Heads turned to us as Devin called them to attention.

"Listen up. Thanks for coming out. We've got lots of work to do, so I'll give it up to the ladies with the plan."

Keesha and Zakia stepped forward. Keesha's gaze lingered on Devin's hand, which was still on my shoulder. Zakia, wearing a black BD Briggs hoodie, jeans, and sneakers, had no problem being heard.

"Okay, people. We all know about this Heritage March and what it's all about. And it's not just locals. This thing is gaining traction from all over the state and beyond. So we need to show up and show out. Let our voices be heard. We will make it clear that not *all* of Ridgeton is onboard with out-of-town agitators"—she paused with a smirk— "coming to our town to intimidate the city council's decision."

I looked out the front glass, where the gusty breeze tickled the awning over the entrance, curling the C-443 flyer tacked to the light pole. Some people stood watching from across the street.

Zakia continued. "We will begin on Fifth and come down, take a right, and go past the monument. We need to stay focused. Stay on the sidewalks and listen closely." She turned to DreShaun. "We *will not* engage these people. We will, however, be loud, be heard, and be seen."

Keesha took it from there. "First, I'd like to take a moment of silence for Reggie Watts. So if we could…"

Everyone bowed their heads. Traffic swooshed outside. A car honked. I couldn't help looking up. A bearded man in a pickup glared at the store in passing.

Keesha raised her head. "That's right, this is our time. A decision has been made to relocate the statue, and some people are looking to change that decision. We already know all too well what they're capable of."

I was surprised at how organized things were. Keesha and Zakia spoke about the laws, codes, permits needed for next weekend. I met a few kids from Briggs and shook hands with some older people who thanked me for showing up. When it got to be too much, being congratulated and patted on the back, I drifted to the back of the store as everyone else stepped outside.

Was I really going to do this? Counter protest at the rally? It had taken everything I had to keep one foot in front of the other last week, at the Unity thing. This promised to be much more than that.

I was staring at the pictures when Zakia came up beside me. "I'm impressed."

I set my hand to my chest and looked around. "With me?"

She laughed. A few kids were still up front, a group was sitting around, playing with the instruments. The store opened at eleven on Saturdays, but Mr. Calloway seemed to be enjoying all the company.

Zakia closed her eyes and bit her smile as she nodded. "Yes, with you and everyone. Seriously, thanks for coming. Does this mean you're joining us?"

"Hmm, well, I do have the Heritage thing..." I cut it short seeing her face. "Okay, sorry, bad joke."

She squinted at me. "You have a lot of those."

"Ouch."

She bumped my shoulder with hers. "Oh, you can tell a joke but can't take a joke? I see how it is."

"Good point. Hey, can I ask you something?"

She shrugged. "Yeah, sure."

"Why does Keesha hate me?"

Zakia rolled her eyes with a laugh. "Hate is a strong word." She nodded toward the front of the store. "Take a walk?"

Outside, Zakia spoke to Keesha and said goodbye to Javier and DreShaun before we started up Main Street. The day was warming up nicely, the leaves in the street flipping and dancing with each passing car. The sky was clear, and the sun was bright, fighting off the morning chill.

Zakia kicked at a leaf. "Keesha and I are both officers in the BSU, and so, you have to understand—"

"Hang on, the 'BSU'?"

She shot me a look. "Yeah, the Black Student Union."

"Gotcha. Okay. Wait, what does the BSU do?"

"Oh, well, I'm going to assume you guys don't have a chapter at Stonewall. Well, it supports," she shrugged, "us. It's a group where we can talk openly about race, discrimination. What we can do for our community. For change. Kind of like what we're doing now."

I nodded. "And that's what Devin and I are trying to do, right?"

"Yes, but..." Zakia, clasped her hands as we waited to cross Eighth Street. She looked left, then right, then pursed her lips. "Hmm, how can I say this? Okay, I mean, our union is open to all students, right? But I think Keesha maybe feels like, here you come swooping in, this cute White guy, football player, ready to fix all our problems—I mean, according to the news and media and all—"

"Did you say, *cute* White guy?"

Zakia blushed. "No, I don't think—"

"I'm pretty sure you said cute."

"Okay, yes. Cute. Fine. Can we get back on track here? Short answer is no, she doesn't hate you. I think Keesha will be okay. At the same time, for us, it's like, here we are, the Black Student Union, working for all of this and now you're here, from Stonewall, and..." She trailed off.

We walked past the construction near the bank. I glanced over to Zakia and realized this was about more than Reggie. More than Devin and me, more than the monuments, even. And, maybe for the first time, I realized what it was Keesha and Zakia needed from me the most.

"Look, I'm sorry about the jokes. How about I don't talk and just listen for a while?"

She nudged me again with her shoulder. "I'd like that."

CHAPTER 24

Zakia caught up with me just before class started on Monday. "Nice hair," she said with a smile.

I ran a hand over my head, where the sides were short but the top a bit longer, cheesing big time yet still trying to play it cool. I'd had it cut Saturday afternoon at the barbershop next to the music shop, seeing how I no longer trusted my old barber with a straight edge razor to my throat. Maybe that was a testament to how weird my life had become, that I felt safer at Briggs and Lower Main Street than I did anywhere else.

Zakia rolled her eyes and strolled into class. As far as reading, I hadn't touched a thing. Not after all the planning or the news about Gunny, hanging out with Parker yesterday. So when Zakia asked about my study guide, I unzipped my book bag and found it smushed down in the bottom.

Her mouth fell open. "Seriously?"

"It was kind of a crazy weekend."

"Yeah, I'll bet. More interviews rolling in?"

"No, not like that," I said, looking away.

"You okay?" Zakia asked, her tone softer.

I nodded. "Yeah, I just…" It was easier for me to joke around. I could do the joking, because if I wasn't laughing it off, I had to face what my life was at the moment. We'd gotten another death threat last night. Devin and I had started comparing them, chuckling like they didn't bother us a bit. But at night, rolling around in bed, the threats always came back to mind. And they weren't so funny then.

Mrs. Johnson swept into the room and slammed the door. "Okay, people. We have a lot to do this week. Oh, and pop quiz time."

Just what I needed. Zakia's gaze lingered on me as the quizzes were passed out. All I could do was turn away and prepare myself for failure.

On the way home my phone dinged with a text from a private number.

> Watch your back and your words. Things are about to happen

By habit, I blocked the number, ignoring the chill rushing down my spine. At home, Mom was working late, and Park and I were on our own for dinner. I smiled at the sweet little note Mom had left for us, like I was ten. But I took her up on the spaghetti in the fridge.

Park was goofing off, rapping *Lose Yourself* about Mom's spaghetti, when my phone dinged again. My chest tightened. Another private number.

This is not a test coon lover

Blocked.

Might want to lock your doors

Blocked.

"What's going on?"

Parker watched me closely.

"Nothing," I snapped. I blocked all the numbers and tossed the phone to the side. I checked on dinner, then flipped on the local news.

Lately, it was all we watched. I plated our dinners while the news went to commercial. When it returned, the reporters were going on about Ridgeton's favorite pastime—our beloved Civil War monument. The big rally organizers were even more worked up now that the city had set a date for the relocation. March 3 of next year.

Great. Announcing a date right before the rally wasn't the brightest idea, in my opinion, not that anyone was asking. The screen flashed to a handful of protestors standing under the great General

Elijah Abner. Red-faced and spitting, these people were not about to let this happen.

It was the usual suspects and the usual talk. The same bearded geezers who were suddenly concerned about our history. Then the news ran some clips, a random mom at the grocery store with a slight smile, wondering if the city council had better ways to spend their time. A guy getting gas who thought the statue certainly wasn't hurting anyone. Seemed everyone they found thought the city was erasing its own history. The screen spanned Main Street. Upper Main, where a couple of businesses had set FREE GUNNY stickers in the windows, then Lower Main, to the sleek little coffee shop and Cal's Music, with *Support C-443!* Signs.

It was like putting a target on the store.

From there it was back to the downtown terrace, the picturesque backdrop of the river in the shot. A reporter on the scene nodded fiercely, as behind her the crowd railed and rallied. But what made me nearly fall out of my chair was Zakia and Keesha standing beside the reporter, taking it all in at the top of the stairs.

The reporter stuck a mike in Zakia's face. I sat up too fast and dumped a meatball on my lap. Parker snorted.

The reporter fired away. "So I'm here with two BD Briggs seniors. Young ladies, what is *your* take on the monuments? Should they stay or go?"

Zakia fiddled with her book bag straps, looked left, then right. "Well, let's see. They were erected in the nineteen fifties, correct?"

Parker smiled. "Isn't that the girl you like? She's pretty."

I nearly flipped my plate over. "What? No. I mean. Shh."

The reporter nodded. "Well, I can't verify, some but..."

Zakia smirked. "They were, I checked. They were a gift from the Daughters of the Confederacy. Erected precisely at the time when the courts were forcing schools to integrate."

She looked good on television. She looked good in person, too, but on the screen her eyes shined, and her smile was all kinds of adorable as she nodded knowingly to the reporter, who blinked a few times.

"So you're in support of the removal of the statues?"

Zakia wasn't taking the bait. "Can you imagine? Wherever did we get our history before these..." She glanced down the steps toward the statue, the great man on horseback, sword drawn. "Statues?"

Parker laughed.

The reporter changed gears. "Some are arguing that if we remove the statues—"

Keesha took it from there. "That what, the Civil War never happened? People can't read books? We don't need a statue of some traitorous general mounted on his horse in a public space to know our history."

There you have it. Back to you, Jim.

I called Devin to see if he caught it. He picked up on the second ring.

"Did you see Zakia on the news?"

He laughed. "Yep. *And* I saw my girlfriend. I'm seeing her now."

I sat up. "You're there?"

"Yeah."

"Why didn't you guys tell me?"

"What do you mean?"

What *did* I mean? I hated the spotlight. I knew this wasn't about me. And yet, I felt left out. "I...nothing. Cool, man, I'll see you tomorrow, all right?"

"Yep. Peace."

I WAS in my room reading *Things Fall Apart* when Devin called.

"Ben." His voice was low, off.

"Hey, man, you okay?"

"Yeah, it's just..."

"Ya'll aren't still at the monument, are you?"

"No, I'm down at the store."

I set the book down. "What's wrong?"

Some movement on his end. "I don't know. This...truck keeps driving by."

His voice was low, very un-Devin like. An engine revved in the background. Then a blast of a trumpet. Max must have been practicing.

"What do you mean?"

"It's, I don't know. Big truck, flags in the back. Guys are talking trash too."

I rolled out of bed. "I'll be down in a few."

Mom and Park were practicing for her next debate. Forcing calmness into my voice, I said I was running to the music store to do a favor for Devin.

Five minutes later, I crossed the bridge and pulled up a block away from the shop, my eyes darting left and right as I searched for any signs of trouble. I found Devin standing outside the store, shoulders hunched and hands in his pockets. He saw me and nodded.

I did the same. "Hey, man, you cool?"

Devin pulled his hands from his pockets, blew into his fist. "Yeah, thanks for coming. I feel stupid, it's probably nothing. Just, after the news and all..." He shrugged.

"Yeah, I know what you mean. Is your pops around?"

Devin nodded to the back. "Yeah, he's got Max and some kids back there."

I smiled. "What, like group lessons?"

Devin smiled. "He wants to do this Christmas jazz thing. It's dumb."

"Damn, it's not even Thanksgiving yet."

"As Pops would say, 'practice, practice, practice.'"

Devin peeked at his phone. I told him about the messages I'd been getting. He glanced up. Of course, he'd gotten them too.

It felt later than only eight. Devin looked around again.

I studied the block up the street before I caught myself. "You sure you're okay?"

"Yeah, I'm good. It's just... I don't know." He laughed.

I knew what he meant. Here we were, two all-state linebackers, scared of our shadows.

He nodded toward the door. "This is stupid, let's go in."

We started inside when the roar of a diesel engine made us both jerk to a stop. An older model pickup barreled down the street. Devin cursed as he stepped forward. The truck, primer gray with a confederate flag mounted in the bed, screeched to a stop in the middle of the street.

My chest tightened and my knees locked. I did my best to stand tall beside Devin as the truck lurched and bucked, spraying black smoke from the exhaust. The driver leaned out the window, his hand in a finger pistol gesture as he pretended to pick us off. *Click, boom. Click, boom.*

The passenger whooped and yelled over the driver. "Coming for you boys, you hear me?"

Devin, who I'd never seen lose his cool, nearly lunged out to the street. "What are you waiting for? I'm right here!"

Both driver and passenger whooped again before the truck grumbled, hitched, then tore up the street to the bridge, leaving Devin and me alone on Lower Main Street, sweating in the cold evening, our chests heaving.

The bell clanged as Mr. Calloway rushed out to us. "You boys okay?"

He had a pistol tucked in his pants. The old timey kind, silver, with a curved ivory grip. My mouth went bone dry. Sure, I'd been around guns, but for a man like Mr. Calloway to come out armed and ready only told me how bad things had gotten.

Devin broke his gaze and turned to his father. "Yeah, just that truck again."

Mr. Calloway looked left, then right. "Come on, why don't you two get in the store?"

Devin refused, and we stood guard on the sidewalk for the next hour, under the clear black sky, only the buzz of the street lamps crackling in the cold. I stuffed my hands in my pockets, hyper alert and looking to spot any sign of danger. Mr. Calloway peeked out every so often until he finished with his lesson. Another ring of the bell as the door opened, and he stepped out again, this time with Max and two other young boys, all bundled up in coats and hats. I couldn't tell if he still had the pistol, as Max begged to stay back with us, but Mr. C wouldn't hear it. He suggested we go inside or go home.

I followed Devin inside, where only a few lamps cast shadows that made the night even more ominous. Devin paced.

I was still thinking about the news. "Hey, so, I've been thinking..."

"Uh-oh."

I nodded. "I, um, I don't have to go on Saturday, to the march."

Devin was fiddling with some guitar picks. He looked up. "You can't let them scare you off so easily."

"No, not that. I mean..." I thought about what Zakia had said. "I don't want to be a distraction. I like what you guys are doing. I wanted to talk to Keesha about it."

He got up and paced to the counter, checked a drawer.

The pistol lay inside. "That your dad's gun?"

He nodded. "Yeah. Just wanted to make sure he left it here."

"You planning on using it?"

Devin looked at me directly. "No. But what you're saying about Saturday, I think you should come, if it's what you want to do. You're as much a part of this as I am now." He smiled as he rolled his eyes. "And for whatever reason, I think Zakia wants you there too. As for Keesha, let me handle that. I'll get her to come around."

"You keep saying that," I said, unable to take my eyes off the gun.

Devin shut the drawer. A car drove past, and we both jumped to attention, then chuckled.

"Okay," I said. "I'm in."

CHAPTER 25

My thoughts were all over the place as I drove home. The threats, the truck, Mr. Calloway, and the gun in the drawer at the shop, all the weird texts. I cranked the heat, but it got too hot. I turned it off, and the cold dread came up feet first, like jumping into the deep end of the pool after a long night's rain.

Another text message. I hit the gas. I was thinking about Mom and Park at home and let up only to roll through a stop sign before I sped up again. I was completely lost in worry when blue lights lit up my window.

"Damn." I smacked the steering wheel, letting off the gas pedal as I searched for a place to pull over. When the cop hit the siren, I gave up and stopped where I was, still halfway out on the street. Cursing under my breath, I gripped the wheel to keep my hands from shaking. I was only two blocks from my house.

In the rearview, I recognized Officer Dave by his dumpy little swagger. My favorite cop from the other day. Damn again. I rolled the window down.

Officer Dave tipped his hat. "Oh, hey, Ben."

He made a show of checking out the inspection sticker on the windshield, then glancing around the truck before he leaned in the window like he was sniffing my breath for any hint of alcohol. "Dave Lewis. Officer Lewis. Remember me from the other day?"

Again, my phone buzzed in my pocket. I thought it might be Mom, or Devin, or another creeper. But the lights from Officer Dave's cruiser were still throwing blue swirls around his cheeks. I sucked it up. "Yes, sir, hi, officer."

"You in a hurry? It's a twenty-five zone through here. You know that, right? And you blew through that stop sign."

I glanced over my shoulder, then wiped my face and tried to stay focused. "Yeah, sorry. I was, um, at the music store." I hesitated, then figured since he was an officer of the law, it wouldn't hurt to mention the truck. "There was this suspicious truck. Two guys, making threats."

Officer Dave reared back. "Hang on. Making threats?"

"Yes. I've been getting a lot of threats recently."

He rocked on his heels a bit. "Now hold on. You mean like the threats from the other day?"

"Kind of. They said they were coming for us next."

Officer Dave frowned. "Hmm. Well, this truck, you get a good look at them?"

It was fuzzy. My mind had been spinning back outside the store. I shook my head. "One had a beard. Both wearing hats."

"Ah. That's about half the town, Ben. What about the truck?"

"Primer gray. I think, it was dark, could have been tan. A flag in the back."

More grimacing. He set his hand on the truck bed and repositioned his gut. "Ben, tell you what, you've had a rough week. I'mma let you off with a warning here tonight." He shifted his weight, leaned closer. "And a bit of advice. Let this go. You hanging around the store the way you were on Saturday, it's not doing you any favors, hear?"

I closed my eyes, half relieved and half confused as to why I had to sit and listen to another lecture from Officer Dave. I opened my mouth to ask what he meant when he waved me off.

"You be careful, slow down. Get yourself home. Have a good night, hear?"

He hobbled back to his cruiser. I watched from my rearview as he fiddled with something inside the car. Obviously, I was to leave first. I put the truck in gear and drove off.

At home, the house was dark but seemingly safe. I shut the front door behind me and double checked the locks. I fell against the door and wiped my face. I took some breaths to calm down. After a few glasses of water, I started downstairs when I noticed the light under Parker's door. A soft hum of music.

I knocked gently. Her music silenced, then she opened the door. One look at me and she opened it wider. "Are you all right?"

I must not have calmed myself down as much as I'd hoped. "Yeah, so, um, you never answered me the other day when I asked. How was school?"

She smiled. "It was fine. I'm fine." She shrugged. "I don't know if anyone's told you, but I can take care of myself." She put up her fists like a boxer.

Parker could always get me to laugh. I smiled, reached out, and tussled her hair like she was eight all over again. "I know, just, sorry."

I turned to leave when she called out. "Dad called while you were gone."

I stopped, closed my eyes. This night would never end. "Yeah?"

"He heard I got suspended, so he figured it was time for a pep talk," she said in a deep grovel, swinging her arm.

She was growing up so fast. I looked up from my feet. "He's good at that sort of thing, huh?" I said. She glanced off. Something was on her mind. "What else?"

Parker rolled her eyes. "He thinks your actions are influencing my behavior." She used air quotes for behavior.

My shoulders slumped, even though it wasn't worth getting upset over. Again, being as headstrong as she was, growing up fast or not, it was easy to forget Parker was only thirteen. "Look, Park..."

She tilted her head, a smile curling at the corners of her mouth. "I told him to shove it. Mom got mad."

"Park."

"Whatever, Ben. You *are* an influence on me, just so you know." She spun away from me. I reached for her shoulders, and she halfway turned, wiping at her eyes. "I'm so proud of you. I hope you know that. For standing up for what you believe. It's, you're amazing."

"Park, I'm not." I looked away, pinched the bridge of my nose. "But thanks. It means a lot to me. It does. I just hate that you got dragged into this."

She snorted, wiped her eyes again with the cuff of her shirt. "Are you kidding?" She put up her fists again. "Bring it on."

I gave her a hug instead. "It's too late to fight. Get some sleep."

Downstairs, I called Zakia. It rang twice, three times, and I was about to hang up because she was probably wondering why I was calling, when the phone clicked. "Ben?"

"Hey, I, uh, how are you?" *Nice.*

"You okay?"

"Yeah, I saw you on the news and just wanted to say you were great."

I held the phone away and dropped my head. So, so corny. I was calling because I needed to know she was all right. The news felt like days, not hours ago.

"Yeah?" I heard her smile. "You sound different."

"Oh, yeah, it's..." My voice was high-pitched and off. It was like all the fear was gassing me up, helium style. I needed to bolt my feet down before I slipped away.

"So, did you want to talk about our assignment?"

I laughed. Because after the night I'd had, sure, okay, I'd talk schoolwork. It sounded like fun. "Yep, it's exactly why I was calling you."

"At eleven." She laughed. Zakia had this great laugh. Deep and confident, but sexy as hell too. "Okay, so you finished the book I assume?"

"Finished?" I looked around for my book bag, under some clothes on the floor. "Well, I'm, almost."

She sighed. "Typical football player."

I sat up with a quick surge of happiness that was all too rare these days. "Hang on, wait. I thought I was different? With the news conference and all?"

"Your fifteen minutes is up, Ben."

"Damn."

"Tell you what. How about we meet in the library tomorrow at lunch."

My chest flushed. It felt good to flirt with a girl. It had been a while. I smiled. "Lunch? It's a date."

"No. Not a date."

"I mean, it kind of is."

"Goodnight, Ben."

Inspired, I kicked the clothes off my bag, dug in, and dusted off *Things Fall Apart*.

CHAPTER 26

I crashed hard, woke up in time to take a shower, get dressed, and have a bowl of cereal at the table with Parker. Things weren't normal by any means, but seeing my little sister so focused, all set for debate in her collared shirt and sweater, things were as close as they'd been in a while.

Mom slept in as she was on swing shift this week. Parker had her face buried in her laptop, going on about Federalists and Anti-Federalists as I slurped the milk from my bowl and stepped outside to warm up the truck. The fall chill had taken a plunge toward winter and the past few nights had dipped into the twenties.

I shuffled down the front porch steps, rubbing my arms, smiling as I thought about the conversation with Zakia last night. Thick frost coated the windshield as I got in the truck and started the engine. I cranked the heat, then jumped out. I took two steps before I saw the gaping rectangle in the back of Mom's car where the window used to be.

I wheeled around, as though maybe someone was standing there and could tell me what happened. My hands shook as I opened the back door to Mom's car, looking for a brick amongst all the diamond-like chunks of glass. Instead, I found some kind of statue.

By then Parker was out on the porch, clutching her elbows. "Ben? What are you doing?"

The statue was one of those porch jockey things, with the black face and red lips, big white eyes. That it was hurled through the back window was bad enough, but what made the hairs on my neck stand up was the small noose around its neck.

"Ben?"

"Get inside, Parker," I snapped.

"Why?"

"Just...get inside."

Mom was in the living room when I came back in. Still in her robe, her hair was matted to the side, and she clutched her phone in one hand. She took one look at what was in my hands and called the police. I forgot about the truck, still running, puffing out clouds of exhaust, when a police officer arrived on the scene.

It wasn't officer Dave but a younger cop who looked like he was barely out of high school. His uniform hung loose on his lanky frame, and he kept adjusting his utility belt and hand-combing his hair. He looked like he'd been napping in his car in the Hardeez parking lot.

"Good morning, Mrs. Hoy."

We met the officer outside. Mom, who'd changed into jeans and a sweatshirt, held up the statue before "Deputy Ballard" could finish introducing himself.

He glanced from the statue to the car as though it took real detective work to figure out what had smashed the window. "Ouch," he said.

Ouch. I glanced at Parker, shivering in the yard, her glare trained on Deputy Ballard, who turned to Mom. "So, uh, looks like some pranksters came by."

Mom's mouth tightened. She spun around, shaking the little statue in his face. "This look like a prank to you?"

Again, he studied the statue, then nodded at me. "Officer Lewis said he ran into you last night."

Mom was aghast. "What does that have to do with anything?"

He ignored her, still talking to me. "Quite a year you were having. Saw that game against Rustburg. You had three sacks."

I blinked, wondering what he was talking about.

He shrugged. "I played at Stonewall. Linebacker, too. Class of 2018."

"Oh, well..."

"I mean, nothing big-time like you, but..." He finally realized I wasn't trying to talk football. "Anyway."

He got to work and ducked into Mom's car, speaking to us over his shoulder. "So, uh, did you see anything suspicious when you got home?"

"No, I saw something suspicious outside of Cal's Music, though." I explained about the truck, the two guys making threats. Parker was taking it all in.

Mom turned to me. "Ben? What threats? What happened?"

Deputy Ballard, still hunched over in the backseat, watched Mom and me. I was stuck trying to downplay it to keep Parker (and Mom) from freaking out, while at the same time trying to convey to the officer how serious things were getting. "There was a truck riding around Main Street last night. Devin called me, said he was worried. I went down there." I looked at the deputy. "I told Officer Dave—uh, Lewis—about it. Gray Chevy, older, jacked up, big confederate flag waving in the back. They're making threats," I nodded at the statue. "And following through."

Ballard frowned. "So you saw them throw this?"

I glanced away with a sigh. "No. It was...these guys, driving past the music store last night, they were making threats to Devin. I know it was them. Look." I pulled out my phone. "I've got these text messages..."

"And you think they did this?"

It was like a bad movie, this guy's refusal to do anything. Deputy Ballard ducked out of the back, wiped his hands on his polyester pants, and looked left, then right, like someone was hiding in the bushes. "Tell you what, I'll file a report, poke around, see what I can find. But at the same time, I'd try to keep a low profile."

Mom launched forward, until she stood only inches from him, her voice quaking with anger. "You're worthless. Absolutely worthless."

I slid over to her, hoping I wouldn't have to restrain her.

Deputy Ballard backed down. "Ma'am. I understand you're frightened, but we're—"

"Frightened? This whole town is about to ignite and you're twiddling your thumbs. What is the police department's plan for this Heritage March, can you tell me that?"

He cocked his head as though he had no idea why the police would need a plan for something like that. While he fumbled around for an answer to Mom's question, Parker turned to me, and I closed my eyes.

We were on our own.

WE HAD to force Parker to go to school. Mom took her in the truck, then followed me to the garage to drop off her car. She said she'd get a ride to work with a coworker, so I took the truck to school. After all the running around, it was going on lunch by the time I got to Briggs.

I missed Zakia in English, which was good because I wasn't in the mood to flirt, smile, or even talk to anyone at the moment. I wanted to punch something, and I was still feeling that way when Devin found me in the lobby and asked what was up.

I shook my head, said I'd tell him later. I couldn't talk, not right now, not even to Devin. I was having trouble with words. I kept replaying the moment in the driveway. Mom's rage, Parker's fear, the indifferent cops that kept showing up at our house only to tell me to lay low. What else was going to happen? I couldn't live like this, waiting for the next bad thing.

Devin asked me to text him later, and I walked off in a daze. Part of me was done with this little experiment. It wasn't working. I wasn't helping anyone. I was only making things worse for myself and my family. But as the bell rang and the lockers shut, another part of me was thankful to be at Briggs. Because if my old friends had any part in what had happened this morning, it meant I was safest within the worn smooth walls of this historical building. Strange times indeed.

It knocked me back to think that Moose or Jeff would do that to Mom's car. But after the messages they'd sent me, who's to say it wasn't them? Or the guys in the truck, or anyone in this town for that matter. Trudging down the hall, I was still stuck on that when I heard my name.

I turned and found Zakia, leaning against my locker, clutching her books. She smiled, but it seemed forced. "Hey, I thought we were meeting in the library."

The library. The phone conversation from a million years ago. I dropped my head. "Oh, right. Sorry."

She pushed off the locker, turned to me, and cocked her brow. "And you missed English. You ducking me, Ben?"

"No, not at all." I laughed, but my heart wasn't in it. Here was this beautiful girl flirting with me and I could only shrug.

Her eyes searched over me. "Well, I've got some time?"

I couldn't say no, not after standing her up already, and so we started for the library, leaving the noise and buzz of the hallways for the sanctuary of books. We took a desk near a window, and Zakia pulled out her book and notebook.

I went in my bag but realized my book was at home, beside my bed. I started to get up. "I um, I didn't bring my book."

She smiled. "Are you serious? Was this all a ruse?"

"No, I..." I smiled. "A what?"

"Here," she patted the seat beside her. "We can share. Just this once and all."

A hint of coconut as she started with the worksheets, going on about Okonkwo's exile and who knew what else. I tried to focus but only saw Mom's smashed back window, the little porch jockey, and most of all, the noose. How the deputy might as well have been laughing through it all. Again, I tried to push through, but my mind kept going back to Devin at the store. Officer Dave last night.

I was in no place to read or study and Zakia could tell. She set the book down. "Ben, what's going on?"

I wiped my face. "Look, Zakia, I'm sorry. It's kind of a bad time."

Her face softened. "You want to talk about it?"

I shook my head. A study group entered the library and took a large table, all smiles and stifled giggles. I looked around the big, beautiful library, remembering my conversation with Dr. Jamerson. "Do you ever... I mean, are you worried about Saturday?"

She closed the book and held it in both hands as she gave it some thought. "Worried, like how? For my safety?"

"Yeah. People are acting crazy. And trust me, that dude, Gunny? He's already there, crazy, I mean. He's been there." I pulled my hand through my hair. "I grew up with his son. It's weird, you know, to suddenly like, detach myself from them."

"Have you tried to talk to them?"

"Um, no. But I think they might be trying to get in touch with me. Last night, they—someone—busted my mom's car window. It's why I missed English."

Zakia's face changed. She set her hand on mine. "What?"

I told her about the store with Devin, getting pulled over, how the cops wouldn't take anything seriously. When I got to the part about the window, I couldn't bring myself to say what was thrown or the noose. It seemed, I don't know, I was ashamed of it. Like it was somehow my fault.

She listened, took it in, and gave it some thought. Then she said something I couldn't believe. "I wanted to warn you, that day at the track."

"I'm glad you didn't. I might not have stayed."

She shook her head. "I don't believe that."

"Seriously, Zakia. I'm not... This whole thing. Me. It's like, they got the wrong guy. I'm not some hero."

She looked off, then back to me with a small smile. "I told you already. You don't have to be a hero. And you don't have to do this alone. There's Devin. And me. And all of us." She squeezed my hand. "I know you just got here, but Keesha and I, Devin, too, we've been working on this for a while now. At town hall meetings, community marches—this is just the first time we've gotten this far."

The strength in her eyes, I found comfort in her confidence. She'd known the stakes the whole time and was still fighting for what she believed in. Most of all, she was right, I didn't have to be a hero. None of us did. We only had to believe.

And maybe that's what made me so afraid.

Zakia's pep talk helped, and as the day wore on, I was able to brush aside some of the fear from that morning. Mom's window was still broken, but it could be fixed. We were okay and that was what mattered. It's what I told myself until I came home to find Moose's truck in my driveway.

I hit the brakes, a bit shocked to see my former co-captain and friend. Even more shocking was seeing Jeff standing beside him. I knew they weren't at my house to play nice, and part of me was ready to get it over with.

Moose turned and squared his shoulders, his eyes narrowing to squints the way they did just before he laid into an underclassman at practice. Jeff's eyes were jumpy and deranged, darting around. Still, I wasn't going to turn around and speed down the road. I parked, got out, half expecting to get jumped, half wanting to hug my friends from an old life.

They seemed in no hurry to speak. Ignoring the drum of my heartbeat in my ears, I reminded myself that this was my house, where Mom and Parker lived as well. I lifted my head and did my best to keep my voice level. "What's up, fellas?"

Moose glanced at Jeff before he spoke. "Hey, Ben, how's Briggs going?"

I shrugged, fixed my book bag. "Oh, just dandy."

Jeff's mouth hung open. His cheeks were gaunt. Sunk deep in their sockets, his eyes held an almost primal gleam. He reminded me of a trapped animal, ready to fight or run its way out of danger.

Moose pushed off his truck, hulking over me as he closed the distance between us. I planted my feet, waiting for whatever was coming next.

He glowered at me, his mouth pursed as though he wasn't sure whether to speak or spit on me. "What in the hell are you doing, man? We've been friends forever, and now you hop off to Briggs? You're on *Good Morning, Virginia*, talking shit about us?" He threw his hand back in Jeff's direction. "Calling Gunny a murderer?"

"I didn't..." I shook it off, forced myself not to hang my head in shame, not to look away from his face. I was relieved Parker had debate and wouldn't come home to this. Mom was at work. This was mine and mine alone. "I've told you and everyone else my reasons. You just don't like those reasons."

Moose glanced over his shoulder to Jeff again, who was muttering to himself. He curled his hands into fists, rolled his neck. It was Friday night all over again. Moose got back to me. "You left us. Left us like we were nothing. And you go on TV and make it sound like we're Nazis or something."

"No, it wasn't like that at all, I didn't—"

"You did!" Jeff screamed out, his face splotchy and red, full of rage. A stream of spit dangled from his lips. "You left us for a bunch of Blacks you don't even know."

Jeff slammed his fist into the truck, his body heaving, retreating back to his shell.

Moose cocked his head, fists still balled and ready. "I can't believe you would do this, not after all we've been through. Coach told us he came here to talk to you and Devin Calloway was here. He the one feeding you all this stuff?"

I rolled my eyes. "Nobody is *feeding* me anything. I'm through with all the *sides*, with all the hate. Look where that got us. We need—"

The punch landed like a brick to my temple. A spark that ignited an explosion in my head. I dropped to the ground. When I blinked, Moose hovered over me, pointing with his left hand, his right still balled into a fist, ready for more. "You don't know a damn thing about what we need."

I tried to blink again but my left eye stayed put. I rolled one way, started to get up, but Moose shoved me down again.

"We stick together. It's what Coach has always said. But no, not you. You run off like a bitch and abandon us all. Everyone sees you at Reggie's thing, when Gunny is in jail. And some of the guys on the team are still talking about that night. You wanna blame someone? Blame yourself. You're the one who went and started all this shit. Remember that."

I tried to get up. Moose smacked me in the face, and I went down again. Two kicks slammed into my side, like sledgehammer blows to my ribs. I gasped, the air sucked from my lungs. I collapsed to the ground. With a grunt, I turned the other way as Moose, huffing and sweating now, allowed me to stagger to my feet.

I managed to stand, hunched and reeling, as Moose came close enough that his nose touched mine. "I should've known you'd do something like this, Ben. I should've known. Tell you what, go to Briggs and take all your self-righteous ways with you. And don't show up at Sal's, ever. That's my free advice for you."

As Moose stalked off, the world as I saw it tilted left, then overcorrected as I struggled to find my balance. But even in the fog, part of me felt like I deserved it. Still, I wasn't going to let him win, let him threaten me and simply drive off. I hobbled after my old friend, spitting blood in the driveway. "What are you saying? You know something about my mom's window? About the truck riding past the music store?"

Moose's eyes flashed when I mentioned the store. Jeff twitched, still looking deranged, like he wanted to finish me off. Moose cocked his head, a begrudging respect in his eyes as I came forward. He didn't hit me again. He recovered, stepping back and shaking his head. "Naw, Ben. I don't know anything about that. I'm too busy winning playoff games. All I'm saying is it wouldn't be good for you to show up at Sal's."

He guided Jeff to the passenger door the way you would a little brother or young son. He ambled around the truck, pausing to let me know what he was thinking. "Just between us, I hope they yank your scholarship." He managed a smile. "Now go get some ice for your eye, and your ribs. And stay away from downtown. Things might get a little hot."

My whole right side drummed with a deep, searing throb. It hurt to breathe, much less call out to him. "What the hell does that mean?"

I took another step toward the truck. Moose held my stare as he slammed the door, revved up the engine, and sped off. I stood there with my eye swollen shut, a split lip, my side feeling like it was caved in, wishing I knew what to do. Wishing for an answer. A way to turn this around.

Instead, I puked in my yard.

CHAPTER 27

I got myself up, looked around, then walked inside. For some reason, I called Dr. Jamerson and left him a rambling message about what I was doing and what was happening in my town. Then my phone buzzed, and I stared at Mom's name on the phone, debating whether or not I could speak to her.

She called again, and once more, until I took the call, an icepack on my face. She'd taken the rest of the day off and wanted to catch Parker's debate, oh, and maybe go by the store. She needed me to pick her up. "Ben, are you there? What's going on?"

"Nothing. It's nothing." I told her I'd be by in a bit, then shuffled into the bathroom to clean up the best I could.

Ten minutes later, I pulled into the plant. "How was work?" I asked as she got in the car, trying to sound upbeat while keeping my head turned toward the driver side window. It didn't work. I looked like a zombie.

She pounced. "What's going on?" She leaned over and pulled me to her. I winced at the shooting pain in both my ribs and around my eye.

"Oh my hell, Ben. What happened?"

Some people were outside, hanging at the picnic tables and smoking cigarettes. They had mesh caps on their heads, holding phones, but Mom's fussing was getting some attention.

I pulled myself away. "It's fine. Can we at least not do this here?" I started driving, ignoring Mom's stare, her raspy breaths. "Hey, look at it this way. Parker's giving out black eyes and I'm receiving them."

"Ben," she said, her voice low and shaky. "Who did this to you?"

No way could I tell her that. Besides, I was still worked up, more over the threats than the punch. Still tasting the blood in my mouth. Still wondering what exactly Moose meant when he'd said some of the guys on the team were talking. Talking about what? The game? Gunny? Reggie? Me? Was that a good thing?

When I didn't answer, Mom only freaked out more. "You need to tell me what happened right now. We need to file a report."

"Yeah, a report." I laughed, tapping the steering wheel. "Because that's been working out so well for us."

So much for normal. Mom demanded to drive. I shrugged my shoulders, swapped seats, and fiddled with the radio that never got reception once we crossed the bridge over Early Creek. Might as well tell her. "Moose and Jeff stopped by the house."

"Moose did that to you."

I nodded. "I think he went easy on me."

I gave up on the radio, left it on an oldies station that was stuck in the static. We turned into the garage, where Mom's Toyota sat untouched where we'd left it, the window still busted out. I turned to her. "Did you call about it?"

She stared at the car. "No, I just figured…"

I unbuckled my seatbelt. "I'll go in and check." I started to get out of the truck.

Mom touched my arm. "It's okay, I'll do it." Her face softened. "And we need to put some ice on your eye." Mom wiped her eyes. "And your ribs," she said, her voice breaking.

"That's what Moose said."

Mom shot me a wet glare. "We're going to talk more about this," she said as she opened the door.

I sat back and exhaled, realizing why she hadn't wanted me to go in to check on the car. Apparently, it wasn't a good idea to show what was left of my face in town.

Mom brushed her hair back before she entered the building, eyeing the cars in the parking lot. For nearly seventeen years I'd grown up here, where everyone knew everyone. Jed, the mechanic, used to smile at me with pride in his eyes as we talked football. Another glance at Mom's car, the broken glass in the back, shards like teeth. Seemed like pride was a double-edged sword.

Or maybe I was overthinking things. Maybe they were backed up. It wasn't until I saw Mom at the counter, jabbing a finger at Jed, that I figured I'd better go check on her. I slid out of the truck and walked around the lot, past the shop, just now noticing the FREE GUNNY sticker on the window. Three guys in coveralls were sitting around a heater, shooting the breeze. One car and two open bays. A guy looked up, his easy grin hardening to stone. I didn't care, I did my best to ignore the throb of pain and strode into the office.

The door dinged as I walked in, although you could hardly hear it the way Mom was letting them have it. "Fifteen years I've been coming here, and now you won't work on my car?"

"Jen, I told you, we're slammed. I'll get to it later."

"You think I don't know what this is about?"

"Mom."

Jed jerked his attention to me. No pride in his eyes now. He took notice of my face then turned back to Mom. "Look, I don't know what you're talking about. We got to special order that window and—"

"It's a Toyota. You probably have one around back." Mom shook her head.

I set a hand on her shoulder, trying to calm her down some, but when I looked through the window out back, I saw a primer-colored truck, a confederate flag mounted to the back. It was the truck from the other night, I was sure of it. My mouth went dry, and I had to force the words out of my mouth. "Mom, let's go. I'll take your car."

She turned to me like she'd just noticed I'd come in. Then she turned back to Jed. "Fifteen years."

Jed knocked his head back, fixed his hat. "You could teach your boy something about loyalty. Looks like he could use the help."

Mom flew to the counter. "Listen here, you prick. My son is the most loyal person I know. He's got the courage to stand up for something he believes in."

Jed never moved, watching Mom without interest. "Like I said, we're slammed."

"Give me the damn keys," she ordered.

Jed set them on the glass counter and slid them to us.

My feet were dead weight. Seeing the truck, I forgot about my throbbing eye and the stab of pain in my ribs as I pulled Mom away and got her turned for the door. She stared him down as we walked outside, then to the truck, past the snickering in the bays. I didn't even look for the guy with the beard. They were here, I knew that much.

"I'll take the car, okay?"

Mom reluctantly handed me the keys and climbed into the truck. Her hair fell over her face.

I tried and failed to calm her down. "We'll find someone else to fix it, okay?"

She nodded, still glaring at the office.

I was worried she might ram the truck through the glass. "Are you okay to drive?"

"Yes, Ben, I just..." She closed her eyes. "Are you?"

She was on the verge of breaking down. I shot her a smile. I knew she thought this was her fault, but it wasn't. I took her by the shoulders. "I'm okay, Mom. It's not as bad as it looks. Are you still going to the school? Parker's thing?"

"It's not right, Ben." I could feel the fight still raging inside of her. This was the avalanche and she only wanted to protect me.

I tried to keep my voice calm. "I know, Mom. But what are we going to do, move?"

"No, they won't win. We can't let them win." She tucked her hair back and wiped her face. A few breaths and I watched the fight turn to tears in her eyes.

I smiled at her, despite it all. I shut the truck door and started for the Toyota, feeling their eyes on me as I cranked the car up. It was cold, with the back window busted out. I flipped the heat on, and something came to me then, as gusts of cold air hit my face.

Mom's determination drove me to face them. I'd been punched, beaten, and terrorized all in a day. I'd switched schools in the middle of my senior year. Now I sat in Mom's little car with the busted window, shunned, bruised, and beaten. I may have even lost my scholarship.

And still I laughed. I set my head back fearlessly, with a little smirk of my own, laughing because they thought they could stop me. My entire body hurt with the movement, but they would never know because I wouldn't give them that. All they needed to know was that I could deal with anything they wanted to throw my way.

CHAPTER 28

A collision of noises came from the back of the music shop. I stifled a laugh, watching Max with his trumpet, his buddies with a clarinet and sax as they rehearsed for the Christmas parade. They were all giggles as Mr. Calloway dutifully strummed a guitar and did his best to steer things along. He'd start, then abruptly stop after things went off the rails, then calmly offer instruction. From there they did it all over again, barreling through *Take the A Train*.

It was more train *wreck* than anything else. And after they crashed and burned once again, shoving each other and cracking smiles, Mr. C waved his hands to bring them to a stop.

"Okay, come on, come on. Let's try that again."

One of the boys whispered something to Max, who broke into a gut laugh, folding over with convulsions. Mr. Calloway only shook his head. "See what I'm working with here?"

"Sounds okay to me," I said.

Mr. Calloway laughed, until he saw my black eye and his smile faltered. He recovered quickly, clearing his throat. "You here for Devin? He's in the back."

"Yeah, I was going to help him with inventory," I offered, which was code for *keep watch on the store*.

Max let his horn fall to his side. "Ben, what happened to you?"

Mr. Calloway shot him a glare. "None of your business about that. Now, from the top, let's go."

I peeked in the door to the back. Devin turned around, saw me, and cocked his head. He opened his mouth, shut it, and closed his eyes.

"I ran into a door?"

He set down the box in his hands. "Yeah? Want to talk about it?"

"Not even a little bit."

I realized I hadn't told him anything about the window the other day, either. I sucked in a breath, caught between letting it all out and keeping it all trapped in. Devin studied me for a moment, until I turned away, picked up a tangle of cords, and started working to roll them up. "Where do you want these?"

He nodded, taking the hint, then pointed to a hook on the wall. "Right there's fine."

The back room was cluttered with storage and antiques. Devin saw me taking it all in and hopped up. "Here, I'll give you the tour."

A huge, dusty organ filled the back wall. Devin said it came out of a church on Fifth Street. The metal pipes spanned high above our heads, and I wasn't sure how someone could move it without taking out the wall. I ran my hands along the keys when I caught Devin staring again. I laughed. "I'm fine, man. Really. Don't want to talk about it."

"Okay, then." He raised his eyebrows. "Well, check this out."

I followed him through the back door and up a narrow stairway, creaking and clicking as we climbed to a drafty attic that held more of the same. Cymbals and brass, old drum sets. A standup bass guitar and a piano. A stained-glass window as tall as me. Devin ducked as he made his way back to the front of the building, where you could hear the traffic through the old windows.

He pulled a string, and a light came on. He pointed to some old trunks lining the wall. "So, my great-grandfather played with Cab Calloway. They toured all over the place. He took these trunks on tour. They've been everywhere. And you should see some of the suits in there."

I'd heard of Cab Calloway. I shot him a look. "He was a jazz guy, right?"

Devin rolled his eyes. "Yeah, jazz guy. He was huge, man. Music, movies, dancing, everything. He was my great-great-uncle."

I glanced over to the trunks, then back to Devin, who was smiling proudly. "Wow, so this really is in your family. Not just the store, but like, the music?"

He looked off in thought, rubbing his chin. "Yeah, it is. Hey, that's kind of deep, coming from you."

"From me? What's that supposed to—"

A crash came from downstairs, and Devin and I jumped up. We heard laughter and Devin sighed. He pulled the light string. "Okay," he said, brushing past me. "That's the tour. Let's see what Max has broken."

We shuffled downstairs. Devin marched over to the boys, who sort of sat taller. "Come on, Pops. You can't get these boys straight?"

Max tilted his head, staring at me. "Ben, for real. What happened to your eye?"

"Max, not now. You got work to do." Devin took a seat behind the three-piece drum set. The boys perked up, stars in their eyes, as Devin snatched up the drumsticks and gave them a twirl. "All they need is a backbeat. Here."

Then it was Mr. Calloway's turn to light up as Devin shifted, counted off the beat, and started things off. *Boom, tis, Boom, tis, boom-boom, tis*

The giggling ceased. Max stopped with the laughing and set the trumpet to his mouth. His friends followed in, and it all came together. *Take the A Train* in full swing. Well, the horn section was somewhat shaky, but after a few curt stares from Mr. C, Max straightened his back and got it going.

They were halfway there when the door opened, some customers walking in, craning their necks as they heard the music from the back. A lady with a little girl walked back and watched the show. Devin smiled and drummed with ease, putting a little solo on at the end before Mr. Calloway ducked out of the guitar strap and welcomed the lady and the girl, looking to rent a violin.

Devin spun the sticks, set them on the snare, and wiped his hands on his pants.

I cocked my head. "So, you play drums too?"

He shrugged. "Man, I grew up in this store. I picked up a bit of everything."

I found a seat with a jolt of pain in my ribs. I shifted in the chair. "So when did you start playing ball?"

"Freshman year."

"You're serious? You didn't play little league or any of that?"

"Nah, Pops wouldn't let me." He glanced down at my side.

I shifted again and tried not to wince.

My dad had pushed me to play football in kindergarten. Moose and Jeff with me, as the Little Rebels went undefeated every year. Then on to middle school, and now here we were. Football was all I'd ever done. There was never time for anything else. And here was Devin, playing jazz in this store.

Thinking of Moose reminded me of my face. Of Mom's car window.

Devin must have read my thoughts. "Man, you gotta watch those doors."

"No, it's..." I laughed.

Max snickered.

Devin sent the boys up front. When they were gone, he swiveled on the stool, his eyes narrowing. "I'm not letting this go. I didn't see you this morning or at lunch. Now the eye. And..." He gestured to my ribs.

I studied the exposed brick wall, slathered with plaster and paint and excess mortar. There was no need to hide what happened anymore. I fiddled with the drumsticks. "Well, my mom is in the market for a back window for her car. And I'm looking for some new friends, because my old ones kind of suck."

Max and his buddies edged back toward us.

Devin shot them a look, then turned to me. "Come on, let's get out of here."

We stepped outside. The chill found my collar, like fingers down my neck. I shoved my hands in my pockets.

Devin pulled his hood up. "So what's going on?"

The cold wind hit my eyes as we hiked up the street. I leaned into it, with my hands in my pockets, and I told Devin about getting pulled over after our watch at the store, then the window yesterday morning, and moved on to Deputy Ballard, the run in with Moose and Jeff, all the way up to Jed's—which reminded me of the truck. I was still mulling it over as Devin rubbed his jaw, already putting it together.

"So your boys stopped by, and Moose did that, huh?"

"Yeah. To be honest, I was kind of expecting it sooner or later, waiting on it, really. I think he took it easy on me."

I thought back to Moose's cryptic warning, that stuff he'd said about things getting hot. But I didn't want to drop that on Devin right now. I was spent, and besides, what good would it do? We were already watching the store. Instead, I told him about the window, what little was being done about it.

Devin stopped and turned to me. "Sorry, Ben. Really, I am."

"Yeah. I mean, I knew my decision wasn't popular, but...I don't like them messing with Mom and Park."

"I get that. That's why I'm so uptight about the store, you know?"

We got up Main Street, the lights changing. Traffic was light. Devin shook his head as I spoke. He'd asked the football team to help watch the store during the Heritage March. DreShaun and Javier said to count on them.

The streets were mostly empty as we arrived at the terrace, took the steps down to the monument. These days there was always something going on down there, but for now, it was quiet.

Devin stared up at Elijah Abner on horseback, sword drawn. "He was one ugly dude, man."

My mouth fell open, because of all the things I thought he might say, *Hang in there. It's going to be all right. You got this.* That certainly wasn't what I was expecting.

And then we were laughing, going on about Elijah and his dumbass name and pointy beard. Devin had told me more about how

Elijah took exile after the war, then once he was pardoned, he came back and wrote several books, fostering the Lost Cause narrative. How he was of the belief God anointed people with dark skin to be identified as slaves. It was all in his writing, out in the open. And dude still got a statue in our town. Crazy.

We were hiking up the steps when he nudged me. "We can get your mom's window fixed. I know a guy, right past the bridge."

"Nice," I said. "Thanks, man."

"Yeah, no problem. But, hey..."

"Yeah?"

"Seriously, though. Moose and Jeff notwithstanding, you think any of your other teammates would be open to help?"

I nearly tripped on the last step. "You want me to ask my old teammates to help *us*?" I pointed to my eye. "After this?"

Devin stuck his hands in his pockets, exhaled a gust of fog from his mouth, and looked me in the eyes. "I think this whole thing works better if we're united. Besides, I mean, all they can say is no, right?"

"And punch me in the face."

He shrugged it off. "I don't think so. I think you have more pull than you give yourself credit. I think some might want to talk, but they're afraid to speak out."

Every time I'd thought back to Stonewall, I saw Coach, Moose, Jeff, and for some reason, my dad. But what about the other guys? The quiet ones? Maybe some of the guys felt like me but were afraid to speak out. Moose had let it slip some guys on the team were talking about that night. With that in mind, I turned to Devin. "Yeah, I'll see what I can do."

We started back down Main Street. The cold felt good on my face, refreshing even, combined with the hope that maybe some of my old teammates might be willing to help. It had me feeling better. Lighter. Just under my breath, I started singing.

"Ebony and Ivory... live together in perfect harmony... I don't know the rest. Do you?"

Devin shook his head. "You're what my pops would call a damn fool."

CHAPTER 29

Dad always dropped in on Thanksgiving Day. It was the same every year, a meal, some football, and we all settled in to get good and uncomfortable. Mom always did her best to play nice. Over the last couple of years, a new tradition had emerged as Parker and I found a loophole. With our stomachs full and our nerves shot, we'd grab the Christmas lights from the basement and escape outside to untangle the strings and cords and start the decorating, knowing we were safe because Dad wasn't about to get up on a ladder and help.

But with the Gunny situation, *my* situation, this Thanksgiving promised to be the worst yet. Parker had already made it clear she didn't want him there. Mom probably didn't either but took the high road. As for me, I sent Dad a text and gave him an out—wishing him well because I knew how the back hurt and all—but he didn't take it. He insisted on coming.

Things would be interesting to say the least.

Mom was up early, prepping and cooking. She'd calmed down some since the window incident. I'd told her about Devin's guy who'd fix it for us, and she'd nodded in thanks. But every time she saw my face, she'd clench her teeth and curse under her breath.

The swelling around my eye was down, leaving only the dark crescent and a little soreness. My ribs would take a bit longer to heal, as it hurt to take deep breaths or cough, but it worked to serve as a reminder of what I was up against.

The parade was underway on TV. I laughed at Parker mashing potatoes in the bowl with the same determination and grit she put into anything she did. She saw me watching and stuck her tongue out at me.

"Help much?" she said.

"What can I do?"

Mom had me drag up some chairs from the basement. I found them in the back, next to the shelf, and I dusted them off. I groaned at the thought of sitting with Dad, listening to the same tired stories to go along with the interrogation about what I thought I was doing, quitting on my team and changing schools. I could almost hear my dad's voice and play out the entire conversation already.

Moose's words came to mind again—about how some of the guys were asking questions. Questions, that's how it started for me. I took out my phone.

On a whim, I texted Ryan Buckley, a junior defensive end. A quick congrats on the playoffs, happy Thanksgiving and all that. Then, before I chickened out, I added that he could text me if he ever wanted to talk about anything. Ryan was a quiet kid who always worked hard, and he'd made some big plays this year. I thought it would be safe to feel him out, see where he stood on things.

A commotion upstairs could only mean Dad was here. I pocketed the phone, cursing under my breath at how he still didn't knock, even though he'd split years ago.

Mom had changed into a sweater, newer jeans, and I think she'd done something with the eyeliner. I knew she didn't dress up to win my dad back, she was past that. I think she liked to look her best just to rub it in.

The walls closed in as the room suddenly got smaller. A blast of tobacco and coffee as Dad removed his coat and glanced around. "Hey, Jen. Sure smells good."

Mom smiled politely. "Thanks. The game's on." She nodded to the TV, wisely sliding out of reach to the sink to avoid a kiss on the cheek.

Dad hobbled over to the couch and plopped down in his usual

place with a grunt, the same way he always did. I brought him a Mountain Dew, hoping we could keep things civil.

"Hey, Dad."

"Thanks," he said, taking the drink. I waited for him to say something about my eye. He didn't. He looked right past me. "Parker, come here, girl," he called over my shoulder.

A pot *clanged* in the kitchen. I didn't have to be there to see it—Parker, glaring at Mom, who was silently urging her to play nice. She appeared at the doorway, stiff and cold.

"Hi, Dad," she said, failing to muster any cheer.

Dad was unfazed. "Don't you 'Hi, Dad,' me. Get over here and give your old man a hug."

I smirked as Parker forced herself forward and bent at the waist as Dad wrapped her up in an awkward embrace.

"How are you? You still stirring up trouble at school?"

I sat at the far end of the couch. Mom sort of lingered at the doorway. We all knew this could go either way.

Parker caught my eyes as she pulled away from him. She took a breath. "Dad, it's Thanksgiving. Let's just be thankful or something."

"I am, sweetheart. I'm thankful for my family, of course. You're getting so tall."

My dad was only thankful for his weed, his bookie, his recliner, and television. But screw it, I'd let him be delusional for a day.

Parker nodded.

Mom clasped her hands. "Well, things are about ready. Everyone hungry?"

The four of us sat down for a nice, excruciating dinner. We dished up, focused on the meal at hand, and only talked about how delicious things were. Thankfully, Grandma arrived halfway in, gushing about her Black Friday plans and beaming along as Parker recapped debate. Somehow, we managed to skirt around the fact that I was not playing in the regional state playoff game this Saturday.

I caught Dad watching me as Mom exhausted all topics not involving school. Wiping his face, Dad set his napkin on the table and said he was looking forward to the big game this weekend. He was doing his best to get something out of me. With gritted teeth, I scooped up thirds and traded kicks with Parker under the table.

Once Dad had his fill, he slid his chair out and sat back, his big gut spilling over his belt. He told my mom how great she was and took his spot on the couch—because he had easy money riding on the Packers. I hid my sigh in my napkin, because this meant two things: one, he wasn't in a rush to leave, and two, I wasn't going to escape this visit without the talk.

At some point, after Grandma bid her farewells, Dad stepped out for another smoke. When he returned, he refilled his soda and took his place on the couch. "I know you don't want to talk to me about it," he began, staring at the TV.

I took a breath. "Nope."

Dad gave me a knowing nod. "Not much else I can do to change your mind, but let me say, I think you've made a mistake. A huge one."

"Well, I spoke to Dr. Jamerson—"

"I don't want to hear a damn thing that uppity intellectual has to say, hear?" he said, a flash of anger in his eyes. "I want you to think about Jeff. Moose. About the friends you've had all your life. I want you to give that some thought."

My chest tightened as the blood rushed to my head. "Oh, I have. Moose gave me a lot to think about."

Dad looked up, getting the message.

I pounced, pointing toward the driveway. "Did you happen to see Mom's window in the driveway?"

Dad spoke to the TV. "What did you think was going to happen, Ben?"

Mom was hawking us from the table, her jaw clenched, eyes narrowed, like she was about to grab a kitchen knife.

I turned to Dad. "Can we step outside?"

We waited until the game cut to commercial before Dad said goodbye to Mom and hugged Parker. At last, we headed outside, where Dad surveyed the yard before he got around to me, his tone a bit softer than it had been inside. "I just don't get it, Ben. You're parading around, on TV no less. How could you do this to your team? Your friends?"

"They left *me*, Dad. I went to Coach first."

He shook his head. Stuck a smoke in his mouth. "It's only going to get worse, you hear? They won't sit for this. That monument isn't going anywhere, it's who we are."

Every muscle in my legs flexed. I stood tight, broiling with anger I wasn't sure I could hold back. "Well, Dad, someone is dead, so that's not going anywhere either."

He shot me a grin. "You just became Mr. Woke overnight, didn't you? Forgot where you came from, what you stand for."

"You know what, Dad? You lost that right. You can't show up and tell me what's right and wrong. You left us. You left Park. Mom taught me to do the right thing, and that's what I'm doing."

I was done with him. Done with Moose, Jeff, and Coach. All of it. I started for the house.

"Get back here, Ben."

At the door, I spun around. "Next time you come here, make sure you knock. Happy Thanksgiving, Dad."

I slammed the door, locked it, and drew back my fist before I set it on my head. When I turned, Mom and Parker were staring at me.

"Sorry."

Mom blinked a few times, grabbing her elbows. I thought she might breakdown on the spot when Parker threw up her hands and said, "Well, that went about how we expected it to go."

I looked at Mom, whose shoulders rose and fell with a helpless laugh. Parker laughed too. "And don't apologize. It's totally okay." She hooked a thumb over her shoulder. "And there's pie."

Later that night, I was in bed when my phone dinged. I sighed, ready for Dad's wrath, or worse, a new threat. Crazy how these guys didn't even take holidays off from harassing me. But it wasn't Dad, it was a text from Ryan.

> Hey man. Happy Thanksgiving.

I sat up and wiped my face. It seemed like days ago when I'd texted him this morning out of desperation. I hadn't been expecting anything back and had almost forgotten about it after Dad's visit. Needless to say, I was still leery, after all the threats, the window, my own dad calling me a traitor. But this seemed like a good start. I texted back.

> Hey Ryan, thanks for getting back to me. I wanted to ask a favor.

I was thinking what else to type, how to word it. Maybe ask if we could meet up for lunch, or at least a call. The dots flashed across my phone as he responded. I wondered what Ryan Buckley might have to say on Thanksgiving.

> I'd like to help. Me and a few others... if that's what you're asking.

Staring at those four words, *I'd like to help*, I exhaled. I threw my head back, blinked my eyes and read the message again. With another breath, I called him.

Before I could back out, he answered. We talked football, a little about school, Thanksgiving, to get through the greeting. He was getting up early the next day to go hunting. After an awkward silence, I went for it.

"So, this whole Heritage March thing."

"Yeah, Moose has been urging us to go."

I winced. Of course he had.

On the other end, Ryan sounded like he was outside, or walking, maybe looking for someplace quiet. "But some of us, a lot of us, really..." He paused, and I sat up straighter, waiting on his next words. "A lot of us support what you're doing, to be honest. It's just... with Coach and Moose and all..."

"Yeah, no, I get it." My ribs ached as I shifted, fighting off the dizziness. My body felt like it did after a run or weights, arms and legs rubbery, a slight burn in my chest. I couldn't believe it, that some of these guys supported me. I felt the need to explain. "That night, on the field. I just couldn't let it go, you know? I didn't want to leave the team, it was the last thing I wanted to do, but I couldn't..." I blinked, squeezing my eyes tight, trying to reel it in and keep it together.

"I still see it when I try to sleep." He said it so quietly I almost didn't hear.

I wiped my eyes. "Yeah."

We talked about that Friday night on the field, like we should've done weeks ago. Ryan had nightmares too, haunted by the visions of parents and fans unloading on each other. Reggie's body in the grass. All that blood. This whole time my teammates, some of them at least, were going through this as well. It made me feel less alone.

After the call, I sat back on my bed, realizing, maybe for the first time, that Devin was right. Maybe we weren't doing this for nothing after all.

CHAPTER 30

Friday night and Mom and Parker were at the dinner table, huddled over a laptop. Pages and pages of study notes were scattered around them as a study session was underway.

Earlier, Parker and I had braved the sales before getting home to finish up the Christmas decorations in the yard. Now, my mom and little sister turned and regarded me with smirks as I tried to rush off.

Parker giggled. "You look nice, Ben. I'm sure your date will be pleased."

I looked down at the new flannel I'd bought. Jeans. Sneakers. I brushed it off. "It's not a date, Park."

Mom and Parker exchanged nods. More giggles. I rolled my eyes but couldn't help my smile. It was almost like old times, at least until I caught the newscast in the living room.

Dennis Darby, our local sports guy, was nearly rabid in his excitement over the weekly high school football section, as Stonewall and Holcomb were set to kick off Saturday afternoon at City Stadium. All smiles vanished in the kitchen. Between the game and the Heritage March, it was shaping up to be a busy Saturday in Ridgeton, Virginia.

Before I could get caught up, headlights swept over the window. My phone dinged, and I pulled myself away from the TV. "Oh, gotta go."

"Have fun," Parker sang out.

"Not a date."

"Tell Zakia I said hi."

"Yep."

They were still giggling as I stepped outside.

I hopped in Zakia's Maxima, relishing the warmth after being outside all day. I had to slide the seat back, as I breathed in the scents—vanilla with a slight hint of cinnamon. Zakia smiled, she had on a little stocking cap, and it was working for her.

"You'd better go," I said. "My mom and little sister might come out, and then we'll be in big trouble. "

She set the car in reverse. "Is that why you didn't want me to come in? I sort of want to meet your little sis. I hear good things."

I laughed. Seemed Parker was already making a name for herself.

Zakia set her arm on my seat as she turned to back out of the driveway. "So, did you have a nice Thanksgiving?"

"Oh wonderful. I saw my dad."

Her eyes went soft. "Oh, how was that?"

"Well, it's over. So that's good."

Zakia froze, waiting for more, but I was all too ready to change the subject.

"Okay, so give me some help with Keesha. I'm determined to get on her good side."

It really wasn't a date. The plan was to meet up with Devin and Keesha at Chili's to grab a bite and hang out. But then again, Zakia had offered to pick me up, so it had a date feel to it. Either way, I was tired of getting the side-eye from Keesha.

Zakia laughed. "She'll come around."

"I keep hearing that."

Pulling up to Chili's, Devin and Keesha were waiting out front, laughing as Keesha poked Devin in the ribs.

Zakia strolled up. "Hey, kids."

Keesha's smile faded.

I did my best. "Hey, Keesha."

"Hi, Ben."

Devin fiddled with the buttons on his pea coat. He looked to the door. "Shall we go in?"

We took our places. Devin and Keesha on one side, Zakia and

me on the other. I was trying to think of something to say when Keesha glanced at Devin, who sort of ducked his head and nodded. It was getting a little awkward by the time Keesha knocked her head back and composed herself. "Ben, I'd like to apologize. I haven't exactly been the welcoming committee for BD Briggs High School."

"Oh," I said, no big deal and all. I looked around like a goofball. "Well, thanks, Keesha." I glanced at Zakia. "And I'd like to say I'm sorry, too. For Stonewall, and everything. I never thought that..."

Our waitress arrived before I could fully humiliate myself. "Hi, welcome to Chili's, I'm Ashley and I'll be your... Oh."

My eyes flipped up. I knew the voice. Sure enough, it was Ashley Goins, one of Liv's good friends. She must have only recently started working there.

Devin threw on a smile. "You all right, Ashley?"

Her mouth hung open. She shot me a nasty glare before she got herself together with a roll of the eyes. "Excuse me." She spun on her heels and marched off.

Keesha glanced at Zakia, then me. "Old friend of yours?"

I shrugged. "Friend of a friend."

Keesha smiled at me for the first time since we'd met. A big, white smile. "Well, so much for going unnoticed."

Another waitress hustled over and took our orders while Ashley hung near the counter and sent death stares my way. Zakia went all in for the jalapeño burger, large Cajun fries, and a chocolate milkshake. Apparently, swimmers know how to do dinner.

Our food arrived, and we talked mostly about tomorrow. The Heritage rally coming to town. Keesha was expecting fifty or so people on our side. A drop in the bucket, but enough to make our presence known.

"Javier, DreShaun, and about fifteen to twenty other guys from the team are going to keep watch on the store," Devin added.

I looked around the table. "Oh, um, about that." I'd been wanting to tell him before but hadn't gotten the chance. "I might have news."

Zakia rubbed her hands together and leaned forward with a smile. "You hear that? Ben has news. Or, *might* have news."

I laughed. "No, seriously." I looked around, swallowed the lump in my throat. Saying it out loud made it real, and since I left Stonewall, I hadn't believed it could happen. "I reached out to an old teammate, Ryan. He said some of the guys want to help."

Devin stopped mid-bite. "Yeah?"

I nodded. "Ryan Buckley. He thinks he might be able to bring ten or so guys. After the game, of course. But... What?"

Keesha and Devin exchanged glances. Zakia looked down.

"Seriously, you guys okay?"

Keesha spoke first. "Don't take this the wrong way, Ben. But is this someone we can trust? Forgive me for being skeptical."

"No, this is legit. I mean, Ryan hasn't spoken out publicly yet, but we talked, and I trust him." I looked directly at Devin. "This is what we wanted, right?"

Devin slid his drink away then nodded. "It is." He turned to Keesha. "Ben's right. This is what we set out to do all along. Unity. We need people from both schools if this is going to work."

Keesha seemed to think it over. But for me and Devin, after that night on the field, then at the press conference, it felt like a step forward. This was a start.

Zakia broke through the awkward silence. "I agree. If kids from Stonewall join us, it will draw more attention to the issue, which is good. Hopefully DreShaun will play nice."

Talking about Saturday, our smiles fell. Same for our voices. I think what we all feared but didn't want to mention was how the Heritage March could turn into another Charlottesville. Images of CNN and hooded men clashing with counter protesters. Blood and tear gas. The fights in the streets. I wanted to make things better, not worse. The last thing I wanted was to see anything like the game again.

I sipped my soda. "To be honest, I'm a little worried about the police. First, there's the football game, then this march. And they don't seem to be taking anything seriously—I don't think they're going to protect us if something goes down."

Everyone's eyes went big. Keesha looked at Zakia, then to Devin, who bowed his head. Zakia too. Keesha stifled a laugh.

I threw my hands up. "What?"

It took a minute. Devin sat up and set his palms on the table.

Keesha tilted her head, her eyes softening. "No, Ben. Probably not."

Their smiles faded. Devin stretched back, his arms reaching for the ceiling before he exhaled and dropped his head some. "My concern is for the store. Other than that, I have no plans to engage these people."

"But," Zakia turned to me, "while protecting the store is our main goal, I'd also like to send a message. Council voted to take the monument down. We won't let one group of people bully them into changing their decision. We have to do something. Even if it's just showing up." She shrugged. "It's our way of saying *enough*."

Keesha smiled. "Yeah. That."

Over refills and dessert, we agreed to meet up at seven the next morning. Devin and Keesha begged off, claiming they had some "studying" to do.

As they left, I slid into the bench across from Zakia so it wouldn't be weird. "What does your dad think of all this, like, you being involved?"

She gave it some thought. "The short answer? Half proud, half terrified."

I nodded. "He seems..." I thought about my dad. "Involved."

She drummed her fingers on the table. "Too involved sometimes."

"Yeah, what's it like? Being the principal's daughter?"

She shrugged. "Well, I mean, when he first took the job on, I was a freshman, so we've kind of come up together."

"Did he teach, before that?"

She sipped her milkshake, nodded. "Yep, American History."

"Makes sense."

She cocked her head. Zakia's eyes sparkled, brown to copper to some color I couldn't explain. "Yeah? *What* makes sense?"

I laughed. "No, I mean, you know a lot about history. Like that interview with the reporter at the monument. It was like watching a professor."

Zakia blushed.

I grabbed a French fry, more to give my hands something to do than anything else.

She wiped her lips with a napkin, looked at me, and smiled. "Hey, I want to show you something cool."

I glanced at the counter. I was more than happy to leave. I didn't want to stay in Ashley's crosshairs any longer now that it was just Zakia and me. "Okay."

We grabbed our things, and I paid our tab. To show there were no bad feelings, I left a decent tip. As we got in the car, I asked Zakia where she was taking me and she only said, "We'll see," until we arrived at BD Briggs and sat in the parking lot.

I looked around. "So, uh, why are you taking me to school, on a Friday night?"

Zakia shot me a wry smile and yanked out the keys. She jangled them at me. "Perks of being the principal's daughter."

"This can't be good."

She opened her door. "Come on, it's fine."

Intrigued, I followed Zakia around the gym toward the tennis courts, where Devin and I had entered that day of the press conference. Zakia talked as though she was giving me a tour. "So, Briggs was built in the early fifties. Cold War and all."

The lights were on over the empty courts, buzzing and blinking erratically. "Ah, a history lesson. Now this is what I call a date."

She nudged me in the shoulder before turning for the other side of the gym and to a metal door where she fidgeted with the keys before finding the right one. With a tug, she wrenched the door open, and we stepped into the darkness. I nearly ran into her, and she laughed. "A date, huh?"

"Sort of, maybe?"

With a laugh she shoved me away. "Typical."

A left, a right, before we rambled down a pitch-black corridor. Zakia used her phone for a flashlight, while I continued to guess what we were doing—ghost hunting, burglary, grade tampering?—enjoying the electricity that hit me whenever her hand brushed mine.

Zakia continued to shush me. I figured it was some sort of initiation as we plunged deeper into the dark, light-sucking tunnel. But it was warm, with pockets of cold, and Zakia seemed fine headed into the abyss, as she hummed along with the drips and drops within the bowels of the old high school. I was beginning to think we were lost when Zakia stopped and turned for the wall.

"Ah, there it is." A click of a switch and lights rattled to life overhead, every other one at least. I took in my surroundings. Cast iron pipes, cabling, brick.

"What in the world?"

Zakia threw her hands up with flourish. "It's a bomb shelter."

"This is what do you do in your spare time?"

She rolled her eyes. "This way."

We continued past the old decorations, streamers, banners, track hurdles, and gym wrestling mats. The small taps of her footsteps were in time with the rhythmic drips and drops of water, the occasional clanging of a pipe. Zakia had obviously done this many times before.

The tunnel came to an unspectacular end. Wooden crates and window frames, some sagging benches, three-legged chairs, and desks below a set of rickety wooden steps leading to a rusted metal door. Zakia broke out the keys again.

I cocked my head. "Does your dad know you come down here?"

Zakia shook her head quickly, a mischievous smile fell across her lips. "That's the best part. I'm not sure my dad even knows about any of this."

She found the right key. The lock clicked and she set her shoulder into the door with practiced efficiency. "Almost there."

Zakia disappeared into the void, the strain of the weak amber light leaking in from the hallway. Then, with a buzz, four overhead lights flickered to life. Zakia spun around to me with a huge smile. "Here we are."

I took in the room. A couch, some old crates, empty soda cans and trash. Stacks of old books and a film projector, chalkboard, Christmas decorations.

"This is wild."

"Isn't it?" She pointed to a banner hanging above an old portable chalkboard—*Seniors '88*.

I roamed the room, breathing in the smells—mildew, musty like a basement with cobwebs in the corners. "So, you come down here by yourself?"

She scrunched up her nose. "No way. This is where I bring my boyfriends."

I laughed, until she cocked her eyebrow, held it, then burst out laughing. "Yeah, I mean, I come down here some, not all the time. I found it when I was a freshman, and well, I was sort of having a hard time with things."

"Yeah?" I flipped through an old Williams High yearbook from the sixties. All Black and Brown faces. "Like?"

Zakia turned away from me and continued. "I was tall and gangly, wore braces. Glasses." She shrugged. "Things weren't so great back then. It didn't help that I was the principal's daughter."

I closed the yearbook, about to say something about how I couldn't imagine her ever having trouble with looks or confidence, maybe remind her she had a terrific smile and stunning eyes. But she wasn't fishing for compliments. Besides, three years ago? Anything could happen in three years. Hell, two months ago my life was completely different.

I dragged a finger over some dusty magazines. "So, you came down here to...read?"

She looked down, smiling at some old textbooks, a set of encyclopedias. "Mmm-hmm."

A smile broke across my face. I couldn't help laughing. I gestured to the shelves. "You read every one of them, didn't you?"

"Shut up. No. Maybe. Yes. But look." She pointed to a sagging shelf stuffed with books.

I glanced over the titles. A few I'd heard of but nothing I'd read. A collection of essays by Malcom X.

It wasn't a bomb shelter but a time capsule. And it was clear this was where Zakia did her research. She plucked a three-ring binder from one of the shelves.

"I studied this town, when the monuments went up and why. About how the town's public pool was filled with concrete instead of integrated. The parades. Like, did you know the Klan marched here almost every year in the sixties and seventies?"

"No." I shrugged. "I mean, I'm not surprised." And up until a few weeks ago, I would have never thought about it or what it meant.

Zakia looked up from the notebook. "Yep, oh it was a nice turnout too. They marched, some on horseback, as they trotted right past Mr. Calloway's music store, up main street to good old Elijah Abner's statue. Left him roses." She set a hand to her chest. "Such a touching sentiment."

I laughed, though it wasn't funny. Where I'd never once given much thought about these statues, only recently I'd realized how they meant many different things to many different people. How had Mr. Calloway's father felt when hooded Klansmen marched past his store? Or what did it mean to set roses at a confederate monument? I wondered how many of my friends' relatives took part in that little tribute? Why was some history so important, with the war and the generals, while other history, forced integration, the Klan and the roses, buried and never discussed?

Zakia watched me mull it over before her eyes lit up again. She set down the notebook and went to the shelf. "Anyway, look at this." She fingered through a yearbook from 1996, found a page, and laughed. "See anyone you know?" She pointed to a kid on the football team.

I looked closer and, sure enough, saw the text beneath it. Andre Ferguson.

"Your dad played ball?"

"Sure did."

"Wow."

"Flip here," she said, and turned to a dog-eared page. "He was on the debate team, the poets' society, literary club, you name it."

"Pretty well-rounded guy."

"Yeah. With high expectations too." She kept her eyes on the page, bit her lip in thought. "I didn't want to say it earlier, but he's not thrilled about me going to the counterprotest tomorrow."

"Oh," I said. "I mean, because he's worried something will happen?"

"I hope it's that. I hope it's not... These days he's always worried about admins, the school board. Or who will show up at a school board meeting and call for his job because his *radical* daughter is out *protesting in the streets*," she said with finger quotes. "These days, my father is about test results, funding, accreditation. He's not much of a risk taker."

"Well, I mean, what about me coming to Briggs? He took that risk."

She laughed. "That was mostly Dr. Jamerson, so my dad went with it."

We stood close, our arms touching. I didn't know what to make of it, but I couldn't move away. Not when Zakia turned to me, our faces coming closer. I held my breath, as she grinned, her lips parting...

Something clanged behind us, and I jumped.

Zakia broke out laughing. "Pipes."

I took a breath, smiled. "Yeah, um, I know."

She laughed again, nudged me with her shoulder. "I hope you're not this jumpy tomorrow."

CHAPTER 31

Zakia had just started her car when our phones started buzzing. She glanced down. "Wow. I'm popular. What in the world?"

There hadn't been much reception in the tunnel. Now I saw two missed calls from Devin.

Zakia drew a breath. "Uh-oh."

"What?"

She stared at her phone, her eyes wide with concern. "Keesha's asking if we're okay."

Another message on her phone.

Something serious was going on. "Are we? Okay, I mean?"

Zakia read the incoming messages. "There's some sort of pre-rally going on downtown." Her mouth went tight. "Looks like the heritage people are gathering at the monument." She turned to me. "Like, right now."

Her phone buzzed again, and she answered the call on speaker, still looking at me. "Hey, Keesha, where are you guys?"

"We're at the music store."

"Everything okay?"

A long silence. "I don't know. They're up there chanting. We saw some torches. Whatever it is, it's getting louder."

Torches? My stomach dropped. I thought back to the game. The taunts, the angry faces. The blood. Zakia put the car in gear. "We're on our way."

"Okay, be careful."

Zakia set her hand on mine. "Do you want me to drop you off, or..."

"No way." I went through the contacts on my phone.

Zakia looked over to me. "Are you sure?"

"Absolutely." I found Ryan's number. "I guess it's time to see who we can trust."

I sent him a text as we neared downtown. Zakia turned on Upper Main Street before I could stop her, and we found ourselves in the thick of the smoke. Trucks on the curb, people hiking down the steps, the glow of the torches surrounding the monument.

A cluster of people on the sidewalk watched closely as Zakia's car edged through traffic. Zakia stared straight ahead. Even with the windows up the chanting and cheering found its way inside the vehicle, sending a shiver down my spine. We were straining for a glimpse of the monument when a truck pulled out in front of us.

"Watch out."

Zakia gasped and hit the brakes, throwing us forward. My back tensed as we exchanged looks, knowing we were helpless if trouble started here. The truck in our way hitched, then backed into a space between vehicles. Zakia hit the gas and we swerved around the other vehicles and tore down Main Street for the Lower Basin.

We found Devin out in front of the store. "Thanks for coming." He glanced up the block, then looked at the door. "I just, I don't know, I got a bad feeling about things. I'd like to keep an eye out, you know?"

I checked my phone. Nothing from Ryan. I sent another text, said we were down at the music store and worried about what might happen as we gathered inside, where the street lamps cast shafts of light through the windows.

Devin locked up, and we fell into the safe pockets of darkness in the store. A lamp was on in the back, near the closet, but we stayed at the door, huddled close, glued to our phones as we reached out to contacts and tried to find out anything about what was happening at the monument.

Every sound, distant and near, pulled our attention. Every passing car had us peeking out the windows. Devin's phone buzzed, and he started pacing, nodding and explaining everything to someone, maybe DreShaun or Javier.

Zakia's shoulder fell against mine as I stared at my phone, willing Ryan to get back to me. Something told me he wouldn't. They had their game tomorrow, the playoffs. There was no time to worry about a former captain who'd quit on them.

Again, my instincts were to call the police, even as I knew Officer Dave wouldn't make us his priority. And I couldn't stop thinking about the gun in the drawer, as Devin paced the length of the store. I didn't know what he was planning on doing, all the jokes and big talk from earlier had given way to something much more serious now.

Devin returned from his pacing, pocketing his phone. He glanced at me. "Should we go see for ourselves?"

His eyes flicked to the drawer, and I knew what he was thinking. I took a breath and nodded, because I was tired of sitting in the dark doing nothing. "Yeah, let's do it."

Devin opened the drawer and reached for the gun when Keesha stepped forward. "No."

We froze.

Keesha shook her head. "Nothing good is going to come from you taking that."

Devin studied the gun in his hand. Then, with a nod, he set it back in the drawer.

Keesha exhaled. "And we're coming with you."

Keesha wasn't asking, and so the four of us set out of the store, locking up before we hiked up the block.

We decided to go around the block instead of right at it. We took a left at the coffee shop and came around one street over so we could try to sneak down from the hill. It was just before ten but felt later. The banks and shops were dark, and the traffic lights changed for empty streets. But the noise from the monument filled the cracks. As we snuck down a side street, a deep, collective voice found my chest and nearly knocked me down.

This is our history. This. Is. Our. History. This. Is. Our. History.

We dipped into an alley and climbed an old driveway entrance, where we took a flight of steps to an abandoned porch on the corner. We huddled there, a hundred feet away, maybe more, well-hidden as the slope of the hill gave us a perfect view. The glow of the terrace lights, combined with the torches, lit up the statue. Still, it felt like one glance in our direction, and we were done for.

The crowd, maybe forty or so, ranging from old to young, was angry and brash. There didn't seem to be any worry of law enforcement or permits.

This. Is. Our. History.

Devin glanced over to me. His face said it all. While we knew the protestors would fight to keep the monument, and we'd heard them talk about history and heritage, seeing them assemble with torches sent my heart into my throat. They chanted through gritted teeth, veins bulging, the power in their voices pulsing with each word. And while I didn't see any rifles or shotguns, I was sure some of these people were armed.

Devin turned away and snickered, but it hardly covered the grip of terror overtaking us. I recognized some of the figures in attendance. These were people of our town—people like Jed and Bus, who lived alongside us. Now they were gathered around the monument with torches, seemingly ready for war.

The chanting turned to cheers as a figure made his way through the bodies and took his place at the sturdy hoofs of old Elijah's horse. He nodded solemnly, then set a hand to his chin and took a few steps with his thoughts.

The man was clean cut. He looked more like a golf pro than a good old boy in his button down and khakis as he opened his arms, as though giving the onlookers a hug. The cheering fizzled out, and this man, with the composure of a politician, seized the moment.

"Folks, the time is upon us. We've been silent for too long as the woke mob, the illegal immigrants, this third world culture has attacked our very way of life and bestowed their beliefs upon us."

Devin turned to me and mouthed "bestowed." I knew what he was thinking: what a jackass.

The jackass continued. "Even here in Virginia, they want to take our guns, our culture, our rights, and now," he paused to admire the old general, "our history. And what I want to know is, where do we draw the line?"

The crowd grumbled. Behind me, I felt Zakia's uneasiness and turned to find Keesha stock still, absorbing the words and reactions. I could only imagine what was going through Devin's mind as he watched intently, his eyes focused, as though he were about to suit up and take the field.

The golf pro/politician guy wasn't through with his stump speech. He studied his loafers as though deep in thought. When he raised his head, his tone changed, his face now a fiery red, like that of a brimstone preacher. He let the spit fly as he ramped things up, his voice breaking. "So, they want to take this down. Rip our history right out by the roots. I say *no*. Not today, not ever. We can't let them keep taking and taking. When will it end?"

He screamed the word "end" so that it ricocheted off the buildings until it found us. The power and hatred in his voice stole my breath. I was still trying to catch it when I spotted Gunny off to the side, within the swell of bodies, nodding with support and cheering him on as though he were a celebrity.

The speaker shook his head, wiped his mouth. "We say no more. No more."

The crowd roared. Back to the chanting. Devin shook his head. These were words I'd heard many times before, but now, hidden in the shadows, I was hearing them differently, seeing the different effects they had on different people.

The chanting died down, and the man started pacing again, cutting a path for Gunny.

"And now they're trying to jail a good man for self-defense."

The booing rained down. Gunny stood almost bashfully, his face solemn, nodding slightly. A few trucks up the block revved their engines and peeled out. Keesha flinched. Zakia and I turned to see where they were headed. Devin only stared off. He didn't move an inch.

I got back to Gunny. I couldn't tell, being so far away, but he appeared to be clear-eyed and sober. His hair was brushed, and he had on a clean shirt. Maybe someone had kept him off the booze.

With his audience riled up, the speaker continued. "This man is a hero. He's a family man, a lifelong citizen of our great town. And what do they want to do? Lock him up? For defending himself?"

Keesha took a sharp breath. Devin still hadn't looked away. The crowd, already agitated, was now ready for war. This ringleader, a guy I'd never seen before, without the slightest hint of a southern accent, had obviously done this sort of thing before. What he was pushing had nothing to do with history or monuments or anything at all. It had everything to do with violence.

Something bad was coming. It rolled off the crowd in fumes. I felt it in the grumbling. I looked off and spotted a police cruiser as a breeze carried the smell of the river to us, and along with it, a waft of smoke.

I wiped my face. I couldn't believe this was my hometown. That this could happen here—was happening here—where I'd lived all my life. It hit me in the chest and stole my breath. Not only what they were saying, but where it was headed. I stood back as Keesha and Devin hung on every word as the crowd sang and chanted and gave Gunny a hero's welcome.

I fought to stay ahead of the fear. I sent another text to Ryan, who still hadn't responded. Zakia frowned at me, as though she knew it was useless. We were alone in this.

"Now, it's time we send a message to this town. To everyone." I looked up again just in time to see the speaker hold up a sign. *Support C-443!* "You see this, you know it's the enemy." He shook the sign. "It's that plain and simple, you hear? This is your enemy."

The smoke. Something was happening. Not here, but close.

Devin gasped. He leaped up and his voice broke. "No. No, no, no, no."

Before I could blink, he was gone. He leaped off the railing and dashed out of the alley for the store.

Keesha called after him. "Devin!"

The speaker shook the sign, the crowd started chanting. I realized this wasn't some late-night march but a battle plan. Everything else had been a diversion. Keesha and Zakia started after Devin. I took one last look at the crowd. The chants. The smoke. These people were about to attack our town.

And there were only four of us to stop them.

CHAPTER 32

We raced after Devin, who'd thrown himself over the balcony and was bounding down out of the alley onto Commerce Street. The steps clattered as we scaled down, chasing after him, looping around in the direction of the music store. The smoke hit full on as we ran, stinging my eyes as the chanting seemed to follow us.

I tore ahead to catch up with Devin. Keesha and Zakia's footsteps slapped the asphalt behind me as the traffic lights flashed yellow. Devin stopped suddenly at the intersection, pausing to look around wildly, just before the boom of an explosion sent me diving to the asphalt.

Devin dropped to his knees and covered his face. Zakia shrieked, and I got to my feet and tried to make sure everyone was okay. Zakia had her phone out while Keesha sprinted past me for Devin. I was too caught up in my own fear to make a decision.

Tires screeched on the next street. The rev of an engine growled before another *boom*, and I hit the street again. Devin staggered back with a scream, before he raced off for the shop again. I gathered myself and started after him when a squad car roared down the street, lights blazing.

A quick chirp of the siren as it came up on Devin, who never looked back but just kept moving. The car slowed to a crawl and trailed him as he came up on the old post office. Keesha called after him.

The officer lowered his window. We were close enough now that I made out the voice of the younger cop, Deputy Ballard. The one my mom had just laid out. Great.

"Stop right there. Right there."

Devin did as he asked. He turned to the officer and pointed to Lower Main. "I have to check the store. Didn't you hear the explosions?"

Devin's voice was torn, shredded with panic. I hurried to catch up, stopping at the edge of the car. The officer glanced back at me. "Ben, what are you doing here?" Before I could answer, he got back to Devin. "What explosion? Hey, all of you. Stop. Now!"

Keesha sidled up to Devin. Zakia said something into the phone then pressed a button. The deputy jumped out of the squad car, leaving it running in the middle of the intersection. Zakia held the phone up to record what was happening.

"Ben. Right there." He motioned to me, waving his hands around to coral us. "You too, all of you." He gestured toward the curb. "Take a seat. I need to ask you a few questions."

Keesha leveled a glare on the officer. Devin was still inching down the road as though pulled by some magnetic force. He remained on his feet, an arm's length from the police car. This wasn't jazz-loving Devin or the philosophical guy I'd gotten to know at the store. His chest was heaving, his mouth open. He didn't seem to realize who he was or where he was, only that he needed to get to the store, and nothing was going to stop him.

Deputy Ballard saw it too, and his eyes wobbled as he set his focus on Devin. "The curb. You, come on. Let's go. Sit on the curb, here."

Keesha cocked her head. "Why? There's no time. Didn't you hear the explosion?" She nodded at Devin. "His father owns Cal's Music. Would you check on Lower Main? It's basically under attack."

"Attack? I didn't hear any explosions." Deputy Ballard pointed to the curb again. He motioned to me, then Zakia. "You two as well. And put that away. We'll sort this out in a minute. Now."

"I'm not putting anything away," Zakia said firmly.

"Sort what out?" Keesha shook her head.

Devin glanced up the street, then took a step for the deputy. "Why are you stopping us?"

Deputy Ballard's hand slid to his hip. "We had a call come in. Four trespassers on the balcony at 21 Main Street. Near the monument. Now sit."

A roar of trucks in the distance, some yelling up at the monument. Headlights swept down Main Street. Another truck came plowing toward us, hit the brakes seeing the squad car in the road, then gunned the engine and tore away.

Deputy Ballard looked back at the truck.

Keesha turned to him, pointing in the direction of the primer gray truck. "That truck just ran a stop sign."

"And made an illegal U-turn," Zakia said helpfully.

Deputy Ballard took a step forward. Keesha met him in the street. Ballard seemed twitchy, and I was worried how this was going to end.

Zakia glanced at Devin. "Devin, let's just sit."

"Sit? No. We need to move," Devin said, his eyes filling with tears. "Can't you smell the smoke? I need to check on the store."

Deputy Ballard's radio squawked. He nodded for the curb. "Let's get this sorted out."

"It's going to be too late by then!" Devin screamed.

Deputy Ballard started for him, his hand brushing his belt, going for the handcuffs.

Keesha yelled out. "What are you doing?"

"I need you to cooperate." He reached for Devin, who ripped his hand away.

"Don't touch me." His voice was raw. "My dad's store. Please!"

Flashes of the news came to mind. How this would have gone down had Keesha not stepped in and told him to leave the gun. Although now, seeing how Ballard was twitching, all I could think about were the headlines. An unarmed Black kid shot by the police. That couldn't happen to Devin Calloway. He couldn't become just another name on a list. He had a football scholarship, pre-law awaiting him. Devin Calloway couldn't die on the street, he had too much to do. He was more than a name in the news. But everything was happening too fast.

Again, Zakia pleaded with Devin from behind her phone, still recording everything. "Devin, please."

Deputy Ballard turned for Zakia and the phone. "That's not necessary."

"I feel like it is," Zakia said calmly.

Devin kept glancing down the street, struggling to regain his composure as he faced Deputy Ballard directly, his voice pleading. "We didn't do anything. Are you listening to me? Those people down there have already threatened me. They're armed. Something's burning!"

When the deputy's hand moved for his holster, my breath caught. He stopped short and cocked his head. "Have you reported the threat?"

Devin wiped his eyes.

Again, Deputy Ballard moved in, and again, Devin jerked away. This time the deputy lunged and wrapped his arms around him.

Devin looked ready to shove him to the ground when Keesha called out. "Devin, no. Just... Please!"

It was enough to make Devin hesitate. When he did, Deputy Ballard turned and shoved him to the street. I called out as the officer flipped Devin on his stomach and cuffed his wrists behind his back. "Are you ready to listen now?"

Devin, his chin on the street, stared straight ahead. His gaze was completely hollow as Keesha screamed at Deputy Ballard, whose knee fell onto Devin's back as he ordered us to stay put as he gasped for breath, fixed his hat, and looked awfully proud of himself for taking down the big football star.

Tears carved down Devin's cheeks as he lay still. Keesha, in a heroic act of self-control, remained on the curb as she let the officer have it about illegal stops and harassment. All the while Zakia held the phone on Ballard like a weapon, as the chants from the monument echoed down Main Street.

"You guys were coming from that direction. Were you on the property of 21 Main Street? Yes or no?"

I didn't hesitate. "Yes."

The deputy looked to me suddenly, still heaving. "Okay then."

Zakia spoke up. "We weren't doing anything wrong. Can you please remove your knee from his back and check on the music shop? There have been threats."

Deputy Ballard was still struggling to catch his breath. He glanced down to his knee, as though he had no idea it was centered on Devin's back. He rocked back some. "We don't have any record of threats. That group has a permit to be here. What we don't need is a clash in the streets. A situation."

Keesha turned her head up to him, her voice clinging onto a calmness I envied. "Sir, you can smell the smoke. Something is burning. Please put your ego away and do something productive."

Devin finally turned, and we locked eyes. He didn't blink, only stared at me full on. It was like he wanted me to understand, to remember this moment, while Ballard, still hunched over but taking his weight off Devin, seemed to consider something in his head as he gazed down the street.

"Remember the threats I mentioned," I said, seeing him shift.

The deputy jerked his head back to us, then down to Devin, still mulling it over. But we'd broken through to him. He looked around, then, with a few deep breaths, he nodded to himself.

Zakia kept recording, but it was the blast of a siren that finally pushed Ballard into action. "Okay," he said. "Okay." He removed his knee from Devin completely. "All right, let's go see."

We stood in the middle of the street, heaving with fear and emotion, stunned into silence as the officer uncuffed Devin and helped him to his feet. Devin stared at him without a word, as Ballard muttered something about once a linebacker always a linebacker. Then we bolted for the cruiser.

All four of us jammed into the plastic backseat. Deputy Ballard hit the gas and we sped through the last traffic light, then cut a quick left against a one-way street. Ballard gunned it down the hill, and the cruiser bottomed out as we came out on Lower Main Street, lunging forward as the deputy slammed on the brakes. The fiery glow of massive flames knocked us back.

Devin let out a wail. Deputy Ballard confirmed something on the radio, but it was too late. Flames tore out of the warehouse—the one we'd walked past only an hour ago. Black smoke plumed out from the new construction, the coffee shop engulfed against the night sky.

The fire was already climbing to the second-floor windows. The entire block was consumed. Smoke and ash hung above our heads, smothering the streetlights, the acrid smell leaking into the car.

Devin screamed in agony, his convulsions shaking the cruiser. Ballard cursed under his breath as he hit the gas. We barreled down the block only to come to a sliding stop at the intersection. By then, Devin was shouldering the door, trying to get out, but it was locked, unable to be opened from the inside. Deputy Ballard fiddled with the radio as he exited the car. After a moment's hesitation, he opened the door, and we broke free in a sprint for the music shop.

From there, it was chaos. Our feet slapped the asphalt. Sirens and screams as the fire truck horns blared. Three trucks barged onto Main, blocking off the street. Another squad car flew past us.

Devin was gone.

Zakia, Keesha, and I coughed on the smoke as we ran for the store, calling after Devin. I heard explosions, but I couldn't tell if it was real or merely the pounding in my head. Again, the deep chanting of voices found my chest. My heart raced all over again. I was dizzy from the screams, the smoke, the wild buzzing in my ears. My eyes blurred as we neared the bridge. We were too late. They'd beaten us here and now the whole street was going to burn.

Keesha and Zakia caught up with me. The chanting grew louder, deeper, almost familiar as we came upon the store. Keesha let out a wail as we spotted Devin, once again on his knees in the middle of the road.

"Devin!"

When I got to him, my legs collapsed. He reached out for the store, and we took in the sight before us. I set a hand on his shoulder as Keesha fell into us and let out a sob.

Devin only stared ahead. "I can't believe what I'm seeing."

I wiped my eyes. My face was wet from sweat, from the tears I didn't know I'd shed. We stared at the miracle in front of us. Devin turned to me, still crying, his mouth open like he didn't know whether to smile or scream.

Cal's Music stood safely behind a wall of wide shoulders and thick necks. A row of football jerseys, arms locked, spanning the entire row of buildings, around the block to the sides, the back, out in the middle of the street. They'd closed the gaps.

We staggered to our feet. Devin folded over again and covered his face in his hands as two figures broke free and rushed over to us.

DreShaun, the quarterback, strode out to us with his gameday smile. He hooked a thumb toward Ryan, who stood beside him.

"Can you believe this shit?"

Ryan chuckled nervously. I couldn't imagine what we looked like by then.

Zakia caught up to us and sort of fell into me. "News Six is on the way, we're going to get all this... Oh, wow..." She smiled brightly. "Wow."

DreShaun slung his arm around Devin. I smacked hands with Ryan and tried to keep my balance, as standing was getting more and more difficult.

"Sorry, man, we were at a pep rally when I got your text. I managed to get some guys together. My phone died, then we got down here and we had to act." He glanced over his shoulder to where several other Stonewall players—Andy, Stephen, and at least ten other guys—stood shoulder to shoulder. All wearing their Rebels jerseys.

"Can't believe these dudes showed out," DreShaun said.

Devin looked at me. We marveled over the scene.

DreShaun only now noticed how shaken we were. "Ya'll all right?"

Devin blinked. He wiped his face. "No. Yeah, just, I can't..."

"Crazy, right? And check it, these dudes agreed to finish the game. Unofficially speaking."

Ryan nodded. "Anytime. Anywhere." He nodded to me for affirmation. "We get Ben, though."

It was hard to match their smiles and lighthearted jokes, not after what we'd seen. Not as the next block was still burning. We were too stunned, too drained, too gripped by competing emotions as we approached the unharmed music store.

The fire department worked to contain the fires up the street. It was bittersweet, how the next block was torched, but here, at the store, everything was mostly intact as what had to be the entire BD Briggs football team was locked in place with the Stonewall guys.

Hands slapped Devin and me on the back, grabbed our heads and pulled us in for quick hugs. DreShaun was almost hopping in place excited as he explained how it went down. "You should've seen it. There was a boom, then two trucks came flying down the street, headed this way. They saw us out there and stopped on a dime. Threw it in reverse so fast..."

Ryan laughed. "Yeah, I think he pissed himself."

"Hope they got insurance," DreShaun said, as not everyone had been so lucky. We all turned our heads to the black smoke pluming out of the second story windows of the new apartments. The coffee shop was unrecognizable.

Devin's eyes were glossy and red. He looked to DreShaun, then to Ryan, and finally back to me. "I think these guys will make good captains next year, huh?"

I nodded. "Yeah, I think so."

CHAPTER 33

Lower Main Street was still a tangle of smoke and lights and yellow tape as police and firemen ran back and forth to work the scene. News Team Six arrived. The warehouse was still ablaze, the coffee shop reduced to a shell of smoldering bricks.

The fire department ordered everyone to stand back. Stacey and her crew set up at the corner and covered what was going on at the music shop.

An hour later, the fire was out but the acrid smell remained in the fog. Remained on my clothes and inside my head. But things were mostly under control. Sawhorses had been erected and the police had secured the scene. Mr. Ferguson ran up and bear hugged Zakia. Then Mom was hugging me. Parker and Max were all over the place. The football guys stayed out front, standing guard, still talking trash to each other but this time with smiles on their faces.

I couldn't help looking out for the Heritage mob, but I knew for now, for tonight at least, we had the numbers.

Deputy Ballard hung back as the commanding officers arrived. Zakia pointed out the police chief, a man she'd interviewed once for the school paper. I watched as he assessed the scene, spoke to Ballard, then conversed with the fire guys. I wondered about the march tomorrow and if that was still on after all this, when Stacey came for us.

She had the camera on and ready behind her, a mike in her hand. Keesha gave her the side eye as the reporter found Devin and set her hand on his arm. "Devin, what are you thinking about right now?"

Devin wiped his eyes. I gazed down the street, where nearly

fifteen guys from my old team had shown up to join what looked like the entire BD Briggs football team. All of them to help Devin. To help me.

Too many to name. Ryan told me again how the night of Reggie's death had shaken a lot of guys. They'd wanted to talk about what had happened, but Coach had shut it down. Moose had made threats. Ryan said it wasn't until I'd reached out to him that he felt inspired to use his voice.

When I asked if he was worried about Coach, Ryan shrugged. "He can't bench all of us, right?"

Devin was still staring at the music store like it was a mirage when Stacey repeated the question about what we were feeling, if we were proud of ourselves for what we'd accomplished.

Devin only stared at the store. "It's hard to put into words," he said. "I'm proud of this whole town right now."

The football guys cheered as Mr. Calloway made his way down the line, thanking each and every one of them before he strode past the window with the *Support C-443!* Logo and inside.

Devin stared at me, as though he too couldn't believe we'd done it. His dad returned with two horns. Devin had one in his hands when Deputy Ballard approached.

"There's a noise ordinance after eleven o'clock."

Devin dropped the horn to his side.

Deputy Ballard shrugged. "I'm sorry about earlier. I, uh, I'm glad how things turned out."

When Devin didn't respond, the deputy took a deep breath and looked past him, up to the store. "Look, I became a cop to help this town. So, that's what I aim to do from here on out. No hard feelings?"

I held my breath as Devin, with more restraint than I'll ever know, closed his eyes and nodded. "Yeah, we're good."

The deputy smiled, then he turned and started to walk away, but Devin called after him. "So what happens tomorrow?"

Deputy Ballard looked around. "Oh, you haven't heard? The mayor revoked the permit. He said we'll call in the National Guard if we have to, but there will be no march. Not after this." He nodded toward the next block, where a heavy cloud of smoke still hung over the store. "There's been enough damage to our town." He gestured to the horn. "Oh, and I think I can look the other way, with the noise ordinance and all."

Devin and I looked at each other, then to the store, at the rivals, locked arm in arm. Devin took a deep breath, just before he put the horn to his mouth. "This one's for Reggie."

ONE YEAR LATER

We were in enemy territory, Charlottesville, Virginia, and the stadium rocked as sixty thousand fans packed the stands. The band swayed and the cheerleaders tumbled out to the field as the battle for the Commonwealth Cup was only minutes away. It was fifty-five degrees and sunny, only a few tufts of clouds overhead as the announcers took to the sidelines for the inside scoop.

I'd been redshirted for my freshman year, and that was fine with me. I was loving college life. The campus, the atmosphere, the new faces from all over the globe. I was hoping to break in next year, maybe get on the field and sort things out from there.

But for now, I soaked it all in, hopping in place with my teammates, scanning the field. Then I saw DC.

Devin stood at the 40-yard line, stretching out. He'd played some and made an impact as a true freshman. The consensus was that he was going to be great, maybe even a pro. That part was up to him.

We'd kept in touch. A few calls here and there, Facetime, Zoom interviews, some random texts. Now I smiled as I made my way over to him, because while everyone hyped him up on the field, I knew his secret. Devin Calloway was going to be a damn good lawyer.

Our eyes met and he smiled. Yeah, the calls and texts left us in touch, but we hadn't kept up like we'd planned. College life was crazy, but I knew where he'd be this summer.

Downtown had been rebuilt. The coffee shop returned, the brick a slightly lighter shade than before, the tile still smelling of grout. Cal's Music had a nice new plaque out front, as it had more recently been deemed a historic building.

The plaque was more of a tribute to the community. After the fire, our mayor had in fact cancelled the Heritage March. The National Guard arrived and camped downtown for a week. Parker brought them cookies. People began speaking up. Soon, it seemed there were more people like Ryan, who'd needed a push from people like Mom and Parker and Zakia. Together, we outnumbered the people like Bus and those at Sal's.

That Saturday after the fires, we'd cleaned up the streets. We worked in the community through our senior year. I started volunteering, started writing. I documented what had happened. I learned my scholarship had never been in danger. My new coach said he was proud of what I'd done.

Officer Dave retired. Deputy Ballard stayed true to his word. He visited schools. He was still a goofball.

Ridgeton was healing. And people gave Devin and me a whole lot of credit for doing our part, which was cool, but today, here we were, on the field again.

"Saw you miss that tackle last week," I said as we slapped hands.

Devin's eyes went big. "Yeah, I learned from the best."

We'd been interviewed too many times to count over the summer. After Gunny received ten years for manslaughter, we'd received more death threats. Jeff never spoke to me again. Moose left for a small school in Tennessee.

Everyone wanted to know about our bond, our friendship, how we'd been linked since everything on the field that fateful Friday night. But now, looking out to the stands, the thousands of cheering fans, it was nice just to be back on the field, to be two kids trying to blend in.

Neither of us were naïve enough to believe Ridgeton had suddenly been cured of its problems. It would take more than the two of us. More than a football game, or even a fire. But Devin and I felt good about what we'd done. We'd tried to make a difference, however small it was.

Devin glanced up to the stands where Parker and Max were

sitting with Mom and Mr. and Mrs. Calloway. Zakia and Keesha were there too. We waved to them, in their direction anyway. "Well, Ben, this is where we part."

We slapped hands again. "Good luck today."

"Good luck to you too."

I turned and started for my side of the field.

"Ben."

I barely heard him over the crowd noise. I turned around. Devin set his arms out as though taking in the stadium, the bleachers filled with fans cheering for his team or mine. I shook my head. He didn't have to say it. No, I couldn't believe it either.

We'd left our town in good hands. With DreShaun and Ryan. With Parker and Max.

It was their turn now.

ACKNOWLEDGMENTS

Two events put this story to motion in my head. First, was the harrowing scenes from the 2017 rally in Charlottesville, Virginia. Maybe I'd been living in a bubble or under a rock, but I never thought, in present times—right up until the moment I turned on the television and saw the hatred live and in color, only an hour's drive from my house—that it would lead to such violence in the streets.

But it did. And it got me thinking

I was still thinking in 2018, on a sunny Saturday morning one fall after my five-year-old son's soccer game. There was a football game taking place nearby, JV or freshman it appeared, and we stopped in to watch. I couldn't help but notice how one side was nearly entirely white and the other black. The parents were taunting one another (nothing like what's in the book but enough to get the gears in my mind working), and a story took hold.

So there it was. My book. I didn't want to take a side, didn't want to preach a lesson. I just wanted to tell a story about two kids who wanted to make things better.

Hometown is more about unity than race. And perhaps I'm still in that bubble, I like my rock, but I wrote Devin and Ben's story with hope for the future.

Thanks to the usual suspects. To Diane Fanning for believing. To Jayy Jacobs for the sensitivity reads. To Jon Perry for the amazing art. To Quincy Cunningham for putting my story to song. To the Immortal Works staff and fellow authors. To Staci Olsen and Jason King, and, as always, Holli Anderson. I never make it easy for you.

To my mom, my dad, Ivy, Liz, and Taylor. To Simon, now eleven and not so innocent anymore. To Bella, the little boss. To my wife Anne for her unwavering belief in me.

ABOUT THE AUTHOR

Pete Fanning is the author of several middle grade and young adult novels, including *Bricktown Boys*, winner of the 2021 Indies Today Best Juvenile Book award. He can be found at www.petefanning.com, where he's posted over 200 flash fiction stories.

This has been an
Immortal Production